*"My sister was named (
whose beauty and grace
Joan after no one in particular, and that worried me as a
child. I also worried about pollution, nuclear war, being
too ugly to be loved, and everyone in my family dying.
In temperament we were as different as water and wine.
She needed to be free, but I needed to be good."*

"There's more than one mystery hidden in this entertaining and
cleverly told story, but the heart of *Only Sisters* lies in Lilian
Nattel's searching look at the idea of family. This irresistible
page-turner is going to stay with me for a long time."
Katherine Ashenberg, author of *Her Turn*

"Lilian Nattel's thoroughly satisfying novel sucked me in from
the very first paragraph to the final perfect lines. Anyone who 's
interested in family dynamics is bound to enjoy this beautifully
written, engaging story about Joan Connor, whose good
intentions lead her astray, but also bring her home again."
Jo Owens, author of *A Funny Kind of Paradise*

ONLY SISTERS

ALSO BY LILIAN NATTEL

Girl at the Edge of Sky
Web of Angels
The Singing Fire
The River Midnight

ONLY SISTERS

LILIAN NATTEL

RANDOM HOUSE CANADA

PUBLISHED BY RANDOM HOUSE CANADA

LIBRARY AND ARCHIVES CANADA CATALOGUING IN PUBLICATION

Title: Only sisters / Lilian Nattel.
Names: Nattel, Lilian, 1956- author.
Identifiers: Canadiana (print) 20220212821 | Canadiana (ebook) 2022021283X
| ISBN 9780735277069 (softcover) | ISBN 9780735277076 (EPUB)
Classification: LCC PS8577.A757 O55 2022 | DDC C813/.54—dc23

Text design: Kelly Hill
Cover design: Kelly Hill
Image credits: (Robin) sylviacphotography/Getty Images

Printed in Canada

2 4 6 8 9 7 5 3 1

Penguin
Random House
RANDOM HOUSE CANADA

For Donna Rhindress, BFF,
who has the gift of always looking truth in the eye

And in memory of Frances Greenbaum

CHAPTER 1

I agreed to become my sister during a polar vortex. It was her fifty-ninth birthday, and we were ten thousand kilometres apart. I was sitting on my bed, and though the city was encased in ice, I had the window open. With the superpower of a menopausal woman, I could melt mountains of snow. The computer was on my lap, a frigid breeze tapping my hot cheeks, while my sister kept breaking up on the screen. It was midnight in my time zone, an hour before dawn in hers. She was a nurse working in rural West Africa, where the seasons were wet or dry but never cold. Her nose was sunburned and peeling. There was a vase of spiky crimson flowers nearby. A fan whirred, stirring her hair.

My sister was named after the movie star Vivien Leigh, whose beauty and grace our mother adored. I was named Joan after no one in particular, and as a child, that worried me. I also worried about pollution, nuclear war, being too ugly to be loved, everyone in my family dying, the callus on my finger (I thought it was a symptom of yaws, a rare tropical disease), getting a B in math, going blind and how to use tampons. (I still worry about going blind. Also, climate change. Flying. And whether I'm ugly.) I wore thick glasses when I was young. Except for that, my sister and I looked very much alike, though she grew up to be a beautiful woman. Even our parents couldn't tell our voices apart on the phone. In temperament, we were as different as water and wine. While I stayed home, my sister travelled the world. She was nonchalant about sharing her bed, picking up and dropping men at whim. I'd had one serious relationship. She delivered babies, bringing life into the world. My patients were dying. She needed to be free, but I needed to be good.

She'd messaged me earlier in the day, while I was on my way to see a patient. I was late because the cold had killed my car battery, and I'd had to wait for a boost. Hurrying along the twelfth-floor corridor of a waterfront condo, I heard my phone whistle. On the lock screen: *Vivien Connor: Skype call tonight at 10 your time?*

It was always Skype—I didn't use social media or messaging apps other than what came with my phone. I wrote back, *Sure*, as if we talked all the time, and stuck the phone back in my jacket pocket. That winter I had a new jacket, waterproof with a removable lining. There was another coat I'd tried on, a black wool that made me feel as chic as a Parisian who only had to lift her chin to stop a taxi, but I visit patients in all weather and so I'd put it back on the rack. As a physician, I could afford both coats, and I'm not stingy, but it seemed unkind to buy two coats when so many people struggle to pay for one. Doing the right thing was a compulsion— my colleagues called me Saint Joan, and they didn't mean it as a compliment.

I'm a physician in palliative care. On the surface, it's like any other form of medicine. Once the cause of a person's symptoms is determined, treatment is prescribed, based on experience and instinct as well as medical training. But there the similarity ends. We don't cure—we heal by easing pain and disability, improving quality of life. Palliative treatment doesn't change the course of a life-limiting illness. It has an unavoidable destination, the same as every person's life. Most physicians can't bear the helplessness of that. Palliative care doctors must bear it and we are expected to do so with professional dispassion. This means hiding my own grief, even though I hold every loss in my heart like a secret child.

I saw Vivien's message just before my first appointment with Eddie Wong. The nurse assigned to his care had warned me that his Yorkshire terrier would jump all over me until it was petted, so as soon as I introduced myself, I bent down to give the dog a vigorous rub along its back and a scratch between the ears. That didn't get me even a small smile from the old man. I would have to work harder for that.

Eddie's apartment, which I subsequently visited many times, had a similar layout to the one I'd sold before moving back home to take care of my mother. Open-plan kitchen and living-dining room, a hallway leading to bedroom, bathroom, den. On the wall were several paintings of the lake view as well as other landscapes—cottage country, the Toronto skyline. A line of portraits hung on the wall next to the dining table, as if they were guests waiting for an invitation to be seated. The living room furniture was sturdy and old. Across from the couch, there was a vintage stereo, a 1960s conceit, large speakers and a turntable built into a wooden cabinet, concealed by sliding doors.

"It still works," Eddie said when he saw me looking.

While he lay down on the couch, I pulled a chair close and hung my jacket on the back of it, then sat. The jacket was navy, like my messenger bag and my pants, my shirt light grey. The bag was spacious—it held a laptop, stethoscope and blood pressure cuff, as well as personal essentials. I unzipped it and extracted my laptop so I could take notes while we talked. I have an unobtrusive laptop—small screen, quiet keyboard—and I've found that as long as I touch-type while keeping my gaze mostly on my patient, it doesn't interfere with the flow of conversation. I like to ease the way with a bit of weather talk or a compliment about something in a new patient's home. Through the window, I could see a fog of steam, like God's breath, hovering over the icy surface of Lake Ontario.

"Do you think the lake will freeze?" I asked.

"It did the year my oldest brother was born," Eddie said.

Afterwards, I googled *has Lake Ontario ever frozen*, and he was right. I put that in my patient notes. I'm known for the thoroughness of my notes. In our practice, we record vitals and medications, but also moods, hopes, resentments, relatives' attitudes and a description of the home environment. These inform us of what's possible and desirable for our patients, so that we can do everything medically feasible to make the rest of their lives worth living and their deaths peaceful. It's what's best about my job—seeing patients light up when they realize that their existence has purpose, their essence still a viable proposition.

But Eddie didn't believe in beating around the bush.

"My niece was skeptical when I told her that you were coming to see me at home," he said. His niece—a dental assistant—had planned to be here, but, like me, she'd had car trouble and was running late. "Doctors don't make house calls anymore. Except when their patient is dying. That tells you something about our world, Dr. Connor." He laughed; he had breath for laughter because the metastases in his lungs were still just scattered cells. He wasn't wearing his dentures and when he laughed his face crinkled around his mouth. There was a wedding photograph on an end table. A young Eddie, shorter than his bride, but barrel-chested.

"Do you think you're dying?"

"I've got Stage 4 cancer." His voice was still deep.

"And you may have it for a while yet."

"No offence, Dr. Connor, but you can cut the crap."

"Call me Joan." From his file, I knew that Eddie was a widower with no children and lived on his own. He had issues with nausea, but he was dealing with the colostomy bag. His blood pressure was higher than I'd have liked, probably due to pain that required better management. I was observing him—skin, nails, lips—not only for signs of illness, but also temperament. He wore loose trousers that pulled above his shins, revealing shiny skin, an indication of edema. His abdomen was slightly distended. (Later, when I examined him, I'd palpate his belly to get a sense of how much of that was fat, fluid or tumour.) Ridges on his fingernails, still pink. A clean odour. He'd obviously bathed before I arrived, but he hadn't put in his teeth. I thought it was a statement.

I asked, "What's your understanding of your disease?" The answer would tell me how much his oncologist had been able to communicate and how much reality my new patient was able to tolerate.

"The cancer is in my gut, lymph nodes, liver and lungs. I'm going to die from the liver before the lungs get too bad. So . . . I'll be able to keep breathing?"

"I think so."

"I don't want to die on a ventilator."

"I'll make sure everyone knows that. We've got a DNR, but your nurse will bring you a DNI form to sign so it's in your record, and she'll go over everything that can be done to make you comfortable. I have to say, Eddie, it isn't often that patients talk with me about their end-of-life preferences at our first visit."

"When you're dying, you shouldn't wait until it's too late."

"You're sick, but active dying is a process. There's nothing I see to indicate that it's begun."

"A *process*. Like turning garbage meat into sausage." His tone was resentful, defiant, adolescent. My elderly patients often say they feel the same inside, that it shocks them to see wrinkles and liver spots in the mirror.

"Not garbage meat. You can't shock me, Eddie. I used to work as an emergency room physician. The ER isn't a nice place."

He pushed himself up to a semi-sitting position. He had the usual turkey neck of the old. A solid chin and a wide nose, cheeks thin but not gaunt, wisps of white hair above his ears. Deep-set eyes and glasses of an older style, square with black frames. "What made you go into this business, instead?"

I weighed how much to share. "Sometimes heroic efforts cause people needless suffering, and I hated that." My tone was more intense than I intended, and I softened it. "Palliative care is a different kind of medicine. We can have an hour or even longer for this appointment. There's no rush. What we're doing here is about the patient, not the meat."

The little dog jumped up on the sofa and lay down beside him. "Time has beaten me," Eddie said. "Even my wife wouldn't recognize me." He pointed to the row of portraits. "That's her, Lucy, the one on the far left nearest the window. In the red dress."

"She looks determined."

"She was."

"Who painted her?"

"I did."

"So you're an artist, Eddie."

"I wouldn't go that far." On his coffee table, there was a pile of books—*Masterpieces of Classical Chinese Art*, *Painting People*, *Kurelek: Collected Works*—and a magnifying glass on top of the pile. "I was a cutter in a shirt factory. The only reason I have a place like this is that a Hong Kong girl liked me and made her father bring me into his business. We got married, and I became his partner. Anyone can pick up a brush. Maybe even a doctor."

"Painting isn't that easy," I said.

He smiled for the first time, a stretch of lips, not revealing his unadorned gums.

"My father painted on weekends," I said, "and more often after he retired. It relaxed him." Like his Scotch, but with no ill effects on the liver.

Eddie shook his head. "No, no, I don't believe that. How could it be relaxing? Sitting on the toilet is relaxing. I miss it now with the bag . . . But art makes you see truth and that is no shit. When I first saw the paintings at the Louvre . . . Have you been there?"

"No." I hadn't gone anywhere in twenty years—I was afraid to fly and worried too much about what might happen at home in my absence. "What was it like?"

"For our honeymoon, my wife wanted Paris, so we went to Paris. She said, 'Eddie, you can't go to Paris and not see the Louvre. It will astonish you.' She was an educated woman, and I don't mean just because she went to college. You see that rock on top of the cabinet? When she found it, she picked it up and kept it. I asked her why. It's just a rock. She said, 'Eddie, it's volcanic rock.' We were in Colorado. It was our fifth anniversary? I'm not sure. She said, 'This came out of the centre of the earth. Imagine how far it's come.' Do you ever think about that?"

"I don't believe I have," I said.

"Before I started painting, I didn't either. Do you think my wife's up there somewhere, waiting for me?"

"The only opinion that matters is yours."

"If you're going to keep me company through this, don't you think you should at least tell me where you believe I'm going, Dr. Connor?"

"Would you like me to connect you with a chaplain?" I stopped because he was already pulling away inside himself, his gaze falling to his hands, his face slack. "I'm not trying to be evasive," I said, and he looked up at me again. "I want you to be able to trust me when I say I know something, so I can give you good care. And just because I'm around death and dying doesn't make me an expert on the afterlife."

"But you come closer than most people."

"That's true." The doctor who trained me in palliative care was religious; my sister was an unshakable atheist; my own beliefs shifted from day to day. "I can tell you what I've witnessed. That in the last few days before they die, people often talk to something or someone no one else can see. They talk about going home. It makes them happy."

"At least that's something to look forward to." The terrier batted his hand for attention. He scratched between its ears.

"Anything else you look forward to, Eddie?"

"Not really. I can't even paint anymore."

"Why not?"

"To stay on my feet in front of the easel, I have to hang on to my walker. I can't hold a brush at the same time. I'm too old to learn how to paint with my teeth."

"You'd have to put your teeth in first."

He smiled broadly, showing me his gums, and I laughed.

"What about a table easel?"

"I thought of it," he said. "But even if I had something like that and could sit, I'm too tired to paint."

"That must be frustrating."

He nodded.

"What makes for a better day?"

"When I can eat. I still like eating. My nieces are good cooks and they bring me food. There's an off-leash park near here where Claude can run around. If I could sit there in the spring. Will I still be here in the spring?"

"We can't make predictions. I can just say what your body is telling us right now. I have your latest scans, and I'll also examine you. Claude . . . named after Monet?"

Another smile.

"So, it sounds to me like we have three goals: eating well, getting to the park and being able to paint."

"You got a miracle in that bag? Or you want to call in the chaplain for that too?"

"Here's another idea. Your oncologist talked to you about FOLFOX."

"It's good if you don't need your fingers."

He was right—one of the nastier side effects of oxaliplatin (the *ox* of *FOLFOX*) is peripheral neuropathy, unpleasant sensations or numbness in fingertips and feet. "Is that why you refused treatment?"

"There are other pleasures I can do without too."

"FOLFOX on its own should be easier to tolerate than the combined chemo you had before. I wouldn't recommend it if I thought the hardship outweighed the benefit." I paused, giving him space to say more, but he just stroked the terrier's back with his old man's hand, so I continued. "People often talk about treatment giving them more time. What would more time mean for you?"

"What it could mean?" He shrugged. "After seventy-five, it goes in a flash. A little more or less doesn't matter."

"Anything in particular on the horizon?"

"My great-nephew wants me at his middle-school graduation. They give out awards."

"You must be special to him."

"You know what goes on special? Junk nobody needs. Do you have children?"

"No."

"Then we're both lucky. Kids cost a fortune and turn your hair grey with worry. And those are the good ones."

I glanced around the living room for something else to help me make a connection. "I see you have a chess set. Do you play often?"

"Sometimes. With the boy." He fell silent again, then said, "Maybe I'll do the chemo. But you have to promise me something."

"What?"

"If I do it, you have to come and paint with me. Don't worry—just once. So you can see if it's relaxing."

"It's a deal." I got my stethoscope and blood pressure cuff out of my bag. "What else do you enjoy?"

While I examined him, he talked about classic movies. I was just about done when a key turned in the door, and several people entered in a flurry of snow and chatter: his nieces and the great-nephew; I recognized them from the portraits on the wall. Once their outerwear was doffed, Niece One—the boy's mother—sent him into the den to watch TV.

"Terrible weather," she said to me. "I can't stand the cold."

"Awful," I said, though I'd been sleeping with the window open. "I'm Joan Connor, the physician from HCPC—Home-Centred Palliative Care. I'm glad you could make it today."

The nieces were blunt-nosed and grey-haired, and prone to talking over each other in rapid-fire bursts. Niece One, the dental assistant, moved around the living room, straightening and shifting things, while Niece Two headed for the kitchen, put a kettle on the stove and plugged in the rice cooker. All through my visits, their roles never varied. The tea-making niece had a more penetrating voice, like a train whistle. Before the kettle boiled, she'd covered pesticides, hormone disrupters, big pharma, and her church friend's lawyer, who cured his cancer with acupuncture and the hand-waving of an ex-priest who did spirit surgery, because it's the chemotherapy that kills you, she insisted. Doctors just blame it on the cancer. On that note, she set a tray with small cups and a teapot beside the books on the coffee table.

I've found that arguing with relatives who want your patient to take herbs or get mud wraps instead of medical treatment gets you nowhere. Focus on common ground, I tell my medical students. Look for tenderness and warmth. If you can't, you're not cut out for palliative care, because your hearts will turn to stone or break, knowing that you're going to lose every patient.

Niece One at last settled in a chair opposite me, a basket of pill bottles on her lap. Her grievances were pragmatic. "My uncle's walker has a wheel that turns in and locks, so it gets stuck on the carpet. I talked to ten people about getting it replaced but nothing is happening. And I can't get through to anyone at the hospital about coordinating his appointments. They've scheduled his MRI at the same time as the Wednesday clinic. I have all his prescriptions; here's the list." She handed it to me and turned toward her sister. "I changed Uncle's sheets. Kevin!" The boy appeared carrying a laundry bag, dropped it by the front door and retreated to the den.

With his nieces present, Eddie was more forthcoming about his symptoms: the pain, his bowel movements, his high blood pressure. As the women fussed, I asked questions: Dull or shooting pain? More after eating or after movement? I made notes and asked about allergies. The boy emerged from the den again to complain that he was bored, and his mother told him to play with the dog, but it whined and huddled against the old man's side. Eddie called the boy over and gave him five dollars for helping with the laundry. The boy pocketed it and said he could take out the garbage too, which he proceeded to do. I adjusted dosages, wrote out new prescriptions. Eddie went to the bathroom, aided by Niece One. It was a long way across the flooring and then the carpet, where the walker was harder to push. The tea-making niece turned sharply toward me. I'd seen that look before, and I braced myself for the attack.

"It was torture when Mum died," she said.

"What happened?" I asked.

She began with the all-too-common accusations: missed signs, the arrogance of the medical profession, the lack of a translator during testing procedures. I tell my students that the health care system is cumbersome. Patients and their families will lay whatever is wrong with it on them, and they shouldn't try to shift the blame because if they do, they'll be seen as defending everything that is hurting the patient. There will be no trust, and without trust, the relationship will be hostile. It's only by having an ally that the unbearable can be borne.

I nodded along as the story unfolded, murmuring sympathetically while Niece Two—Cecilia was her name—enumerated mistakes that piled on top of each other, then described in fierce detail her mother's grotesque suffering followed by her brutal hospital death. I'd heard it all before, or much the same, but there was something in her story—a detail—which one? Maybe it was how she took her sister's hand, the feel of their palms clasped, the heat of it, the sweatiness of it, that made me suddenly think of myself and my sister. The pair of us, pimpled and ignorant, stretched to the breaking. It was unexpected and inappropriate, this indulging in personal reflections. My patient and his family deserved the dignity of my full attention. And so I took a breath and shut away my memories.

"I'm so sorry," I said. "That must have been awful for you."

"When my father broke down, Uncle Eddie took care of us. Not Aunt Lucy. She wasn't maternal. He deserves better than this."

"What do you want for him, Cecilia?"

"Peace, not pain, and no strangers. At home, comfortable."

"That's my job. To keep him comfortable. Dying is usually a gentle process. It's easier than giving birth, because labour hurts and dying shouldn't. But it's like birth—there are signs it's coming."

"My sister thinks it should be in hospital. With experts. She also says it'll be easier to sell the condo because nobody wants to buy a place someone died in."

"Your sister is practical."

"You could say that. I just don't want him to go through what Mum did."

"He won't," I said. "Not if I can help it."

"Can you really help it?" Her tone was scornful, but I didn't take it personally. Many people have been scarred by a medical system that's ungentle in its zeal to cure while understaffed and underfunded.

"Most of my patients die at home," I said. "Their bodies weaken, but right up until their last moments, we can usually give them everything they need, including pain relief, medication for anxiety, even oxygen. However, if there's a complication—"

"Like Mum's pneumonia?" Cecilia asked.

"Yes—and when I've had to transfer patients to the hospital for intubation or other procedures that can only be done there, sometimes the patient isn't able to come home again. So, we make sure there's a plan for that too. If we know your uncle's wishes—and the family's—we'll have everything in place to implement them as far as possible. We support complementary therapies, except where they're contra-indicated. He could do acupuncture."

"Maybe. I've heard good things about vitamin IVs too. We'll see."

Cecilia got up then and carried my cup into the kitchen. I put away my laptop. Eddie was pushing the walker back across the carpet, Niece One—her name was Linda—following him. "Kevin!" she called, and the boy came out of the den to help. He crouched in front of the walker, unjammed the wheel lock, then crab-walked backwards in case his assistance was required again. When his great-uncle was lying on the couch again, Kevin threw himself at Eddie's feet. The dog jumped into his lap. Linda bent to wipe a drop of spit from the corner of her uncle's mouth, then seated herself across from Cecilia, who poured her a cup of tea. Their affection was palpable; even as an outsider I was warmed by it.

After reminding Eddie and his nieces how to reach me, I made my departure, wondering what my sister and I would see in each other when we were old and sitting together at a kitchen table.

There are 37 trillion cells in the human body, constantly replicating. Red blood cells have a life of four months. Cells in the small intestine last four days. Taste buds ten. Fat cells renew a few at a time—it takes eight years for a complete changeover. So, when Vivien and I were at the table in that future time, every cell in our bodies would be new. Could we speak, then, of what we'd lost?

CHAPTER 2

saw four other patients that day. At the end of it, I hoped my car would start. It was a hatchback and silver, the colour least likely to be involved in an accident. I didn't love it. I'd learned very young that it's best not to love things, because you lose a part of yourself when they are taken from you.

Darkness had settled on other cars in the parking lot, muddying them to a uniform dullness, but mine glinted under a street lamp. My car was immaculate. It had to be so I could take my mother to her appointments—she wouldn't step foot in it, otherwise. I unlocked the door and climbed in, turned the key in the ignition, and after a few seconds of sputtering, the engine settled into a purr. Waiting for the windshield to defrost, I scrolled through the notifications on my phone. A real estate newsletter from an old friend named Augie. Delete. News headlines. Scan and swipe. A text message from a colleague asking for a ride to our team meeting. I replied, *No problem. Pick you up at 8*. I put it in my calendar along with Vivien's call, on the off chance that she'd make it.

In the village clinic where she worked, access to internet and electricity was unreliable.

Confession: I don't do highways. I have a horror of going fast. Instead of taking the Gardiner Expressway and the Don Valley, I headed out of downtown on city streets. While I drove, I listened to *Docs Outside the Box*, my shoulders tightening as streets widened and houses were spaced farther apart. Getting closer to home.

I lived with my mother in the suburban bungalow where I was raised in East York, a neighbourhood squeezed between prosperous old Toronto and scruffier Scarborough. Most of the neighbours on our street were elderly. They'd all moved in when the development was new and having a house with your own yard was exciting. When my parents, Sheila and Hugh Connor, bought our back-split bungalow, my mother was beautiful and my father hopeful enough to plant trees, overriding her aversion to the mess of falling leaves, though he didn't go as far as flowers or vegetables because they attracted bugs, which made her shudder.

Dad, a veteran of the Second World War, was twelve years older than Mom. When she started working for him as a receptionist, she thought he was glamorous—a former pilot!—and she looked up to him. Her father had been an angry drunk, and she'd never known what it was like to feel safe with a man until she met Dad, who never hit anyone no matter how wasted he got. Dad felt incredibly lucky to have a gorgeous young thing like Sheila on his arm when they went dancing. After they married, Dad wanted a son but loved his girls, especially his first, my sister, who'd clenched his finger with her tiny fist as if she'd hold on to it through eternity, her innocent trust a sign that the war hadn't broken everything. Neither of my parents grasped that what they valued in the other was intertwined with trauma. Dad had nightmares about friends who'd been shot down. Mom had insomnia. To cope, he drank and she cleaned.

Dad was in business with his best friend, "Uncle" Jack to us. A war buddy, Jack had been a navigator in Dad's bomber squadron, an RAF unit with a mix of Canadians, Brits and Aussies. After the war, Dad and Uncle Jack had looked around for something to do and pooled their resources to acquire a colour printing press, which became J&H Printing ("Producing Flyers and Brochures You Want to Frame"). Uncle Jack was short and broad-shouldered, a good dancer. He had wives, not all at once, but in sequence. The first, Aunt Peggy, had been Mom's closest friend. A year after Aunt Peggy died, Jack married again and had two sons—Augie and his big brother, Steve. A divorce followed, then another marriage. Through it all, he and the boys remained in their house and we remained in ours, across the street from each other.

Uncle Jack had bought his first. Then Dad talked to the developer about building a back-split for us with large windows. (Ever since being confined in those bomber cockpits, Dad avoided closed-in spaces.) The printing business did well enough to support us, and eventually the sale of it funded Dad's retirement. But what had initially seemed like a lot of money dwindled over time. After he drank himself to death, I moved back home to help Mom out. I told Vivien it would just be until Mom adjusted and we figured out her finances. My sister, who'd made it her life's work to stay as far from home as possible, had laughed. That was twenty years ago.

Mom couldn't stand the garage being cluttered with stuff, even a car, so I parked in the driveway. At the door, I stamped my feet on the doormat to loosen any grit. Then I unlocked the front door, pushed it open, kicked off one boot, stepped over the threshold with the unshod foot, hung on to the door while I repeated the process with the other foot, picked up both boots and wiped the soles with the cloth in the pail beside the doormat, then returned the cloth and placed the boots on the mat inside the entrance.

Mom stood there, watching the procedure anxiously. "Did you wipe your boots thoroughly?" she couldn't help asking.

"Yes, of course."

She was wearing the bathrobe I'd bought for her. It was soft and warm and I thought she'd enjoy it for a little while at least.

"Give me the rag. I'll do it again."

"You don't need to."

Mom was already reaching for the rag. She picked up a boot and scrubbed the sole—still the mom I'd always known. Even congestive heart failure couldn't stop her.

"Wait till you see," she said, wheezing as she set the boot down and wiped the other one.

"See what?"

"The living room."

"I can't wait." I pulled the messenger bag off my shoulder, hung my coat in the hall closet and settled the bag on the floor below it.

"I did it this time."

"What did you do, Mom?"

"Look." She shuffled the few steps to the living room. "It's perfection."

"You always say that."

"But this time it's just right. Don't you think so?"

The living room floor was bare, the subfloor exposed as it had been since I was a teenager and Mom ripped up the carpet. In the middle of the otherwise empty room sat a white leather recliner. It matched the blank walls, also white.

My mother had been a tidy child. She'd shared a room with her sister, who was not, and they'd fought about it until my aunt moved to Australia. Mom was lonely without her, but at least she had the room all to herself. It was her sanctuary. She found solace there after her father's rampages and she forgot all her problems when she worked on improving it. That was her hobby, her preoccupation. She'd move things around, sand furniture, and paint, making sure all objects gleamed. Still, she never considered throwing everything out to start fresh. That came later, and when it did, a new realm of obsession opened to her.

The mom I knew had a volatile relationship with the stuff of life: her possessions, ours, and how to contain them. When she felt secure, making sure the house was immaculate kept her satisfied. But stress made her other compulsion flare. This disorder—compulsive spartanism—is the opposite of hoarding, but like hoarding, it's difficult to treat because it seems so reasonable to the person in its grip, even socially acceptable.

Doesn't everybody love Marie Kondo? My mother was Marie Kondo on steroids. In certain moods, she'd look around the house and decide that everything in it was junk and clutter that was sucking the air out of the place, making her sick. Soon, she'd feel like the walls were closing in on her and she had to make space. So, she would purge, slowly to begin with, then in a panic.

First, she'd give away clothes that didn't fit, books she wouldn't read, gifts she had no use for. Still feeling claustrophobic, she'd return her most recent purchases. After that, she'd discard everything that wasn't absolutely necessary. I tried to anticipate what was necessary and what wasn't, but Mom's ever-expanding definition of *junk* always caught me off guard.

When she was done, all our things swept away, she'd relax. A cleared house was a blessed house. It was a world before creation with the potential to be made perfect. In a house stripped to the walls, Mom could ponder her next move. Nothing would be decided until she was sure of doing it right, her restlessness building. Eventually, she'd erupt in a flurry of activity and an influx of acquisitions. Her enthusiasm was infectious, and until the spending got out of control, it amused my father. When she was done redecorating, she'd be so pleased. We'd all hope it would last. And it would. For a while. Then the cycle repeated.

As a child, I'd find Mom standing at the window, hyperventilating or crying, and I'd try to comfort her, believing that she wanted to create the perfect home because she loved us so much. My sister scoffed at that. She said stuff came into the house just so Mom could have the satisfaction of getting rid of it: pictures hung to be removed, nails pulled out, the walls repainted white. It was only later, after Vivien left home, that I realized my mother was as addicted to her compulsion as my father was to drink, which was why, when she had no more things of her own to throw away, she went after others'.

Sometimes she denied it. I'd ask her, "What happened to my pencil case?" and she'd say, "What pencil case?" I'd tell her, "The pink zippered one. I wrote my name on it, I drew a flower on it at school, with a Magic Marker," and she'd say, "You never had a pencil case like that. I don't remember it at all." She'd sound so sure, I'd wonder if I'd dreamt it. If the flower and the name weren't real, then maybe I wasn't either until someone made me so.

Mom did that kind of clearing out at night. She was stealthy, gliding into rooms and sliding out drawers that she scanned with a penlight. I didn't think it was strange until Augie, the younger of Uncle Jack's sons, came for a sleepover. I was six, in first grade, and Vivien was nine. It wasn't long after the first moon landing, the wonder of it still occupying a place of honour in my mind. Lying in the darkness, with Augie asleep in the other twin bed, I watched my mother drift in, wearing white pyjamas; she looked like the grainy image of an astronaut in the moonscape, and I felt a kind of pride in her. Someone out of the ordinary. Floating. A higher being glimpsed dimly like a space walker or a fairy, gracing the earth but not of it. I went back to sleep, the smell of trees and the creek wafting from the ravine behind our yard.

The next morning, after we woke up but weren't yet out of bed, Augie asked, "What was your mother doing?" Clearly, he hadn't been asleep. The question made me feel like one of the weird kids who had accidents in class. Panicking, I told him that Mom had to practise sneaking around because she was a space spy. It seemed like a plausible explanation, I thought—the moon was free of clutter, and so Mom would like it there.

Augie said, "I don't believe you."

Vivien appeared in the doorway. She wasn't beautiful yet—we were both ordinary and nearly as alike as twins. Even our parents could mistake a picture of Vivien at five for me before I needed glasses. I saw my sister as a bigger, badder self with perfect vision.

She said, "Mom was testing her new invisibility spray. Where are you, Augie?"

She walked blindly forward and dropped onto the bed on top of him. I was amazed that she'd chosen my side over a boy's, especially one of Uncle Jack's. Augie cried. Dad took him home.

When Dad came back, my parents had what they called a discussion. Mom discussed punishing Vivien with no TV for a week, and Dad discussed that his kid was just standing up for her little sister and she wouldn't have had to do that if Mom didn't prowl through the house at night. Mom wanted to know why he always took Vivien's side, why he'd been at Uncle Jack's for so long, and whether he'd been drinking. Dad had fewer questions: he just wanted to know if she was planning to replace everything that had disappeared from the kitchen and overdraw their bank account again. As usual, the discussion occurred at high volume, and Mom cried.

While they were at it, I lay on my bed, fingers plugging my ears, face squashed into my pillow. Then Vivien tapped my shoulder and shoved a tiny teddy bear at me. It had movable legs. It had happy eyes. Vivien said, "Put that in your pocket and let's go." We crept down to the basement and out the back door, ran across our lawn to the ravine. The trail we followed led us up on a ridge above the creek, which then gradually sloped back down. No houses could be seen from there. Nothing but trees and the creek. We saw a fox cross the trail and trot into the bushes. We listened to crickets. We tried to skip rocks on the water.

By the time we got home, it was as if the argument had never happened. There was music on the hi-fi, and our parents were swaying to it. Mom's eyes were dreamy, her arms around Dad's neck. He had one hand on the small of her back, the other cupping her head, which rested on his shoulder. When I went to the bathroom, I saw their bed was unmade and knew that meant Dad would be grilling burgers for dinner so Mom could relax and do her crossword. It did not mean I could skip my bath after dinner.

I needed to find a hiding place for the teddy bear. During bath time, Mom would put my clothes in the washing machine, first emptying the pockets and tossing out any junk. I wasn't sure whether a small teddy bear was junk, but I suspected that it could be. The best place to hide something was in the basement. It was Dad's place, and Mom wasn't allowed to touch anything down there, not the old radio or his bookcase or the Ping-Pong table or his chair, and especially not the locked cabinet where Dad kept his Scotch. I could have hidden something small in the cabinet if I found the key, but I was too scared to go down to the dark basement. Instead, I slid the happy teddy under my pillow, forgetting that my mother would find it when she changed the sheets, which she also did during bath time.

As soon as I was in bed that evening, I reached under the pillow, but my skinny, scrabbling hand felt nothing. I should have taken the teddy to the basement. Vivien wouldn't have been scared of the dark. Why had she given a present to someone as careless as me? *I didn't deserve it*, I thought, and then, *Maybe I just dreamt it, like the pink pencil case.* I wanted to ask Vivien if she remembered giving it to me, but I was afraid she'd say no. Feeling sick to my stomach, I got up and tore the corner of a page in the school exercise book where I'd been practising printing. On it, I drew something like a teddy bear and wrote, *Vivien.* As I kissed it, a spark passed between myself and the bit of paper. I folded it into a tiny square and hid it in a crack under my window ledge. Knowing it was safe, I fell asleep.

Dad left for work early the next morning, as he always did, and Mom stayed in bed. So, Vivien fixed us breakfast, pouring me a bowl of my favourite cereal, Frosted Flakes, and adding a handful of Smarties. I ate quickly before the flakes got mushy, the double hit of sugar coating my tongue while I read the back of the cereal box. (I loved Tony the Tiger, who looked like a happy drunk and was always saying, "Grrrreat!") Then I asked Vivien how to spell *pencil case* and wrote it on another scrap of paper, which I slid into the hiding place in my room. Vivien didn't make fun of me, but told me that when I ran out of space for my scraps under the windowsill, I should get an extra school notebook from my teacher and keep it in my schoolbag. Vivien was still in a good mood, so we walked to school together. I imagined that she carried an invisible, magic umbrella, and I had nothing to worry about as long as I was near her.

I knew better than to tell my mother that the white recliner wasn't any improvement over the furniture she'd gotten rid of. So, I just asked, "Is it comfortable?"

"Very. I ordered it online. Same day delivery."

As I put an arm around her, I looked down at the top of her head and noticed how much her hair had thinned, the vulnerable pink scalp showing through.

"Are you hungry, Mom?"

"A little."

"Pasta?"

"Sounds good. I wouldn't mind the paper now."

"Okay."

She got settled in the recliner while I opened the front door and leaned out to reach the mailbox. I always left the newspaper in the box until she asked for it, so she wouldn't be bothered by it lying around. For the same reason, I dealt with the mail after she went to sleep. These were small things that kept Mom calm with so little effort from me.

When I gave her the newspaper, she said, "Have you heard from Vivien?"

"Not really." There was no reason to tell my mother about the Skype call. She'd just be disappointed if it didn't happen. Over the years, Vivien had kept her distance, visiting every couple of years before Dad died and less often afterwards.

"I sent her a message, but she hasn't answered," Mom said. Through every clearing, she was careful to hang on to her phone so she could stay in touch with my sister. It was a necessity—unlike, say, furniture or Advil. Mom's naked need pierced me with its poignancy.

"She must not have internet where she is," Mom said.

"Or else the electricity's gone out." There was always that excuse.

"True."

"And I'm here."

"Yes, you are," she said, her face still full of longing.

"Dinner will be ready soon, Mom."

There was pasta sauce in the fridge from a big batch I'd made on the weekend. Over the fridge, in a cabinet too high for her to reach, I kept a large stainless-steel pot and a couple of smaller ones, along with a kitchen knife, the blender and the food processor, so I wouldn't have to replace them when Mom got into her next clearing phase. I took down a couple of the pots, filled the larger one with water and set it on the stove to boil.

I often had imaginary conversations with Vivien while cooking dinner. I'd start off with something like, *What harm is there in stashing a pair of folding chairs and collapsible trays in the trunk of my car so that we always have something to eat dinner on?* Or . . . *Mom isn't fussy about the bathrooms anymore. She just cleans the one in her room and leaves the other one to me as long as I keep the door closed.*

I thought Vivien would say, *She doesn't have the energy, that's all.* And I would say, *What's the difference, she's mellowed. It's been too long since you've seen her. Come home, at least for a short visit. Mom misses you.* Even in my head, I wouldn't admit how much I missed Vivien too—that I had never gotten over her deserting me, that I'd never understood why she had, that it haunted me. I glanced out the window, but all I could see in the winter darkness was my reflection. Against the imperfect mirror of night, it looked like my sister's.

As soon as the water came to a boil, I threw in two handfuls of spaghetti. In the other pot, I poured sauce and set it on a burner to warm. I got a can of chickpeas from the pantry to add some protein. But when I pulled open the utensils drawer to find the can opener, it was empty. This morning the drawer had been full. Now, nothing. No can opener. No spatula or tongs or salad servers. The sudden void reminded me of a recurring dream: coming home from school to find my house gone, a single brick left on the lawn.

I was confused and upset. My mother was in the collecting phase. She'd just *bought* a piece of furniture. The only reason she didn't drive me totally crazy was that I could depend on the methodical nature of her obsession. Fill, fill, fill. All done, then rest. After a while, clear, clear, clear. It was as predictable as that death follows dying, and the predictability made life with Mom bearable.

When I walked into the living room, I saw her sitting in the recliner, footrest up, legs stretched out, reading the newspaper. She wrote letters to the editor. Sometimes they were printed, but of course Mom never kept a copy. She was happy just knowing that her views had been published. In her letters—like the one about needing a street light at the corner—she came across as articulate and reasonable. She'd always been able to maintain a facade for outsiders. To her cardiologist, Mom was a neatly dressed old lady, spry for someone with such a serious heart condition, intelligent, wry. To her hairdresser, she was the customer who tipped fifty dollars at Christmas. Mom was well-spoken, she donated money to conservation efforts, and she loved the beauty of wild animals, so long as they had the sense to remain at a suitable distance.

"Mom! What happened to the can opener?"

"It wasn't any good." She folded back the newspaper and put pen to the crossword as if the conversation was over, the obvious having been declared.

"It worked fine!"

"It left too sharp an edge on the can."

"Because it's a can opener."

"I was worried you'd cut yourself. I'm going to order one of those new ones that go around the side instead of through the top. It's better. No sharp edge."

"And the spatula?"

"What?" My mother had some hearing loss, which she invoked at convenient times.

I raised my voice. "The spatula. That's sharp too? And the wooden spoon?"

"Soft plastic is full of carcinogens. Wood splinters. Do I really have to point out the risks? You're a physician, for heaven's sake."

"I cook for you every night, Mom. I need a can opener."

"You know I can't stand junk." My mother's eyes cooled. All my life, I'd backed away from that look. It said, *Threaten my spartan space and I can get rid of you too; I'll clear you out of my life like a carcinogenic spatula.* "Seriously, how can you live with it? If you don't care about me, you should at least have some self-respect."

"Do you hear yourself?"

"You're shouting." Mom put her hand on her heart.

It was a gesture that went back to my earliest memories, a stop sign that I obeyed as I did all rules of the road. Vivien was the rule-breaker, the vagabond, the one whose scarce and brief communications my mother longed for. Not Joan, good old Joan. Even indentured servants were released after seven years; I'd been here for twenty. I'd given up my home, a good man, the stepdaughter I'd loved—suspended my life to take care of hers.

This time I couldn't stop. "What's next, Mom? My book-case? My bed? Are you going to give it to Goodwill? It won't be the first time."

Mom shook her head.

"I put a lock on my door once. I can do it again."

"Don't, Joanie, don't." Mom was breathing quickly now, her nostrils pinched. "I can't stand locked doors."

"Patients depend on me. I have to eat. I have to sleep."

"I know." Mom was wheezing, trying to catch her breath and failing. She reached into her pocket for the inhaler, put it in her mouth, pressed the release button and breathed in. It didn't help and Mom's eyes watered with effort as she sucked air. My anger collapsed.

I said, "Mom, forget it. Just breathe."

She put the inhaler in her mouth again. The lines of old age formed a ruffled ridge above her pursed lips, a serrated cliff below it. A hair grew on the cliff. She'd forgotten to pluck it and would be mortified if she realized I'd noticed.

I said, "I'll get over to Metro and pick up some takeout."

Mom nodded. She breathed. Her eyes dried up. She tried to smile and the effort of it was worse than when she was trying to catch a breath.

I opened the closet door and pulled my coat off the hanger.

"Just remember," Mom called, "no chicken, dear. They're defecation machines."

At the car, I paused to get hold of myself. The back seat of my hatchback was down to extend the cargo space. It had enough room for everything we'd need if my mother emptied the house. An extra-large bag of road salt to deal with ice on the walk; folding chairs and trays; a queen-sized air mattress in a bag; an ultralight double sleeping bag that rolled up into a pack smaller than a basketball; toiletries; a change of clothes for me and one for Mom; a pair of stainless steel camp sets with cup, bowl, and cutlery on a ring; a crate of liquid meal substitute (strawberry—the only kind my mother would drink); and a painting by my father—a small one of me and my sister playing in the ravine—packed in bubble wrap for protection. All of it was tucked under a tarp, neatly tied so that Mom wouldn't see any of it when I took her to appointments. Slung over my shoulder, the messenger bag—which I always kept near—held smaller, crucial items: not only my laptop and medical gear, but a travel kit, my wallet, reading glasses and the key to my storage locker. In my pocket: phone, car keys. Minimal living. Didn't people take courses to figure out how to do that?

I drove to the twenty-four-hour Metro and picked up a couple of vacuum-packed frozen dinners, as well as a couple of can openers, one for home and the other to keep in the car. I checked my phone. There was just enough time to get back, heat up dinner, and clean the kitchen to Mom's standards before Vivien called.

CHAPTER 3

My sister and I fought throughout our childhood. Over the last slice of peach pie, the top plate in a stack of identical plates, who got to use the bathroom first. Of course we fought: we were sisters and we were so different. Vivien played Ping-Pong with Dad, they watched hockey games together, she hung around him and his friends. She liked the timbre of male voices, the smell of their cigars, the greasy food they ate, the sips of beer they gave her, the slap of cards when they played poker at Uncle Jack's, the hair-raising stories they told.

Dad and Uncle Jack and their veteran friends would drink and place bets—penny stakes, none of them were rich—and regale each other with memories of the air base in Yorkshire. When they'd drunk enough, they'd mourn their lost comrades. Mom didn't like Uncle Jack. Out of his hearing, she called him "that little Jew" and Dad let her. He called Uncle Jack a little Jew too, but it sounded different coming from him, usually after several glasses of Scotch, as in, "Other guys didn't make it back, but we had our Jack. Just follow the little Jew, he'll get us home."

Dad's parents, like Uncle Jack's, were working-class immigrants, Dad's from Britain, Uncle Jack's from Poland. They couldn't afford to send their kids to college, needing them to go out to work as soon as they could. In the Royal Air Force, men from their background were usually ground crew. If someone showed aptitude, he might become a gunner or a navigator, like Uncle Jack, but rarely a pilot. In his unit, Dad had a reputation for nerve under fire. His parents were proud of him—he'd even won a medal. But at dinner parties held for the pilots by local English notables, the others in his squadron were witty and worldly, while Dad sat like a lump, tongue-tied, knowing they all thought he was beneath them.

A few months into his service, Dad began to fly under the command of a fellow Canadian, Captain Edwin, who came from money but—being gay—was something of an outsider himself. He befriended Dad and Uncle Jack, and the three of them would take off in Captain Edwin's car to the nearest city, Leeds, to make the most of their leave. For Captain Edwin, a painter, that meant art galleries, jazz clubs, opera and theatre, and he introduced Dad and Jack to all of it.

After the war, Captain Edwin became a professional artist, living year-round in a cottage on the shore of a lake north of Toronto, where Dad and Uncle Jack were welcomed as brothers. Uncle Jack went for the fishing, but with Captain Edwin's encouragement, Dad started painting there. He looked different at the easel, his face more expressive. I'd wonder about that, and why, when people set off fireworks for holidays, he would stiffen and go blank—I knew nothing about PTSD back then. All the time I was growing up, he continued to paint at the cottage, where messes were allowed, just like they were at Uncle Jack's house.

When I was little, Mom came up to the cottage too. In the twilight of a summer evening, she'd sit near the campfire with me on her lap while Vivien toasted marshmallows. Nursing his beer—it was only ever beer at the cottage—Dad would direct my sister: "Viv, honey, not in the fire, point the stick down near the coals so your marshmallow doesn't burn." I'd nag my father to tell us a Barky story. He'd pretend to be too tired until I begged, promising not to interrupt, though inevitably I would, unable to stand the suspense: "Oh no, Daddy, are they going to get caught?"

They were his own invention, stories about the dangerous escapades of Barky the dog, Chippy the chipmunk, and Wingy the butterfly. Wingy was the leader, flying ahead to search for the Bad Guys who'd invaded the forest. When they were found, Chippy would get inside their pant legs and bite, and Barky would pretend to be a Bad Guy dog and lure them toward a camouflaged pit. Barky was always trying to keep Chippy out of trouble, especially when he got distracted by a cute chipmunk (Uncle Jack would snort at that), but they always prevailed, and Dad would say, "The end. Until next time." Then Vivien and I would brush our teeth and go to the kids' room in the cottage, which had two sets of bunk beds, and talk to Augie and Steve until we all fell asleep.

By the time I was nine, Mom preferred to stay home and clean in peace. The rest of us went up in Uncle Jack's station wagon, and because I got carsick, I had to sit in the front seat while Vivien and the boys squeezed in back. When we pulled out of Uncle Jack's driveway, I'd see Mom standing on the porch by herself. She'd look so solitary, waving goodbye, that I'd feel guilty about abandoning her. All weekend, I'd jot down in my diary everything that bothered me about being at the cottage: mosquito bites, the toe-sucking squishiness of the lake bottom, smelly boys. Convincing myself I didn't like anything about cottage life, I ended up staying indoors, playing Candy Land by myself.

Vivien wasn't bothered by the lake bottom. Like Dad, she loved the water, and they'd dive off the dock, competing to see who could swim underwater the longest without taking a breath. Sometimes, Dad let her win. When she crowed and punched the air, his smile was ear to ear. On rainy days, she drew pictures of animals that she copied from an encyclopedia that belonged to Captain Edwin. Dad kept one framed on his desk at work. Years later, I found it—a drawing of a whale—in Uncle Jack's attic. Stuck to the back of it was a photograph of me and Vivien playing Candy Land.

Until I saw the picture, I'd forgotten all about that day. At breakfast, Vivien had said that if I went into the water that morning, she'd spend the whole afternoon inside with me, playing board games. She bet I wouldn't. I said I would, but after she went out, I thought about it for so long I figured that by the time I walked down to the lake, put my towel on the sand, my glasses on the towel, and blindly tiptoed into the water, she'd given up on me. Vivien and the boys were heads bobbing in the distance, but when I called, she swam back to me. She got me to dunk so we could talk like whales underwater, making bubbles with our speech. We came up for air and sank down again. I opened my eyes and saw my future self reflected in my sister, what I could and should become, hair lightened by the sun, skin darkened by it, impervious to lake monsters hiding in the muck. I reached out with my hands and Vivien took them. I kicked out my legs and we floated nose to nose until we ran out of breath.

In my storage locker, I have a few photographs that I managed to save from Mom's clearing. If there were more, I could have remembered other things. If I'd remembered, then maybe I'd have understood Vivien, and I could have found a way to bring her back to me.

No matter how much we squabbled, Vivien and I had always been on the same side. It didn't matter that she found reading tedious and the only subjects she liked were Gym and French, while I was a bookworm who loved every subject but those, or that she was Dad's favourite and I wasn't—we'd had each other's backs. But during the fall when I was nine, she changed. I don't know which came first, Mom refusing to go to the cottage or Dad drinking more heavily. I realized later that he'd just learned that his RAF squadron had dropped bombs on civilians—not factories, as he'd believed—and he started having nightmares about mothers and babies buried under rubble. It felt like our family was falling apart.

Vivien had hit puberty. She was always fighting with Mom over how long she was on the phone, what time she had to come home, how she got home, who her friends were. She hated her clothes, she hated her hair. She took the bus downtown by herself to go to a rock concert. The next time, she got a ride with older friends. Every so often, Mom said to me, "At least I don't have to worry about *you*," and I lived for the rare sugar jolt of her attention.

My mother had no emotional support. She hadn't had any close friends since Aunt Peggy died. My father was always at work or drinking, sometimes at Uncle Jack's, other times down in the basement while he listened to the radio.

Once in a while, he made an effort to stay sober, have dinner with us and play Ping-Pong with Vivien. But it didn't last, which seemed to make Mom angrier than if he hadn't tried at all. She'd stalk through the house, eyes blazing as she examined the things in it.

One night between Christmas and New Year's, Dad didn't come home. Even Uncle Jack didn't know where he was. I wrote over and over in my diary—five pages of it— *Please God, don't let Dad be dead*, while Mom called every hospital in Toronto. The next morning, Dad walked in with bowed shoulders as if he was carrying a tragedy, but all that had happened was he'd stayed in a bar till closing and then passed out in his car.

Mom said it was a miracle he hadn't frozen to death.

Not long after, she said the Ping-Pong table took up too much space and sold it to a neighbour, trespassing in Dad's space for the first time. Then she sold the dining table and the couch too. For Vivien's thirteenth birthday, Mom ordered pizza and cake, and there was a brief truce. We had a birthday picnic on a blanket laid out on the living room floor. Dad had soda unmixed with alcohol, and we played Vivien's favourite records. After the next time he got drunk, Mom sold the hi-fi. The records, which she said were scratched, went to Goodwill before Vivien could object.

On a cold Saturday, with Dad absent as usual, I wrote in my diary: *February 3rd, 1973. It snowed this morning. Vivien came home with a stray cat. I think it was white but it's hard to say for sure under the dirt. It was big. It scratched her. She didn't mind. If she was a cat she would scratch too. I'm not a cat. I'm a fox. I look like a girl, but I'm really a fox. You can't tell what someone is just by looking at them. That's the secret.*

The cat was loud and furry, and as soon as Vivien put it down, it ran madly, banging into walls and yowling.

Mom said, "Are you trying to give me a heart attack?"

Vivien yelled, "Other kids have pets! You don't let me have anything."

"Vivien Leigh Connor, you get rid of that filthy animal."

"He's not! I won't! He's mine, and he's beautiful."

"You'll do as I say."

"Why should I?" By now, the cat was crouched in a corner, back arched, fur on end, hissing. "You want him too, don't you, Roo?" That had been her nickname for me when we were little. From Joan to Joey, and when she learned that a joey is a baby kangaroo, to Roo.

I glanced from my sister to my mother, not wanting to choose. "I don't know."

Mom's face was drawn. "I can't do this." She put her hand on her heart.

Cat hair was already floating in the sunbeams that came through the window, warming the living room as if it wasn't well below freezing outside. Clumps of cat hair settled like dandelion fluff. The pallor in my mother's face frightened me, and so I dragged out the vacuum cleaner, a heavy old brown Hoover that I'd never used before. I plugged it in and pushed it back and forth across the carpet, desperate to get rid of the cat hair before Mom's heart gave out. The cat fled from the Hoover, tearing across the carpet and then skittering along the wood floor of the hallway.

Mom escaped to the backyard. I found her lying in the snow without a coat. I lay beside her, putting my head on her chest so I could listen to her heart and make sure it was still beating. I kissed my mother's hand. She smelled of soap, something lemony, as she touched my cheek. It could have been summer except for the snow and the wind.

Inside the house, Vivien was calling, "Kitty, Kitty, I love you!"

That afternoon, Dad returned home from wherever he'd been, caught the cat and carried it away while Vivien moped in her room. When I knocked on her door and opened it a crack, she growled, "Go away!"

To celebrate Valentine's Day that year, Vivien got herself the first of her tattoos. She'd looked up tattooing in the library and made a boy do it in exchange for a sexual favour. The way she put it to me was, "A boy will do anything for a girl if she's *nice* to him." Though I didn't understand what she meant by *nice*, I felt it in the heat of my face.

The tattoo was a *V* for Vivien or victory. It was small, blue, on her upper left arm. No one could take it away. At school, in the girls' washroom, I sat in a stall and used a ballpoint pen to draw a *J* on my arm. I knew that I'd never be brave enough to ink it with a needle. I wasn't like my sister— I wouldn't be able to withstand the look of disgust and disappointment on my mother's face.

That wasn't long after the last moon landing. In school, I was learning that the moon is actually blanketed with dust, called regolith, which formed when rocks were broken into minuscule fragments by the impact of meteorites. The layers of regolith are as deep as several men stacked on top of each other. Without atmosphere or water flow to wear them down, the dust particles are jagged and sharp. Astronauts tracked it into their spaceship, and the fine bits scratched their lungs when they breathed them in. I imagined my family on the dead moon and my mother clearing the spaceship of its dust, coughing as she worked to save us from harm.

I stopped going to the cottage then, staying home instead to keep Mom company so she wouldn't be sad. Vivien kept going and started rowing across the lake to explore the other side. In another year, she was routinely breaking curfew. My father got control of his drinking and then lost it; my mother cycled through the phases of her compulsion. Vivien acted indifferent to it all. For her, there were more tattoos, cigarettes, flasks, weed. The bigger the reaction, the more it energized her—proof she was her own person. At fifteen, she had an older boyfriend from Quebec who had a prison record and helped her with French. After she dumped him, she got involved in protesting seal hunts and was picked up by police for throwing paint on a woman's mink. (Dad cashed in his life insurance to replace the coat and the charges were dropped.) The worse she behaved, the better I did, which only made me less visible. The harder I tried to get my old sister back, the further she receded.

I knew Vivien was working the night shift in a village clinic in the Democratic Republic of the Congo. Ten o'clock came and went without her call. By midnight, which was six in the morning her time, I'd finished editing and uploading my patient notes, sitting cross-legged on my bed. I was just about to close my laptop when Skype burbled. I accepted the call, and Vivien's face came into view. How long since I'd seen her in person? Three years—no, closer to four. She'd stayed for a day, on her way to a conference in Buffalo.

"I'd given up on you," I said.

"I couldn't get here any earlier."

Even with the lag and blur of poor WiFi and a low-resolution webcam, my sister was vivid. Her tattoos: birds of paradise on the right arm and poisonous amphibians on the left. The blue-inked *V* was now embedded in the tongue of a frog. Her hair was burgundy and her nose sunburned, her cheeks were pink and her eyes blue as a doll's. She wore a white T-shirt and denim shorts. Behind her, I could see yellow curtains and a vase of flowers on a filing cabinet.

"What happened?" I asked.

"There was a motorcycle accident. Young guy, maybe nineteen. No internal bleeding, but he has an open femoral shaft fracture. And the other leg smashed to bits."

"The clinic isn't equipped for that."

"His friends brought him here because he can't afford the hospital. It makes me so angry. We did the best we could for him, which amounts to a patch job and giving him antibiotics."

"At least it's a change for you."

"It was—all I've done recently is deliver babies. What about you? How's work?"

"I started with a new patient today," I said. "Crabby but interesting. I like him. His family not so much. His niece wants him to do vitamin IVs instead of chemo."

"Canadians are spoiled. They don't appreciate free health care. Why didn't you answer my email?"

"You sent pictures. I didn't know you expected an answer."

"Even on my birthday?"

"I didn't forget." (I just wanted to see if she cared.) "I was busy and now I can tell you in person. Happy birthday!"

"I'm not too busy to write *you*."

"Well." Sometimes she worked for weeks at a time in remote places where communication was impossible. I'd reassure Mom that Vivien was fine, while I'd pray for her safe return, hoping there was a God to hear me. "It would be nice if you'd visit."

"You could meet me halfway. Morocco or even Spain."

"Why Spain?" I'd never told her how bad my anxiety about flying had gotten.

"Raoul taught me some Spanish. *Cómo estás? Que te folle un pez.* I'll buy the tickets."

For my fortieth birthday, she'd promised a holiday together in Cuba, and in case she'd meant it, I tried hypnotherapy to conquer my fear. It didn't work, but that was fine—Vivien never had time for the holiday. I wondered why she'd suggested it at all. "You'll never get around to it," I said.

"What if I did?"

"I've got Mom."

"Your excuse for everything."

"At least you know where I am."

"I always tell you when I get a new assignment," she said.

"Unless you don't."

"I try to. Just a sec." Vivien looked up. I saw a hand touch her shoulder and heard a male voice asking her a question in French (among the two hundred languages spoken in the DRC, it's the official one). "*Un peu plus de temps*," she said to him and then turned back to me.

"Who's that?" I asked.

"A colleague."

"So, how's Raoul?"

"We're not together anymore." This was her version

of decluttering—leaving people behind. She did like to travel light.

"He lasted what—two months?" I'd thought it would be a bit longer; he was a buff physician and younger than my sister.

"Seven."

"Must be a record."

"At least I'm getting some on a regular basis. You?"

"I've got other priorities." The breakup with my ex had been hard and messy; in the aftermath, he'd cut me off from my stepdaughter. While living with Mom, I'd only made the occasional stab at dating. It always looked better than it tasted, which was honestly a relief. I couldn't imagine how I'd meet one more person's needs.

"Joan . . . you worry me. Living in that suburban desert with Mom. A slave to her sickness."

"She's eighty-four," I said. "She has congestive heart failure. *Someone* has to take care of her."

"That's not the sickness I mean. What are you going to do with yourself when she's gone?"

"Know that I did everything I could for her."

"I'm sure it's a long list." Vivien sighed. "Speaking of assignments, I'm leaving the clinic and won't have any cell service or WiFi for a while."

"What's a while?"

Vivien replied, but I couldn't make it out.

"You're breaking up."

Her face disappeared. "I turned off the camera," she said. "Can you hear me now?"

"Yes."

"There's been a new Ebola outbreak."

"Where?" Far from her, I was hoping.

"A village about three hundred kilometres east. Just a few cases."

"Good."

"It has to be contained. So, anyway, I volunteered to go."

"No, Vivien." I was picturing my sister hemorrhaging from every orifice. "Don't take this one on."

"I'll be careful."

"Mom—"

"I'll message her that I'm going away with a vaccination team again. Like I did last fall."

"And what do I say if something happens to you? How much time do you think she's got? You want her to spend her last months in pain? Is that it? You still hate her that much?"

"Joan, stop. That's ancient history."

"If that was true, you'd come home." She was quiet for a moment, and I pressed her. "Mom is fragile."

"I know. I've been thinking about that. It's just that . . ." Vivien's voice slowed, and I thought we might finally talk about the rift between her and Mom—between us—and then I could tell her how sorry I was. "But I just can't leave right now," she said. "There's so much to do here."

"That's it, then." I wouldn't say more. I was afraid if I did, Vivien would stop talking to me altogether.

"No, listen to me. I'm aware of the risks I'm taking, and of Mom's condition. I don't want her to suffer." I heard her flick a lighter and inhale. This was new—she'd quit ages ago. "So, I came up with a plan."

"Which is what?"

She hesitated, then said, "I want to send you my passwords so you can access everything. My social media accounts, my email, the cloud. Then if I'm sick . . . if I die, you keep posting, and Mom lives in peace for as long as she's got."

"That's crazy."

"It'll work. You'd send her messages from me. Share pictures on Facebook. She enjoys seeing them. It's easy—they're all in Google Photos—and you won't run out, I like to take pictures."

"Vivien . . ."

"I mean it. When have I ever asked you for anything?"

My sister pleading . . . It made me sweat.

"I've never even had a Facebook account."

"You'll figure it out."

"But if something happens to you, won't one of the doctors post about it?" I asked. "Or be in touch with someone who does? What are the chances this won't explode?"

"I move around a lot, and the village is very remote— only accessible by water. I'm an independent nurse now. There's no organization to notify. Only next of kin. You."

"I hate this," I said.

"Promise. Be me, Joan—be a nicer me."

"That shouldn't be too hard," I said.

Vivien laughed.

"Turn on the webcam again." I wanted to see her.

She did, and in the last few minutes of our conversation, she was the sister I remembered, the one with the magic umbrella. She called me Roo.

CHAPTER 4

On a rainy autumn night when I was thirteen, Vivien put a hand on my shoulder to wake me up and then crawled into my bed. I didn't ask her what was wrong—I was just so pleased and mystified that my sister wanted to be close again. It had been years since she'd let me into her bed because I'd had a bad dream, or invited me to a sleepover in her room. I was anxious that I'd inadvertently say something to make her leave, so I stayed quiet, and we lay on our backs silently, side by side, for a while.

Then she whispered, "I'm pregnant."

I held her hand; she put her head on my shoulder. Keeping her voice low in case Mom was up, she said that she'd wanted an abortion. That scared me—abortions were illegal and I knew that women died. Trying not to show any fear, I asked how she'd get one, and Vivien said she knew someone whose aunt could take care of it.

"She does it in her house. I went," Vivien said.

"Without telling me?"

"You're too young."

"I'm not. What happened?"

"I couldn't go through with it. I thought of Aunt Peggy."

We'd seen pictures of Aunt Peggy, who'd died before we were born, in an old photo album at Uncle Jack's. Pasted corners held the snapshots on thick black sheets: Uncle Jack and Dad, their squadron, Mom and Aunt Peggy standing arm-in-arm. They both wore one-piece bathing suits that skirted their thighs, the lake behind them. They looked alike—blond, tall, curvy—as if Aunt Peggy was more closely related to my mother than we were.

Until high school, my mother hadn't had any real friends because her father was a drunk who didn't like strangers in the house. And then Peggy—originally Aagje, but no one could pronounce it—moved in next door. Peggy Schaft's family had immigrated from the Netherlands, and she asked Mom for help with her English. So, after school, they did homework together and discovered they had a lot in common: both neat, both liking science and puzzles—which didn't endear them to other kids their age, boys or girls. They'd talk and listen to the radio and practise dancing together, and any time Mom's father locked her out of the house, she now had a refuge at Aunt Peggy's.

Mom's parents split up when she was in grade ten, and she got Aunt Peggy to help her clear out everything her father had left behind: the ceramic ashtray he'd thrown at her mother and glued back together; the screwdriver he'd used to pry open the lockbox where Mom kept her babysitting money; the armchair where her mother had sat once and learned not to do again after he twisted her arm behind her back, dislocating the shoulder; the old workboots he'd worn when he kicked my mother; the knife he'd used to trim his fingernails and also to hack off a section of Mom's hair, which had, for some reason, offended him. They hauled out the couch. And then the bed he'd slept in. Mom moved on to her own room next, bagging up the clothes he'd called her a slut for wearing. The dresser went too and then her bed because he'd paid for them. When they were done, the house that had suffocated her was airy and bright.

As soon as my grandmother returned from work, she made Mom bring everything back into the house—except for the ashtray—but Mom never forgot the tranquility she'd felt, standing in her empty room.

A year later, Aunt Peggy had an abortion. As soon as we got our periods, Mom told us the story as a warning, sparing no detail. Aunt Peggy passed out after she got home. Mom found her on the bathroom floor and put newspapers under her to soak up the blood. "It just about killed her," Mom would say.

Aunt Peggy met Uncle Jack when she was twenty-one and came to pick up Mom at J&H Printing, where Mom was the receptionist. They became a foursome—my parents, Aunt Peggy and Uncle Jack—Mom swallowing her disapproval. She helped Aunt Peggy sew her wedding dress and later wore it at her own wedding.

Aunt Peggy and Uncle Jack lost their only baby to SIDS when he was four months old. She believed it was a punishment for her abortion. No one could convince her otherwise—not Mom, not Uncle Jack, not her doctor, who could offer no other explanation, the cause of SIDS being unknown. She was afraid to get pregnant again, so Uncle Jack suggested they adopt. The day before the social worker was to meet them and begin the process, Aunt Peggy dropped off the balcony of their eighth-floor apartment. Uncle Jack said she fell; my mother thought she'd jumped, and blamed Uncle Jack, as if it was his fault that they'd lived in an apartment with a balcony someone could leap from.

She was the one who packed up Aunt Peggy's things. Uncle Jack told her to keep anything she wanted as a memento and she chose Aunt Peggy's favourite teacup. It didn't seem right to her to shove it in with all her other dishes, so Mom cleared out everything else. When there was nothing in the cabinet but Aunt Peggy's china teacup, imprinted with roses, Mom felt her friend smiling from above. It was her first time "decluttering" (as she put it) since she'd tried to get rid of her father's things. And now that she had her own home, there was no one to stop her from revelling in it. Having cleared the kitchen cabinet, she moved on to other cupboards and drawers. For years, Peggy's cup survived all of Mom's purging.

My father rarely swore. He was a stickler for manners as if *please*, *thank you*, and *yes, sir* were army salutes and omitting them could get someone busted down to private. Even drunk, he'd say, "Excuse me," before vomiting. The suit he wore to work, his appreciation of art, his books, his manners—these were the signs he'd moved into the middle class during the postwar boom. His parents had had dirt under their fingernails. He was the first in his family to own a home and a new car, and he was saving up to buy Mom a mink coat. None of this gave him a sense of security, though.

He couldn't shake off memories of his childhood: his father, laid off, waiting for hours in line at the Toronto House of Industry, a charity that supplied food to the needy, for a handout of oatmeal and beans. Even after being soaked and boiled, the beans were so stale and hard, Dad said, he swallowed more than he chewed, and then cried because there wasn't enough for him to have a larger helping. As an airman, he'd learned that hunger wasn't the worst a person could endure.

He believed that war might come again, or some other disaster, and in a tempest, all our suburban newness would fall apart like the three little pigs' house of straw. He thought some people were blown about by the wind and others were the wind. Dad wanted his girls to marry the wind. He hoped we'd have Mom's looks, that we'd go to university and find husbands there among the sons of men like his fellow pilots, and we would dance at country clubs, surpassing him as he'd surpassed his parents. Instead, we took after him, not our mother—dimpled jaws, wavy hair, our pale skin the white of shock. It hurt him that he had no connections to ensure our future. Still, he thought Vivien—the stronger of us—would make her way in the world despite that.

My father loved me, but he didn't see who I was until I was in middle school. At the time, I was methodically making my way through the bookcase in the basement. The laundry and furnace rooms were unfinished, but the rest was carpeted and bright, with sliding glass doors that led out to the backyard. The bar was at the back, the bookcase opposite. Near the glass doors, there was an armchair and a table with a radio beside it. I spent hours lying on the carpet, reading my father's books on the sly, nervous that he'd be angry with me—this was his sacred space. Ever since Mom had gotten rid of the Ping-Pong table, even Vivien didn't spend any time down here.

One weekend, immersed in a novel about a doctor, I didn't hear my father's footsteps and was startled when he appeared in front of me. He asked what I was doing, and I mutely held up the book. He nodded and sat in his armchair, waving at me to continue. I tried, but I couldn't focus on the words while he was watching me, so I told him I didn't care about marrying a doctor, I was going to be one. Dad said, "Don't you want kids?" I told him I'd do that too, and he said, "I don't know any women doctors. I guess you'll have to get better grades than the boys." Then he reached over to the radio, always tuned to a classical music station, turned it on, retrieved the book he'd been reading, and opened it to where he'd left off.

After that, whenever my father and I found ourselves together in the basement, we'd talk a little. Dad told me the story about the oatmeal and beans. He asked why I wanted to be a doctor. I said it sounded more interesting than answering phones like my mother did before she was married. Also, I wondered—I was shy to say this, but I did—if God wanted me to do it so I could fix people. I asked Dad if he believed in God, and he said he wished he did, as believing seemed to give other people comfort, but what he saw in the war only confirmed that hell and heaven are in human hands. He talked about the Yorkshire air base and being invited to a weekend at a country home where he was expected to shoot skeet, which he'd thought was an edible bird. He'd been sorely disappointed to miss every shot until he learned that he was aiming at clay discs. I laughed at that, and my father looked at me in a deadpan way that made me laugh harder. Soon, a history of medicine turned up in the bookcase.

That spring, when I was in grade seven, and in the summer that followed, my father only drank when he played poker or watched a game. He took Mom out to movies, a concert, even the opera. My mother dressed up for him, showing me how she applied foundation and blush and a touch of mascara to the tips of her lashes. Even Vivien was mellowing. She got a summer job at J&H Printing and she seemed to like heading off to work with our father in the morning.

Then she got knocked up, and the world went sideways.

I'd have skipped my piano lesson if I'd known that Vivien was going to tell my parents she was pregnant. When I came home, they were all in the living room, Dad pacing, Vivien sitting on the couch, Mom next to her. My sister's head was bent, her cheeks red.

"All summer, I thought, *Hey, I got my little girl back*." Dad's voice was hoarse. He'd pulled his tie loose so he could yell without constraint. "The trouble you got into before—never mind that. Wipe the slate clean. So what if I had to pick you up at a police station? So what if Mom never got a fucking mink for herself because I had to pay for the one you wrecked? You learned your lesson. You were back on track. That's what I thought—because I'm only your dumbass father."

It was a Saturday in December, not officially winter yet, but there'd been an early snowstorm, and it was nearly as cold as the day Vivien had brought home the stray cat. Our backyard was pillowed with snow and reflected sun gilded the living room. The couch had a pattern of flowers the same shade as Mom's hair. She'd just been to the salon, her hair voluminous and wavier than mine. At first that was all I could see, her hair lit gold and a hint of golden cheek. When I stepped closer, I was surprised at her calm expression and the tender way she stroked my sister's hot cheek.

"You have shit for brains," Dad said. "You get that? Throwing away your future! Like a stupid cunt!"

"Hugh! Watch your mouth," Mom snapped.

My father stopped short, as if he'd realized he'd gone too far, then shook his head as if thinking he hadn't. "I want Mark's number."

It had been a summer romance. My sister's boyfriend had returned to his home in Florida before school started.

"I'm calling his father, and he's going to do the right thing," Dad said.

I expected Vivien to laugh in his face, but she just stared at him. It was my mother who said, "What right thing?"

"I don't fucking know! Get married, I guess."

"You're not serious," Mom said.

"It *was* Mark, wasn't it, Viv? Or are you a tramp, too?"

"Hugh!"

When my sister didn't reply, Dad paused in his ranting to shout at me, "Get to your room!"

After I slammed my door, stupidly calling through it, "I can still hear you," he dropped his voice and I missed the rest. At some point, I heard the garage door open and then close. Half an hour later, it opened again, and Dad called us to dinner—he'd bought rotisserie chicken. It was in the centre of the table, still in the paper bag lined with tinfoil. Vivien turned green at the odour, then Mom refused to touch it. Dad told me to get the poultry shears—spring-loaded like his pliers—out of the drawer. After I handed them to him, he took the chicken out of the bag, cut off the string and divided up the meat into breast, wings and thighs. I was the only one who ate, and when I was done, I sucked the barbecue sauce off the string. Dad's dinner was largely liquid.

When my parents retired to their bedroom to fight, I cleared the table and got a plate of crackers for Vivien, who said she felt better with something in her stomach. We went down to the basement, away from the shouting. At the top of the stairs, I turned on the light, and at the bottom, Vivien turned it off. We sat on the shag carpet, huddled together for warmth.

There was a girl at our school who'd gotten pregnant. Her parents had kicked her out, and she went into foster care. She had to switch schools, but the days of expelling girls for being pregnant were finally over. Instead, we had sex-ed classes that were all about the ruined lives of teen mothers.

"Dad shouldn't have talked to you like that," I said.

"I don't care."

"Why didn't you just tell him it was Mark?"

"Mark's a shit. He'd say it isn't his fault and Dad would believe him. Anyway, I'd still be pregnant, so what's the difference? Dad hates me, Roo." She hadn't called me Roo since she'd had to let the stray cat go.

"Dad's just mad," I said. "He'll get over it."

"He doesn't get over anything. He just gets hammered."

"So, you think I'll become his favourite now? Go to work with him next summer? Learn to operate the switchboard? Get in on the poker games while you stay home with Mom?"

"God," Vivien groaned.

I dragged my fingers through the carpet and found a Ping-Pong ball cached there. I pinched it, marvelling at its escape from Mom's vacuum cleaner. How many times had suction pulled at the shaggy pile and missed the fragile egg within?

"What's it feel like?" I asked.

"Like the flu, with bigger breasts."

"I wouldn't mind the bigger breasts part." I was thirteen and a half, still flat-chested. My sister was four months pregnant; we would celebrate her seventeenth birthday in mid-January.

"Are you going to keep it?"

"How am I supposed to be a mother? I don't want a baby, and I can't wait to get out of this stupid house and see the rest of the world." She paused. "But I felt it yesterday. Like a butterfly. I don't know what to do."

"Mom could help."

"I wasn't planning to tell them today. She guessed."

"How?" I'd been spraying room deodorizer in the bathroom whenever Vivien threw up, and she had been hiding the small mound of her belly under oversized sweatshirts.

"I quit smoking. I just don't want cigarettes anymore. Mom said the same thing happened when she was pregnant with me."

"Mom smoked?"

"Yep. She noticed that my clothes had stopped smelling of cigarettes. How did she notice that? She never pays attention to anything except when she's in the mood to toss it."

"Well, she does like things clean."

"She likes to clean. There's a difference."

"Mom took your side."

"You don't think that's weird?"

"She just cares about you. And the baby." My mother had been protective—I'd never seen her like that, not for me.

"I don't know. Maybe."

She sounded hopeful, and I squeezed her hand, ashamed of my jealousy.

The day after that Skype call with my sister, I took my bookcase and the books in it to my storage locker so Mom couldn't get rid of them like she had the can opener and the spatula. The locker was large and well organized, and I soon found a spot for the bookcase beside a purple armchair rocker and a silver lamp, which made the storage locker homey even though there was no power outlet to plug into. My journals were housed in an antique oak filing cabinet. As a child, I'd lost a few to Mom's purging—as vigilant as I was, it was never enough to prevent her tossing out a year of my life now and then. But I still had 1977 in a yellow school notebook, which I pulled out of the bottom drawer. With my coat to keep me warm and a flashlight to provide illumination, I settled myself in the armchair to read. That year, I was putting a heart instead of a dot over *i*'s and *j*'s.

Monday, March 7: Vivien has a double chin! She asked me if she's gross, and I told her she's just fat because she's pregnant. She saw the doctor today, and I got to listen to the heartbeat with a fetoscope that looks like a horn. Vivien wants a boy. I'm worried about his soft head, babies have these fontanels so the skull can grow, but she isn't scared of dropping him. We're going to backpack through Europe and Vivien will carry him

*in a sling. I'm reading Travels with My Aunt. The aunt
is wild, she has no fear and a lot of lovers, and it turns
out she's actually his mother. The librarian wouldn't
let me take it out, so I got it from a used bookstore.
People think they know everything about me, but they
hardly know anything. Vivien is worried about Dad,
he's in bad shape, but Mom's the one to watch. She's
getting ready for something big. There's a look in her
eyes. I'm not supposed to tell Vivien that Mom bought
a christening gown. It's too pretty.*

The gown was white satin and frilly, though we didn't
know if the baby would be a boy or a girl. In any case, Vivien
was already committed to atheism and didn't want the baby
baptized. (She had been and so had I, *just in case*, according
to Mom, who never went to church but always put a crèche
under the tree at Christmas.) Mom used to dress Vivien in
frilly baby dresses, and said she'd looked like a little doll
until she was about eighteen months old, when she'd
started wriggling out of her clothes and her diaper to run
around butt-naked.

When my stepdaughter, Zoe, was a baby, Mom bought a
ruffled velvet dress for her, which Zoe loved, not for the frills
but the feel of the velvet. When I put her in pyjamas, she'd
hold on to the dress as if it was a blankie, and we'd sit in the
purple armchair while I rocked her to sleep. Vivien had
helped me pick out the armchair on one of her visits home.
In the store, she sat in the chair to test it out, and got me to
squeeze in beside her, holding my stepdaughter. I still
remember the warm pressure of my sister and the baby, as
close as if we shared a common skin.

CHAPTER 5

Vivien died on March 20, which was a Wednesday, two months after the Skype call. I was notified by email forty-eight hours after the fact. The delay made me angry, and I blamed my sister for living in a place where she could die while I was going about my day, knowing nothing.

I read the email in my room after dinner, sitting cross-legged like a kid, my knees covered by the white quilt my mother had ordered online for me. I made some weird noise, and she called from the living room to see if I was okay. "I'm fine," I shouted because I had no control over the force of my voice. The email triggered a hot flash that set my skin on fire and a river of sweat couldn't douse it.

I got up and walked down the hallway past Mom, who made no comment, likely assuming I was collecting mail or doing some other routine chore for her. I opened the front door and stepped outside to stand in the frozen slush, which crackled under my stockinged feet. I gulped the cool air. A neighbour was wheeling out his compost bin, and I didn't want him to hear me sob, so I choked down my grief without a sound. Death is a natural process, just the other side of birth, except when it's the death of someone you love.

Vivien didn't die of Ebola. She'd fallen out of a dugout and cut her leg on a rock in the river. It was something that would have been easily cured with antibiotics, but there weren't any to be had at the clinic; the meagre supply had run out. Because of the Ebola outbreak, there was a travel ban in the region. No one could get in or out. When the fever started, it rose rapidly, and she became too delirious to call home even if there had been service. And then she died.

I should have been there. I'd have put my arms around my sister and held her to this world.

The next day, I went to work—nobody could know I'd lost my sister. I'd given her my word. Between patients, I sat in my car, trying to force back my tears. Sometimes they rolled down anyway, and I pressed the heels of my hands against my eyes, talking to Vivien in my head. I didn't have a lot to tell her. It was mostly, *What the fuck, Vivien! What the fuck.*

I put off going home after work and went to my storage locker instead. I rocked in the purple armchair and cried, wishing I could stay longer, but I had to make dinner for my mother. When Mom saw my red eyes, she asked if I'd been drinking. (Living with Dad had trained her to suspect intoxication as the explanation for everything amiss.) I told her I had allergies, and she seemed to accept it though the house didn't have a speck of dust and the leafless trees were bare of pollen. Mom was noticeably short of breath that evening; she had just enough energy to hobble from her recliner to her bed and to tell me that Vivien still hadn't replied to her message.

"She will," I said, "as soon as she has internet again."

When Mom was in bed, watching the TV that had arrived with the white quilt, I took my laptop down to the basement. After Dad died, I caught Mom trying to pull up the shag carpet, which was glued to the concrete floor. I told her to stop, but she kept yanking at the carpet, pulling up tufts until I put my hands over hers and held them. "Leave it alone," I told her. "It's still Dad's." The basement remained as it had always been: the carpet, the wood panelling, the built-in bar, the liquor cabinet opened by the old key I kept on my key chain. Mom hadn't been down here in over a year, since she couldn't manage the stairs anymore.

I sat on the floor and opened my email, looking for the one with Vivien's user names and passwords. She'd told me to post a picture—Mom would like that. I logged into her social media accounts—Facebook, Twitter, Instagram—switching back and forth between the tabs. I had no idea what I was looking at or what my sister got out of it. Across the top of the screen were symbols with mysterious functions; below that, too many boxes with names and faces I didn't know. In every tab, her profile picture grinned at me, her nose peeling, and I left the laptop on the floor and ran into the laundry room. I closed the door and turned on the washing machine. When it was noisily swooshing water around an empty drum, I crouched next to it and cried, smacking the cement floor with the flat of my hand. The last time I saw my sister, her image was wavering, her voice out of sync with it, the yellow curtains framing her hennaed hair. Did I tell her I loved her before we said goodbye? I think so. I'm almost certain.

When the cycle was done, I washed my face, using the

hand soap next to the laundry sink, checked my eyes in the mirror—not too red—and returned to my laptop.

Having closed every tab except Facebook, I slowly scrolled across the icons. There—the dark circle with the squiggle in the middle. I recognized it from helping Mom install Messenger on her phone so she could stay in touch with Vivien. I clicked on the squiggle and a sidebar popped up with Mom's name at the top of the list. I clicked on that and typed in the box, *Hi Mom. All good. Just stopped in a village store with WiFi. Still away with the vaccination team. Going to have no service for a while. Back in a couple weeks. By your birthday latest. XO.*

Send.

A box with Vivien's belongings arrived two weeks later. I opened it, saw a backpack with a phone sticking out the side and her hairbrush on top, then closed it up again. Unable to bear the sight of things she'd so recently touched, I took the box down to the basement, where it just fit into Dad's liquor cabinet. I shut the door and turned the key in the lock. That night, I dreamt Vivien was sleeping in my bed. When I woke up, I lay still, feeling her there next to me. The impression was so real, her arm around me, and it lasted until the grey light of an overcast dawn filtered in. That was the day Mom couldn't catch her breath and ended up in the emergency room of the nearest hospital.

On Mom's second day of lying on a stretcher in emergency, I cancelled my patients' appointments to stay with her and nag staff about getting her a bed. Mom's chart showed systolic dysfunction with decreased left ventricular ejection fraction: her heart wasn't contracting enough to fully pump the blood her body needed. In response, her heart was beating too rapidly. Blood was backing up, fluids pooling inside her. She was at risk of cardiac arrest.

The cardiology wards were full, but at last they admitted her to nephrology, alongside patients with kidney disease. The room was small, with four beds crammed into it and no space for a bathroom. The patients had limited mobility, and beside every bed was a commode: a simple chair with a removable basin under the hole in the seat. (Dealing with bedpans was too much for staff already run off their feet, and sitting upright on the commode was easier for the patient, too.) The ward reeked of urine, but Mom coped as she had when Dad was at his worst, by creating a mental bubble in which there was no talk of anything unpleasant. To fend off the assault on her senses, she kept the curtain closed around her bed and a bottle of hand sanitizer under her pillow. When sounds came from other patients using their commodes, Mom hummed for the duration, dumping sanitizer on her hands.

As the doctors adjusted her medication, Mom's blood pressure moved toward normal, her heartbeat slowed and fluid retention was reduced. She stabilized, but even so, she was too frail to go home. I contacted every facility that provided good care, but none of them had space for her, and so she remained on the ward. We were told that other patients were lying on stretchers in the ER because her bed was occupied, that she was costing taxpayers thousands of dollars a day, and that we should accept a transfer to any long-term care facility, however far away, however terrible. We were asked—ordered—to be "flexible."

I'd used the same tone myself in talking to the families of patients waiting for a space in hospice. That made it no less objectionable when I was on the receiving end. In fact, it was worse, because I felt remorse on top of resentment. I swore to myself I'd never use the word *flexible* with my patients again. I was afraid they would transfer her when I wasn't there, but I couldn't be with her all the time. I had patients, and I had to sleep. On the eighth day, just as Mom was going to be shipped off to a vertically stacked storage locker facility—a notorious long-term care "home"—I got the call that a space for her had opened up in Valley View. A relatively new rehab facility, it could provide a range of therapies to build up her strength: physio, occupational, medical. Thank God. I'd been about to lose my mind.

Constructed on the site of an old hospital for vagrants and the dissolute, Valley View was connected to the old jail, which had been converted to serve as the rehab's administrative wing. (Death row had been preserved, and it was open for tours on special occasions.) Mom's room had windows overlooking a park, and it was gigantic—I'd never seen anything like it in a health-care setting—but it was also semi-private. There was a bed at each end, with a nightstand and dresser. Now that her own crisis was over, my mother grew cranky about the accumulation of things around her roommate's bed. The woman was a relentless knitter who had already completed a heap of baby hats. A basket overflowed with yarn. Skeins were piled up on her dresser and along the window ledge between get-well cards and pots of flowers.

Mom turned eighty-five the Saturday after she got to Valley View. As requested, nicer "Vivien" sent her an e-card and lemon cheesecake—Mom's favourite—to celebrate. We ate it together by Mom's bed, and when we were done, I tossed all the "clutter" in the wastebasket by the nursing station, not in the room.

As soon as I was seated beside her again, Mom pointed her chin toward her roommate and hissed, "Why doesn't she ever stop knitting?"

I could barely see her roommate at the other end of the room. "You've got up to six weeks in rehab here," I said, "so just do your best to ignore her."

"I want to go home."

"That's why I need you to do everything your care team asks you to do. So that you're able to."

"I'm not comfortable. I want my things."

"What things? You don't have any."

"I don't know. *My* things."

"Your recliner?"

"Yes. And my bathrobe."

"You're wearing it. I brought it for you."

"And my phone. Where's my phone?"

"On your lap. You're scaring me, Mom."

"I'm worried."

"About?"

"Vivien. Something's wrong. She never writes so much. Look." She handed me her phone.

Dear Mom, I know we haven't always seen eye to eye, but today, I want you to share this little dream with me. After all, your birthday is just once a year! Imagine a lovely lemon cheesecake with white icing. On it are eighty-five candles plus one for good luck. You and I are blowing them out together, whoosh, in one big breath. That's a lot of candles, but when we do it together, it's easy. And then you feel me give you a kiss on your cheek. Remember how I'd do that when I got really excited and then I'd frown because I'd been too mushy? I don't frown anymore. Life is too short to bother frowning. I wish I was with you today, but the patients here rely on me and have no one else. I think of you often, and the fact that I'm not physically there doesn't mean you're not in my heart. You are, Mom, and I hope that someday soon I'll be there in person to give you a great big hug. Have a good day and ignore doctor's orders. I asked Joan to bring you the cheesecake. Love, Vivien

I'd expected Mom to be over the moon. For her eighty-fourth, the real Vivien had messaged her, *Happy birthday heart-emoji.* Just like that, written out. When I handed back her phone, Mom took it tentatively, frowning as if I was offering her a sandwich bag of dog poo.

"She was just emotional," I said nervously. "She knows you're in the hospital."

"This isn't like her. The card—it's pink. And it sings."

"She remembered. That's the important thing, Mom."

"Do you think Vivien is in trouble?"

"Stop worrying." My tone was too shrill and Mom still looked uneasy. "She asked me to send you the e-card in case she couldn't."

"Has she talked to you?"

"When she asked me to send the card. She was sorry to miss your birthday."

"She was?"

"Yes, Mom."

"And you're sure she's all right?"

"I'm sure. Do you need help to reply?"

"Don't fuss. I'm not crippled."

"All right, then."

"Did you clean the kitchen?"

"Yes."

"With bleach?"

"Yes." (No.)

"And you recycled the newspaper?"

"I've got it with me." I took it out of my bag and unfolded it. "There's an article about the Magellanic Cloud."

"The Large Magellanic Cloud. It's going to crash into us in 2.5 billion years. So sad about the polar bears."

"What about them?"

"I don't like my toothbrush. The bristles are too big. You'd think they wouldn't allow plants in hospital rooms."

"Why not? Having plants improves outcomes."

My mother's rapid change of subject was something new, like her mash-up of acquiring and decluttering, as if she was sprinting from one target to the next and back again to cover it all while she had time.

"They attract bugs. Don't be ignorant. People rely on you to know things because you're a physician. They're under the impression that doctors are scientists." She shook her head.

"The polar bears," I prompted to move her away from her roommate's clutter and my sister's fictional well-being.

"With the melting ice . . ." Mom's eyes became wet. I wondered if she was crying over the bears or if she was thinking of Vivien, and I was afraid I might start to cry and give everything away, and then where would we be?

"It's hard," I said.

"They're starving. They're eating their cubs. Not the mothers—they'd die first—but the males are killing off the future of their species. Can you imagine the deprivation that would cause that?"

"I can, actually."

My mother looked at me for a moment as if still waiting for an answer, then jumped back to the subject of colliding solar systems—Andromeda might come later, perhaps after the sun's death—and after that moved on to the Arctic and issues of sovereignty and endangered animals. "I want to increase the amount of my monthly donation to the World Wildlife Fund. Add another five dollars," she said. "Can you do that for me?"

"You can do it yourself when you're up to it."

"Good. I am now. Let's go home."

"Mom, please. We've talked about that already."

"Don't *Mom, please* me. I'm not a child."

"Don't act like one."

"What did you say?" She didn't seem to notice the sound of clicking had stopped. Her knitting neighbour had lowered her needles—another family's arguments are always good entertainment.

"Nothing important." Her hearing loss was as convenient for me as it was for her.

"Not nothing—what was it?"

"We'll discuss it later."

"You're such a . . ." Just as Mom was about to escalate, the nurse came in. My mother's forehead immediately smoothed into placid wrinkles. "Hello, Ruby. What's up? Not my blood pressure, I hope."

Ruby, who was round and dimple-cheeked, chuckled. "Your mother is so funny," she said, smiling as she rolled the stand with the vital-signs monitor to Mom's bedside. Mom had found out that at home in the Philippines, Ruby had majored in psychology, but when her husband was disabled in an accident, she'd quit her studies to work abroad as a nanny. Her children were conceived during visits home and raised by her parents. After she'd done the required stint as a nanny to qualify for permanent residency, Ruby went to nursing school while working nights. Finally, she was able to become a citizen and bring her children here under provisions for minors, though her husband hadn't yet been able to join her. This all emerged in response to my mother's sympathetic questions. Mom was always interested in the details of other people's lives, almost as much as she was interested in their failings.

As soon as we were alone again, Mom said, "I don't understand how Ruby can be overweight. I mean she's a nurse! You'd look so much nicer, Joan, if you coloured your hair."

"I don't need to." My dark hair, not yet grey, was the single thing I was vain about.

"Blond would bring out the blue of your eyes." I have hazel eyes, more brown than green. I might have been concerned that Mom was getting confused if she hadn't been in the habit of looking at me and thinking of Vivien ever since the day my sister left home.

"Vivien's the one with blue eyes," I said.

"Blond looks good on anyone."

"I prefer my natural colour."

"E. coli is natural too. Have you been buying romaine lettuce?"

"No—I'm not doing anything you wouldn't if you were home."

Mom smiled at that, then said, "Can you turn on the TV for me?"

"It's going to be connected later today. What about the crossword?"

"I'm too tired."

"I could read the clues to you and write your answers in."

"All right." My mother looked at me then with love, and I melted like wet paper.

After the crossword, Mom dozed. I sat in a chair next to her bed. When I moved back home, I'd started keeping my journal on my computer, backed up on a flash drive. Now it was in the cloud, where even Mom couldn't reach. I thumb-tapped on my phone: *How am I supposed to be a nicer Vivien? I'm not even nice myself. It was ridiculous for me to agree. What am I supposed to post? Mom's practically guessed already. I've got to figure this out.*

The sentimental tone had been a mistake. I'd have to study my sister's social media more closely to catch her voice. If I couldn't be a nicer Vivien, I'd be a better one: not thinking only of herself, but still recognizable as herself. Just a shift in angle. A Vivien who left and came back. Who knew what she left. Who was making up for it. That was a Vivien I could get behind.

While Mom was napping, her roommate's children and grandchildren showed up. They goofed around, trying on each other's new hats and mitts, laughing and shushing each other, whispering so as not to wake my mother. I wondered what it would be like to be so much at ease in a family.

Mom didn't doze for long. She sneezed and snorted, then sat up and grabbed her phone. She checked Facebook religiously, as if it was a lifeline. "Why hasn't she posted anything?" Mom asked, and I reminded her that Vivien was travelling through remote areas, doing a vaccination blitz. The physiotherapist arrived. He was tall and blond, which pleased my mother, and after he helped her into a wheelchair so he could take her off to her session, I kissed her goodbye and left.

CHAPTER 6

ocial Media Allows You to Do Four Important Things. That's what I learned when I searched online. *Discover new ideas! Develop your brand! Drive traffic! Connect with your audience!* Nothing on how to impersonate your sister.

For the next few days, I went to work, visited Mom at the facility, and watched YouTube videos on how to post, share a picture, comment, react, message. I learned that capital letters shout. Also, that sexual innuendo had made eggplant and peach emojis risqué. Then I methodically logged into Vivien's accounts on my laptop, opening a new tab for each, and carefully compared them. She seemed to have abandoned her Twitter account, and on Instagram, she just reposted the photos she'd uploaded to Facebook, adding random hashtags like #peoplefocus and #earthjustice. I could do that, couldn't I? If she wrote anything, it was brief and emphatic, every word followed by a period.

But. Facebook.

There were lengthy posts, groups, pages and friends. Apparently, she liked Weird Nature, Tattoo Spirit, ZXY Films (which I won't describe and unfollowed), World Soccer, World Midwives, all the *Ocean's* movies—Eleven, Twelve, Thirteen, Eight—and also Ocean Sea Life. There were other movies, books, heavy metal bands. No surprise in that. She had 561 friends and belonged to two groups: Nurses against FGM and Knitting for Life. My sister knitted?

I found gaps in her timeline when she'd been out of touch, but many of her friends also worked in developing or war-torn countries and periodically vanished. As soon as someone popped online again, they were welcomed back. Vivien posted photos of tropical flowers and baby goats and skin lesions. Some of these were in direct messages to people I'd never heard of.

My sister's words. Her images. Meant only for the recipient.

And me.

She had to have realized that I'd see these when she gave me her passwords, and I wondered why she hadn't deleted them. No time? No capacity for embarrassment? An overriding desire to leave a remnant of herself behind if something bad did happen?

Her most recent chats in Messenger: with a colleague discussing a case; some flirtation between her and Raoul Delgado—her ex, and the only name I recognized; Oscar Karlsson, a researcher in Sweden, who'd just gotten a grant to expand his lab; a nurse in Nigeria named Grace Musa, saying, *Hello luv, saw you were online. Praying for you.* Vivien had replied, *Fighting words, dear.*

She'd also been in regular contact with Augie Rosenstein—Uncle Jack's younger son—though he used to be *my* best friend. Now I only ever saw him at weddings and funerals, like a cousin. But he confided in her; they bantered; she called him on his bullshit.

Her last conversation with Augie on Messenger:

THU, JAN 17, 12:04 AM

Vivien: Face it, Augie, you're short

Augie: Happy birthday. And five foot eleven is taller than average

Vivien: Maybe in the Philippines. Not, say, in the Netherlands

Augie: How was I supposed to know my date was six feet tall?

Vivien: Wasn't it in her profile?

Augie: I thought she was exaggerating

Vivien: Because you did?

Augie: A man's got to be over six feet to get any swipes. I told her one of my vertebrae had collapsed. She didn't buy it

Vivien: Did you really expect her to?

Augie: When you're pushed into a corner, you say the first thing that pops into your head

Vivien: Ha! Men pulling shit like that must be what turned my sister off dating

Augie: I haven't seen much of Joan for years. Not since she broke up with that guy. Paul, right?

Vivien: That was a shit show

Augie: Say more

That was the end of the conversation. Vivien went away and didn't come back. So, I was left wondering—what was she going to say about me and Paul?

Augie had known Paul slightly—when we bought the condo, Augie was our agent. He'd even found it for us in the building where Paul and I were renting. It was downtown, I could bike to work from there, and I loved that place for its view of the lake. Later, when we had to sell, Augie handled that too, and he recommended the storage locker where I moved my stuff, thinking that would only be temporary.

I had met Paul in the elevator of that building. His sleeves were rolled up, his jacket off and draped over his shoulder, and I noticed his muscular arms. I was twenty-six and had just moved in. He was thirty. I started the conversation—maybe the only one I've ever initiated with a man who wasn't a colleague or a patient. I saw the Air Canada pilot wings on his jacket and told him my father had been an RAF pilot. We chatted until he got to his floor, then he stood for a minute, pressing a button to keep the elevator door open, and invited me out for a drink. I supposed he was interested in knowing more about my father. I'd long since traded my glasses for contacts, but I still saw myself as undesirable and Paul as too cute. He worked hard to persuade me otherwise. That wasn't the only thing I liked about him. When we went for a drink, he meant a drink— he only had one. He'd been everywhere, but when he was off duty, he enjoyed simple things. And he put his child's needs ahead of his own.

Paul was born in Hong Kong and so was his ex-wife. She'd married him to please her parents. They'd tried to make a go of it, but shortly after she got pregnant, she left him. Because of his job—extended time away, irregular schedule—she got custody. He had his daughter, Zoe, every other weekend, alternating holidays, and for a month in the summer, which he didn't consider nearly enough. All through our relationship, Paul fought for joint custody.

Zoe was just a baby when Paul and I got together, but she knew her own mind and was choosy with her affection, so that when it was bestowed, it felt like an honour. I loved her. Even as a toddler, she had a quirky sense of humour. Once, when I took her to a music group, she refused to march around to the beat, laughing at the other toddlers as if to say, *Are you really doing that just because everyone else is?* For a while, at five or six, she was obsessed with dinosaurs. At ten, she was enthralled by horror stories and had a penchant for sarcasm that sometimes got her into trouble. During her last summer in Toronto—we had her for August that year—the three of us made a movie using the new video camera Paul had just brought home from Hong Kong. Zoe assigned the parts—she was the monster, Paul the monster hunter, and I got to be the victim, my face and arms smeared with gore made by mixing food colouring with corn syrup and water.

Dad had been sober for eleven years when I met Paul, and he liked him. The feeling was mutual. They had a love of flying in common, and Dad found Zoe enchanting. Mom was chilly. She referred to Paul as "your Oriental friend," which made me cringe. When I was out with her and my stepdaughter, she quickly made clear to all and sundry that the Chinese baby wasn't her real granddaughter. I tried talking to her about it, but she was resistant, so it was easier to just visit her on my own.

Paul and I used to fight about his dirty socks (he left them everywhere, as if they were seeds he expected to grow into fresh ones), about my schedule (he hated when I took night shifts), more seriously about Zoe (I couldn't say no to her, which created problems with his ex) and most intensely about his best friend, who was a pig (no offence to the animal). But the nature of his job—keeping him away for a week at a time—made each return another honeymoon. I wore red pyjamas because it was his favourite colour; he brought me kitschy souvenirs, which I treasured because they were wholly unnecessary. I took several trips with him, white-knuckling the flights, Paul's calm voice coaching me through them. I thought we'd have kids together as soon as the timing was right, and then we ran out of time.

He won joint custody of his daughter when she was eleven—we'd been together ten years by then. During March break, Zoe got her period. It was her week with us, so I showed her how to use a pad and took her out for a girls' night to celebrate. We saw a movie (her choice—low-budget horror), and afterwards we had poutine and milkshakes. A few days later, Paul's ex announced that she was going to be moving to Vancouver with Zoe so they could be closer to her family. Paul could either live there too and retain joint custody, or see his daughter during school breaks. We consulted a lawyer, who informed us that Paul could fight his ex-wife over the move, but it would be expensive and drag on, and he'd probably lose because his job was flexible and his ex had gotten a promotion, which meant she could afford tuition at a private school for gifted children, where she intended to enrol Zoe.

So, Paul asked for a transfer, which was soon in the works. Theoretically, I could work anywhere because there was always demand for ER physicians. But my parents were in crisis. Dad had relapsed, and the effects of his renewed heavy drinking had been physically devastating. He was now in a coma, the result of hepatic encephalopathy, a brain disorder caused by liver damage. It was too late for a liver transplant—even if he'd been a better candidate for one, his illness was terminal.

Mom poured all her energy into cleaning the house so that when Dad came back, he wouldn't get sick. When I tried to gently prepare her for the reality that he wouldn't, she always got angry. She didn't eat unless I shopped for groceries, cooked for her, and stayed until she got down a few mouthfuls. She neglected her bills; I found final notices for utilities in her trash, and if I hadn't paid immediately, she'd have been sitting in a cold, dark house. To make it easier for me to deal with her bills, we went to her bank so she could add me as an account holder. That's when I discovered that their savings were considerably less than I'd expected—Dad had started on his principal to make ends meet. She wouldn't be able to survive on what was left of his investments.

I broached the possibility of bringing Mom to Vancouver, but she wouldn't leave her home and Paul didn't particularly want the woman who'd rejected his daughter in his. I suggested we visit back and forth, but he'd be spending all his off weeks with his daughter, and I couldn't afford to work half-time. Worse, he didn't believe in long-distance relationships; his daughter needed stability. Our arguments grew so heated, they made Zoe cry. Paul accused me of putting him last. I said it was his way or none. We yelled, we slammed doors. And Zoe went to stay with her mother until they moved.

Just before Paul went off on his next long-haul flight, we had a terrible argument about his best friend, Andrew. It was one of those inexplicable friendships between men who have nothing in common but that they've been friends their whole lives. They'd go to a sports bar and watch a game while Andrew got shit-faced and harassed the waitress. He'd screw any woman with two legs and would take pictures if she only had one—his words. Paul said Andrew was only trying to get a rise out of me. Mostly, I avoided Andrew, but when I couldn't, he'd always make a pass at me. The one time I told Paul about it, he refused to believe that his old friend would be that disloyal; I had to have misinterpreted a convivial gesture because I disliked Andrew in the first place. I was so angry, I was speechless. I stalked into the bathroom and locked the door behind me. When Paul banged on it because he needed to use the toilet, I told him to piss in a bottle.

While he was away on that long-haul flight, I was home one evening after a long shift and was already in pyjamas when Andrew buzzed the intercom. He was here to pick up a cordless drill, didn't Paul tell me? No, he hadn't. But I was on my second large glass of Scotch, so I was thinking, *Who cares, let him up*. Andrew came in, helped himself to a drink and joined me on the couch. When he moved in to kiss me, I didn't push him away. Did I realize he'd boast about it to Paul? That the decision I'd been avoiding would be made for me? Probably. But not that Paul would cut off all contact with my stepdaughter when he left me. I spoke to my lawyer only to learn that as a stepmother, I had no parental rights.

Grief-stricken, I confided in Vivien, thinking she, of all people, wouldn't judge me. She had spent time with Zoe whenever she visited and knew how much I loved her. But all she said was "Nobody loves a martyr, Joan. You should have gone to Vancouver. You fucked up your life and, what's worse, you abandoned that child."

My journal, 1999, the last one on paper: *You gave away
your kid, Vivien. I just followed your example. That's what I told
her. She hung up on me.*

After the breakup, I couldn't get on an airplane.

So, was she going to tell Augie about all that mess?

I stared at his chat box. There was a green dot beside his
name, which I had learned meant he was online, open for a
reply. I could message him as my sister. I could be as blunt
as she had always been. I needed the practice, and after all,
I'd *promised* her.

WED, APR 17, 11:40 PM

Vivien: You're a slow learner, Augie. No wonder your
mother didn't want you to start kindergarten with
everyone else. Good thing she held you back

Augie: Ouch.

Three smaller dots wriggled while he typed.

Augie: I don't hear from you for three months and
that's the first thing you've got to say. Are you trying to
quit smoking again?

Vivien: I love smoking. Why should I quit?

Augie: What's going on?

Vivien: Nothing

Vivien: Why would there be?

Augie: You're talking so fast

Vivien: You mean typing

Augie: Whatever

I pictured a cigarette between my fingers, brought it to my lips and took an imaginary drag, then typed with slow deliberation, using only two fingers, like Vivien did when we were in high school, the clickety-clack from her room giving Mom a headache. Vivien took the typewriter with her when she left home. It was portable. It had an orange case, like her travel clock. I don't know how she saved either of them from our mother.

> **Vivien:** Mom's in the hospital. Was. Now she's in rehab
> **Augie:** Sorry, I didn't know. Joan never calls me anymore
> **Vivien:** Should she?
> **Augie:** Maybe I could help
> **Vivien:** You know Joan. She's the helper, not the helpee
> **Augie:** If the house needs to be retrofitted
> **Vivien:** Might have to be sold to pay for Mom's care
> **Augie:** I'll shoot her an email
> **Vivien:** Let me know how it goes

I went to bed thinking, *What now?*

The summer Vivien got pregnant, since she was working for my father, they left the house together, early in the morning before traffic was heavy, and took the long route, avoiding the highway, so that she could practise driving. If she was not quite the Vivien before the stray cat and tattoos, she was vibrant, as if work suited her better than school or boss-Dad was more congenial than home-Dad. At dinner, the two of them now had inside jokes. And though she acted indifferent to—even irritated by—Dad's compliments (about her steady hand at the wheel or how customers liked the sound of her voice on the phone), I was envious and couldn't wait until I was old enough to work or drive or both.

I had nothing to do that summer. My friends were both at camp, but I wasn't allowed to go because it was unhygienic. They sent me letters in envelopes with *private and confidential* scribbled all over them. They wrote about boys— one of them had got to first base. I wasn't sure what that entailed, precisely. I would have asked Vivien, except that she was always with Mark or working or telling me to go away. I worried that my friends, having become sophisticated at camp, wouldn't talk to me after they got home.

I spent hours watching the news. It was the summer that Israeli commandos freed a hundred hostages in Uganda, Lebanon's civil war kept dragging on, Jimmy Carter was running for president, and Montreal hosted the Olympics.

We watched the games on a colour TV, the first on the street. Mom was reaching the peak of a collecting phase, and the new living room broadloom, plush and beige, was still off-gassing. She'd acquired a golden-brown loveseat with a matching armchair to go with the floral couch. Mark sat in the armchair, and Vivien sat on his lap, an arm around his neck. Mark's father—an American—had just married Augie and Steve's mother, and Mark had no one to stay with during the extended honeymoon but his stepmother's ex-husband, so he was there for the whole summer. His main attraction—as far as I could tell—was his hair, which he wore in dreadlocks. That tormented our mother, who wanted to approve of him—so handsome and blond—but couldn't because of the dreadlocks.

Still, Mom was flying high on having made the house perfect, and the Olympics started auspiciously, reinforcing her good mood. She was a fan of royalty in general, and the Queen in particular. She starred in the opening ceremonies all in pink—what could be more feminine—and at fifty, she was as slender as Mom. Also, Princess Anne was on the British equestrian team, the only female athlete at the games who didn't have to take a sex test to prove she was female. It was Mom's idea to invite Uncle Jack and the boys to watch the games in mesmerizing colour with us.

I wasn't sure how I felt about that. Augie and I had drifted apart in middle school. He played guitar in a band, and I spent my free time reading in the basement. He hung out with his group of friends, and I had my two friends who weren't popular either. I didn't want him to come over if he was reluctant—it would be too embarrassing.

On the first day of competition, Vivien and Mark laid claim to the armchair. Augie and Steve sprawled on the floor with a large bowl of popcorn and a newspaper spread out under the bowl to protect the carpet. Uncle Jack, between wives, carried a kitchen chair to the exact spot, he said, with the best view of the TV. I took over the loveseat, where it was easy to reach down for popcorn, while Mom and Dad had the couch. When Mom's face lit up, so did Dad's. She sat like a girl, knees up, leaning into him.

The next day, Uncle Jack and the boys came over again. Augie pushed the popcorn bowl closer to me; he smiled; our hands touched in the bowl. We watched little Nadia Comaneci set a world record with her perfect ten in gymnastics, though the board showed a score of one because it wasn't designed for that many digits. Mom was so excited, she clapped her hands. I knew when to press an advantage and asked if Augie and I could pick up pizza for everyone. She told me of course, and to get money from her purse.

It was late when we set out, and the walk to the plaza seemed long, maybe because I felt shy again. Augie's hair was long, not as long as Mark's, but shoulder-length and a nutty brown. Musician's hair.

Every lawn had its sprinkler going as usual, but dusk made the streets look strange, the spray of water—broken by shadows—hanging mid-air, the squatting bungalows secretive behind the mist. Augie said, "Remember *Day of the Triffids*." We'd read it at school the previous year. "Watch out for ambulatory, man-eating plants."

I was impressed by *ambulatory*, and I didn't correct *man-eating*, though the plants ate women and children too. After a time, I feigned exhaustion and slumped onto the grass of somebody's lawn. Augie slumped down beside me.

He said, "I hate middle school."

I said, "Me too."

He said, "I should be in high school. I'm fourteen."

I said, "Yeah."

He said, "I want to go to a high school for the arts, but Dad won't let me."

"Really? But he always tells Dad to keep painting."

"Dad would let me go if I wanted to paint, but he says all musicians do drugs."

"That sounds like my father, not yours."

"Your father doesn't sound like your father when he's talking to me, either."

I said, "I think I need a piggyback ride the rest of the way."

He said, "Okay. Let's go."

Augie crouched and I put my arms around his neck. He reached back to grab on behind my knees and hoisted me up. We were both breathing quickly. He trotted at first, then slowed to a walk. Pressed against his back, soon damp with his sweat or mine, I felt his spine through my cotton shirt. I imagined writing my friends a letter: *He doesn't stink, I think he takes showers. If he tries to kiss me, I'll kick him.* A few minutes later, I decided I wouldn't kick him. At the plaza, I slid off his back. I rubbed my sweaty palms on my shorts before reaching into my pocket for money to pay for the pizza. With the change, we got Popsicles—grape for me, banana for Augie. We cracked them in half and shared as we waited for our order.

After a week of hosting the Olympics watch party at our house, Mom's ebullience diminished. Popcorn rolled off the newspaper onto the new carpet, and the kitchen chair left marks. When the Canadian women's basketball team lost to Bulgaria, she said, "No more." So, Uncle Jack and his boys watched the second week of games in black and white, the flickering of the television visible through their front window.

Every evening, while Vivien and Mark were off to the beach or a party, Dad went across the street, ostensibly to talk business with Uncle Jack, then toddled home late, smelling of Scotch. Mom sat on the couch without him, watching athletes leap and roll. I felt obliged to keep her company from my perch on the loveseat. During the commercials, she leafed through home furnishing catalogues. Sometimes, she'd call my attention to a shiny page. Lonely and bored, I'd say, "It looks nice," and she'd shake her head, "Not quite right."

My diary was full of yearning and complaints about missing my friends. I wasn't paying attention to Vivien and Mark except to be glad I didn't have to see them necking all the time anymore. At the start of September, Mark's father and new stepmother returned and took him home to Florida. In school, when Augie and I passed each other in the corridors, we'd nod and move along.

CHAPTER 7

The day after I messaged Augie as Vivien, the world didn't shatter, no one called me a fraud, and so, as usual, I dialed into the morning check-in. The other members of the practice in my district, South-Centre Toronto, were on the call: Larry Klieger (one of the practice's founders), our nurses and the social worker, who told us that, during the night, a patient of mine had gone to the ER and from there had been admitted to the ICU. I spent the next hour on the phone and online, uploading files and filling out forms to complete the transfer. When I checked email, I found one from Augie offering to assess the house. I suggested he come over on Tuesday evening. By nine thirty, I was done and on my way.

It was a beautiful spring day, and I left the car windows open to pick up the scent of trees in bloom. I was able to see four patients, including the one in the ICU. The hardest was a child, his family Syrian refugees. After I left their apartment, I cried in the car, ashamed to be so self-indulgent. While I was trying to get control, my pager beeped with a message. My mother's case manager wanted me to come see her as soon as possible.

The case manager was British, Martha something—I don't remember exactly. She had rosacea, which burgundied her cheeks, and naturally silver hair that curled to her shoulders. In my journal, I referred to her most often as the Toothy Woman. She was always smiling, as if that would sweep away the concerns of anxious relatives.

Her office was windowless, the desk dominated by a computer monitor, and she typed as I spoke, her eyes on the screen, shielded from my distress. Occasionally and at random, she smiled at me over the monitor. The gist of this meeting: my mother was uncooperative. As soon as she exerted the minimum effort required to improve her condition, she complained of being tired. That morning, she'd refused to get dressed. No one could force her to get better, Martha informed me, and so we should be considering "next steps."

It was an ominous phrase. Next steps were never an improvement.

As a physician, I had some slight advantages, but I had no power to put my mother higher on a waiting list at a decent place. And I couldn't halt her decline.

In the desert of suffering, compassion is water. Every day, I dole it out to my parched patients and their families, careful to save enough for each one. That day, with the child, his mother and his sister, I'd drained my reserves. I had nothing left. I was thinking, *I can't do this.*

The phone rang. Martha picked it up. Her side of the conversation: "Hello . . . I'm in a meeting . . . Yes . . . Daughter is here." (Social workers refer to a patient's relatives by their family role, not their name—Mom, Sister, Nephew—as if that's the sum of their identity.)

Martha put down the receiver. She smiled at me. "I have to deal with a situation. Just think about next steps. I'll be right back."

Once she was gone, I scooted around to look at her computer screen, but it was locked. I sat back down and took out my phone, but there was no one I could call. Did I have enough data to download the Facebook app? Messenger? Solitaire? I always saw people in waiting rooms playing Solitaire. Did it require data? Kids always know these things. I thought of my young patient, whose family had saved their children from bombs and were now losing him to illness. "But you have medicine in your hospitals," the older sister had said to me. "There's nothing?" My eyes welled up. I needed Solitaire.

Martha returned, smiling, but she didn't speak until she'd reseated herself behind the monitor. "Your mother requested a bedpan."

"That doesn't sound like her. She's fastidious."

"She's deteriorating."

"She seems awfully alert for someone whose condition is going downhill so rapidly."

"Sometimes it happens like that," Martha said.

I nodded, ignoring the condescension. It wouldn't help for me to say that I thought Mom was playing for pity or taking revenge on staff for pestering her.

"There's a waiting list for this facility. If your mother continues to be non-compliant, we have to move her out."

"When?" I asked.

"Not today, but you need to make your mother understand that this isn't a hotel. Either she complies with the program or she leaves."

My mother's roommate was making her way along the corridor, using a walker. I said hello as we passed. In the room, there were more flowers and cards than ever, crowding the window ledge on the roommate's side, joined now by spools of thread and bolts of fabric. Mom was in bed in her nightgown and bathrobe. The head of the bed was raised, the tray in front of her. While she ate, she was watching TV. Her bedside table was bare; I knew better than to bring her flowers. She raised a fork in greeting. "Hello, dear."

"How's dinner?"

"Good." She muted the TV. "I told them I'm a vegetarian."

"But you're not."

"The food is better. *She* ate chicken." Mom nodded toward her neighbour's bed. "I doubt she's going to get better with that sort of diet."

I pulled a chair close. "What are you watching?"

"A documentary about dreaming. How was your day?"

"A young patient wrote a story for me."

"What about?"

"Birds that fly to the stars and make a home there."

"Then what happens?"

"No one can see them except in dreams."

"When you worked in ER, the patients never gave you stories."

"I like doing palliative care."

"But it makes you sad."

"Sometimes. But it's also a privilege. Being with people at the end."

"The sacred journey," she said.

I must have looked surprised, because she pushed the tray away. "You girls thought I didn't understand anything because I was just a housewife."

"That's not true. We always knew you were smart."

"I wouldn't have guessed." She pulled her bathrobe tighter around her chest.

"Cold?"

"A bit."

I opened my messenger bag and took out a scarf. "This is light, but it'll warm you up." She leaned forward, and I wrapped it around her neck. I said, "I always wondered what you'd have done if you'd grown up in a different time."

"You did?"

"I had this idea you could have been a spy."

My mother laughed. I rebuckled my bag.

"Mom, we need to talk about something. Your case manager called me in for a meeting."

"Whatever for?"

"You're not making any progress. They say you stop the exercises as soon as you start."

"Because I'm old and sick."

"She says you have to stop treating this place like a hotel."

"Hardly a hotel. It's a mess, and strangers are always going in and out. I told you I want to go home."

"So, you think that's where you're going if you get kicked out?"

She didn't bother to reply. To her, the answer was obvious.

"I work all day. Who do you expect to take care of you?"

"What are you saying?"

"I'm not saying. *You're* telling me that you're too tired to do physio."

"I guess so."

"Now you won't even get up to go to the toilet. Anyone that incapacitated needs long-term care. That's what your case manager talked to me about. She can get you into one of the larger facilities on the outskirts of the city. It always has beds. I'm sorry it won't be one of the places we prefer—"

"*You* prefer! You can't wait to get rid of me."

"It'll probably be far away," I said patiently. I could have said, *It'll be a fuck of a distance to get to.* "But I'll visit as often as I can, and hopefully a space will open up somewhere else."

"Absolutely not. If I want to go home, then I go home."

"I can't take care of you. Not in your current condition. You're too fragile." (And also, I think I said, *You never listen to anyone. I give in, but the nurses don't. That's why you're using a bedpan, isn't it? To shit on them?*)

"You want me out of the way so you can get that junk of yours out of your storage locker and throw it all over the house." She crossed her arms, as if the facts should give in to her as easily as her daughter, who—at that moment—wanted to shake her.

Instead, I breathed in and out, trying to act like a professional, not someone who cries in the car. It took a few more breaths and then some more until I could speak in my calm doctor voice. "What are you hoping for, Mom?"

"That Vivien won't see me in a place like that."

"What else?"

"That she'll come home."

"She will."

Mom looked at me, agony in her eyes.

If I couldn't motivate her, maybe Vivien could.

At home, I shared a couple of my sister's photos to Facebook. In one of them, a crocodile was attacking a baby hippo. The other had been taken by someone else, maybe the man who'd spoken to her in French during our last Skype call. She was sitting on a bench outside the clinic, and her eyes had the shine of surgical steel. She might have been thinking about the danger she was facing. Or hooking up with that French-speaking colleague. Several of Vivien's Facebook friends welcomed her back. I clicked the "Like" icon on their comments. Then I messaged my mother.

THU, APR 18, 08:04 PM

Vivien: Hi Mom, I'm back

Sheila: About time. Thanks for the card. It was very pink.

Vivien: Matches my sunburn

Sheila: Sunburns cause cancer. You should take better care of yourself.

Vivien: So should you. Joan tells me you're not trying to get better. I was talking to her about coming for a visit

Sheila: When

Vivien: Follow the program and we'll figure it out

I was about to exit the app, but the three dots were wiggling, and so I waited for Mom. It took a while—the dots wiggled and stopped several times as if she was deleting what she'd written and starting again.

Sheila: I'm sorry about the bed
Vivien: What bed?
Sheila: Yours. You know.
Vivien: The one you gave away when I was pregnant?
Sheila: Yes that one.
Vivien: It's okay, Mom. That was a long time ago
Sheila: Okay. I'll try harder. Come home soon

The green dot beside my mother's name winked out. As usual, Vivien had succeeded where I'd failed. But instead of sparking my old resentment, I started to wonder what else could be accomplished this way.

So, that bed. Mom always believed that's what drove Vivien away, but obviously, it had to be the crib.

Mom's gentleness when she found out Vivien was pregnant had puzzled me at first. Usually, my parents were in sync, their compulsions escalating and dropping away in tandem. But for much of Vivien's pregnancy, Mom acted as if she lived in a house that Dad just haplessly stumbled through now and again.

Dad's own anger soon ebbed. Now, he looked at Vivien sadly. I caught her, once, crying in the bathroom over it, though she insisted she was just hormonal. As she'd predicted, his drinking escalated. He'd never missed work before, but he did now, and Uncle Jack covered for him. There were no more conversations between us in the basement; to make up for his hungover mornings, Dad put in long hours, then drank for long hours to "unwind" from all that effort.

Mom didn't say a word about his drinking. All of her attention had shifted to the coming baby. The *new* baby, she would say, beaming. She assembled a trousseau of baby things: little clothes wrapped in tissue paper, rattles, chew toys, picture books, cloth diapers, diaper pins. She was always talking about the baby—how they'd go to the park and the pool and the library for crafts—as if this fresh start was better than any purged house could ever be. At Christmas, Vivien found a crib under the tree. Mom bought books on child rearing, which she not only read, but underlined. While reading, she'd drink tea, always out of Aunt Peggy's teacup.

Then it hit me: Vivien was Peggy. Sixteen, pregnant. Mom hadn't been able to help her friend—not enough to prevent her suicide—but she could help Vivien, and this desire now over-rode every other. At thirteen, I had trouble putting all this into words, or even teasing out why it made me uneasy.

My sister alternated between distrusting Mom and soaking up her care. She still called me a pest—though almost affectionately—and undertook to educate me about women's liberation and reproductive rights, showing me the illustrations in *Our Bodies, Ourselves*. Sometimes, she had bad dreams. Once, on my way to the bathroom, I heard her crying in her sleep. I went into her room and woke her up, and she asked me to stay. After that, I slept with her every night, and she said that kept the bad dreams away.

During Vivien's sixth month, Dad crashed into a stop sign—luckily it wasn't a tree or he'd have died. He'd been speeding, a habit he had when he was drunk, as if going seventy kilometres an hour in a thirty zone rendered him invisible. The police officer in the cruiser idling at the corner apparently disagreed. Dad lost his licence, and Mom refused to drive him to the office. If Uncle Jack wasn't able to give Dad a lift, he had to use public transit. His car in the driveway was a continual reminder that he—a veteran with the Distinguished Flying Medal—was now a man on foot. The indignity stung, and he drank diligently to blunt it.

In her seventh month, Vivien dressed for a school dance, wearing one of the pretty maternity dresses Mom had bought for her. When the school principal made her leave the dance, Mom was outraged. She was ready to drive to the school and confront the principal, but Vivien stopped her. She didn't care about the dance, she'd just wanted to annoy the principal. Mission accomplished.

Despite Mom's solicitousness—maybe because of it—Vivien made a point of behaving as if pregnancy hadn't changed her. She spit at one of the popular kids who'd called her a slutty blimp, and was suspended for a day. She hung out with boys who wanted to dismantle capitalism. They travelled by bus to an anti-nuclear protest, skipping school, which led to Vivien being suspended again. Then, in her eighth month of pregnancy, she and her friends went to hear a speaker from Doctors Without Borders.

"They call it guerrilla medicine," Vivien said to me afterwards, still exhilarated. "They don't care whose side anyone is on. I'm going to do that. I'll be a nurse, and when you're a doctor, Roo, you can come with me."

That night, Dad shook me awake at four a.m., saying he had something funny to tell me, and then threw up on me. The next morning, I stepped over his body, slumped in the hallway where he'd blacked out.

A jumbo-sized box of extra-large trash bags appeared in the garage. Sometimes, I'd catch my mother standing in front of a closet, clothes draped over her arm, or bent over a drawer, a little pile of things on top of the dresser. She'd put everything back while asking me something ordinary, like "How was school?" then she'd walk off halfway through my answer. I started keeping my diary in my schoolbag. One Saturday, Mom sat in the kitchen for hours, drinking tea from Aunt Peggy's china cup.

The next day, a Sunday, Dad was in their bedroom, sleeping off a binge. I was in Vivien's room, the two of us on her bed playing gin rummy. I was just about to pick up the card that would give me a winning hand when Mom appeared in the doorway and said she wanted to have a chat with Vivien. We both followed her to the living room. She sat on the couch and patted the seat beside her. Vivien joined her, as she had the day my parents found out she was pregnant. It had been bright and wintry then; now the windows were grey and spring rain pattered against the glass.

"Let's talk, honey," Mom said.

I perched on the arm of the couch, my feet touching my sister's legs.

"What?" she asked.

"You want to be a nurse and travel, right?" Mom said.

Vivien nodded.

"So, we should plan for you to do that."

"Okay, I guess."

"You can't take a baby with you."

"It'll be a while until I can go. I have to get into nursing school and graduate first. You said you'd help."

"I've been thinking about how best to do that. You're always full of ideas."

"So?"

"Shouldn't you be free to do whatever comes into your head, go anywhere, any time?"

"How?"

"Give us custody of the baby."

"What do you mean custody?" she said. "Like adoption?"

"I was thinking just custody, but yes, adopting would be better. More stable for the child. There'd be no wondering where its mother is."

"And Dad would be—"

"The father."

"*My* dad. Who's a drunk."

"Don't call him that!"

"Why not? It's true."

"Your father works hard. He provides us with everything we have."

"And you're thinking I'd be what? My child's *sister*?"

"If you aren't here, we need to be able to make all the necessary decisions."

"That's never going to happen, Mom."

"It's not entirely up to you."

"What's that supposed to mean?"

"You're a minor. I'm responsible for your welfare."

Vivien snapped her fingers. "News flash, Mom. Pregnancy gives you legal rights. I'm the one who decides."

Mom scoffed. "Where did you get that idea?"

"My guidance counsellor. She talked to me about going to a maternity home."

"You wouldn't!"

"I could if I want. I'm over sixteen, so I have the right to live anywhere I choose."

"And you'd go there instead of your own home?"

"She just wanted me to know all the options."

"She doesn't know anything. I'm doing this for *you*."

"For me? Taking my baby?"

"If Aunt Peggy's mother had done this for her, she'd be alive today. What's wrong with you?"

"I'm not your fucking Peggy."

"So true." Mom's mouth twisted as if she'd opened a drawer and found something gross in it. "You're a selfish child."

"This baby is *mine*. Not some drunk's and a crazy lady's."

Mom's eyes went cold. "What did you call me?"

Vivien stared right back. Then she manoeuvred herself to a standing position, waddled out of the house and slammed the door. Mom got up and stood at the window, trying to catch her breath, her hand on her heart. When she'd calmed down, she turned, walked to the garage and brought in the box of trash bags.

Mom attacked the house as if it had to pay for all the months she'd wasted holding back. Her cleaning was an assault—she pushed the vacuum cleaner back and forth so hard it flipped over; she sloshed water all over the kitchen with the string mop. Over the next couple of weeks, she got rid of every book, including those she'd previously considered necessary, like the dictionary and encyclopedia. Ashtrays disappeared and so did the occasional tables on which they'd perched. One day there, the next gone. The kitchen set, the couch.

Nothing was safe. Dad's radio, his bookcase, even the contents of his liquor cabinet—all of it went, his weak protests barely slowing her down. There were more firsts: Mom ripped up the living room carpet and got rid of the beds. We slept on camping mats that she rolled up and stored in the car after we got up. Then she packed all the baby things, intending to donate them to Goodwill: knitted outfits, receiving blankets, rattles, the christening gown, and the crib, pristine in its box.

Vivien tried to stop her from removing the crib. She stood in front of Mom, blocking her way, and Mom said, "This is *my* house. I decide what's in it. Like you said—you're old enough to go anywhere you want. Now move."

Shaken, Vivien did.

The last thing to go was Aunt Peggy's teacup. When there was nothing left in the house but us, Mom stood amidst the emptiness, hands on her hips, breathing heavily.

That night, she couldn't sleep, as if—despite surpassing all previous efforts—she needed more to clear. Prowling in the dark, she scoured drawers, though there was nothing left in them. I lay awake, uncomfortable on the mat in my room, listening to her drag out the vacuum cleaner she'd borrowed from a neighbour, then pass it back and forth over the sub-floor in the living room. When the roaring ceased, followed by a loud thump, Vivien and I both emerged from our rooms. We found Mom on the floor, her hand on her chest. The sound of the vacuum must have woken Dad, who was crouching next to Mom, looking at us in confusion.

"Call 911, Joan!" Vivien yelled, and I ran to the phone, almost pulling it out of the wall, the cord stretching as I tried to get closer to my mother. "What do I tell them?"

"That Mom's having a heart attack."

I dialed. The nine took so long to circle from the notch, the ones short, snappy, and I thought, *Why don't we have a push-button phone?*

"Nine one one. What is your emergency?"

While I described Mom's pain and shortness of breath, Vivien knelt on the floor and cradled our mother against her large belly. Dad was crying and vowing to quit drinking if Mom would just be okay. I gave our address, making sure the dispatcher noted it was Crescent, not Drive, because there was another street with the same name nearby.

EMTs came and put my mother on a stretcher. Dad went with her, saying he'd call us from the hospital. I told him that we'd be at Uncle Jack's. This was what people did before cellphones, before email, before answering machines. They went to the neighbours'. I wasn't waiting with my sister in an empty house for my mother to die.

The ambulance left. Vivien and I got dressed and then crossed the street. Standing on the porch, we held hands, waiting for Uncle Jack to answer the doorbell. When we told him what had happened, he offered us the bed in the guest room, but we wanted to stay up, in case Dad called, so Uncle Jack made us cocoa and then watched TV with us, the volume low because the boys were sleeping.

Vivien finally dropped off, exhausted. Uncle Jack put a cushion under her head and covered her with a blanket. It was almost morning.

In a cluttered kitchen—bowl of bananas, knapsack hanging on the back of a chair, notes and pictures under fridge magnets, cookies out on a plate (not even in a cookie jar), mail on the counter, a can of WD-40 on top of a bill— I helped Uncle Jack make a stack of ham and cheese sandwiches for breakfast. If you're not going to eat kosher, he said, you may as well go all the way.

Uncle Jack said that everything would be okay, that

maybe Mom had just gotten dizzy from breathing in cleaning fumes, and I said, "Uh-huh." He'd noticed the Goodwill truck appearing in front of our house a lot, he said, and added that in the war, guys did all kinds of weird things to cope with stress. A buddy of his had kept all his nail clippings in a sack in his duffle bag, and another got naked, covered himself in mud and walked into a bar for a beer.

I told him Vivien didn't have a bed anymore and asked him if sleeping on a mat on the floor could hurt her or the baby. Uncle Jack put down the knife he'd been using to cut the sandwiches into triangles. He said it was high time his sons got up, and he roused them with swearing on both sides. Then Augie and Steve helped him dismantle the bed in the guest room, carry the pieces over to our house and reassemble them in Vivien's room.

Around noon, my parents came home. Mom's heart was undamaged—she'd had a panic attack.

CHAPTER 8

As I was heading from my car to the office for our monthly meeting, a painting under my arm, Martha called to give me an update on Mom. The "Vivien effect" had run its course: Mom was back to resisting all their efforts to help her. "I'll speak to her," I promised the care manager, but I was worried.

I climbed to the second floor of the house where our offices were located, in a residential area around the corner from Toronto General Hospital. It was my turn to present, and since I was already too hot, I opened the windows in the conference room. Outside, a bicycle courier was splashed by a car driving through a puddle. In the sky to the west, a rainbow was fading.

These meetings were a chance for staff from all three districts to get together, and the conference room was full. Larry, the head of the practice, had been my mentor in palliative care. He'd taught me that patients are people, alive or not, and to speak politely to the deceased while removing IV lines. The office had wide aisles to accommodate his wheelchair, which he parked beside the front row of chairs in the conference room.

Though we didn't socialize, I knew my colleagues had confidence in my expertise and always looked forward to what I had to say, but I didn't enjoy being a presenter. Uncomfortable with all eyes on me, I got through the slides showing Eddie Wong's medical history. He'd chosen to do chemo, and as a result, his mobility had improved. He was painting again and had given us a thank-you gift: a view of Lake Ontario during the polar vortex, frost smoke obscuring the city's skyline. After I showed everyone the painting, I spoke about my relationship with the patient, my voice emotional as I described the first time he'd fully smiled at me, showing his bare gums. Then a hot flash started at my feet, as if creeping up from the earth's molten core, and made me think of climate change. "Nothing occurs in isolation," I said. "The melting ice cap is altering wind currents, so we had that frigid air hovering over us all winter. Hence the polar vortex. And Eddie's painting."

One of the nurses said, "Hence Saint Joan," and chuckled.

Our planet is five billion years old—in galactic terms, middle-aged. A menopausal woman. Throwing off a furnace of heat can produce a cold flash, as I knew myself. After the presentation, I needed a sweater. I stood around for a few excruciating minutes while my colleagues scarfed the usual bagels and coffee, then escaped to a coffee shop where I could get a bite in peace.

I'd decided to increase my data plan so I could use my phone, not just my laptop, to post for Vivien. I'd had it turned off during my talk, and when I turned it on, it immediately started chirping. The notifications didn't stop until I muted it. Facebook loved my sister.

Several of her friends had messaged things like, *Where'd you go?* and *Are you okay?* and I replied to each of them, *Internet down.* Under the latest picture of Vivien, Mom had commented, *Wear sunscreen!* I tapped on the reaction button, chose the heart, then unselected it as too sentimental, and replied, *Remember our deal.*

While I was doing that, a chat head popped up on my screen: Grace Musa, the Nigerian nurse. *Are you mad at me?*

I tapped on the chat. Vivien's last message—*Fighting words, dear*—was sent in January. I scrolled up. Their conversations were intermittent, but they addressed each other with affection, using lots of *luv* and *dear.*

Who was Grace to her?

I tapped on her profile, then photos. Grace had an oval face and wore cat-eye glasses. Her uniform: a white cotton dress, sleeves rolled up, which she wore over a T-shirt. In one photo, she was holding a newborn, silicone gloves on her hands. To her right, I saw a metal sink with the umbilical cord in it. Grace looked younger than my sister, maybe in her forties, hair still dark. I tapped "About." Grace didn't like heavy metal. She preferred gospel, and her favourite movie was *The Shack*—based on the book about a despairing father who meets God in the form of a Black woman. (I'd read it myself and liked it, but Vivien said the blurb on the back was enough to make her nauseous.) Nothing in common there.

Grace was currently working as a flying midwife with UNICEF, commuting by helicopter to clinics in the northeast of Nigeria, a dangerous region subject to attacks by Boko Haram fanatics. It was one of the few hot spots where Vivien had never been posted. But before that, I saw, Grace had worked at a trauma hospital run by Doctors Without Borders in Port Harcourt, which was in the south of the country. I checked the date on the photo—2007—and yes, Vivien had been a surgical nurse in the same hospital then. They must have met through their work and the intensity of it had bonded them. It appeared they'd both gotten burnt out around the same time. Grace had remained in Nigeria but turned to midwifery, while my sister had gone to the DRC with a focus on vaccination and stints in rural clinics largely devoted to women and children.

Careful, careful, I thought.

TUE, APR 23, 12:08 PM
Vivien: No, never mad at you, was just kidding
Grace: Glad you're back safe. You take too many risks
Vivien: You're one to talk
Grace: I'll be okay
Vivien: You can't be sure, not where you are
Grace: I should be, as long as I behave
Vivien: Counting on it dear
Grace: ❤

It seemed I'd passed. At least for the moment.

After my last appointment of the day, I headed directly to Valley View. Mom sniped at me the entire visit, complaining about her roommate, the food, and the light coming through the large windows, which woke her up too early in the morning. Every time I tried to talk with her about physiotherapy, she pretended not to hear me. I couldn't stay long because

Augie was coming over to assess the house, and I left Mom fuming at her helplessness.

Augie was divorced—unlike his father, just once—and, like me, didn't have kids. From his messages to Vivien, I knew that he wished he'd pursued music instead of becoming a real estate agent. He arrived, wearing jeans and a sports jacket, friendly below and formal above, covering all bases. He was still attractive in a low-key way: neither square jawed nor rounded, not balding, no hair sticking out of his nose. Just an ordinary man with warm, brown eyes and a direct gaze, who could laugh at himself, as I'd also seen in his chats with Vivien. I wore sweatpants and a T-shirt—my uniform at home—and was surprised to find myself regretting it. We greeted each other with a cousinly hug.

"You're looking good," he said. "Tinted contacts?"

"Thanks. Just my eyes. I had laser surgery."

"Nice. How's your mom?"

"Frustrating. If she doesn't start making progress, I'm going to have to find a place for her."

"So, the house . . ."

"I need to know what I'd have to do to put it on the market."

"Right," he said. "Let's have a look."

We started with the kitchen. Mom had disposed of the table set just before she went into hospital, and I'd replaced it with a folding chair and tray stand from my trunk. The dishes were washed and put away, and while waiting for Augie, I'd been reading the news. The folding chair was padded under the vinyl and having the newspaper to myself for as long as I liked was luxurious. No rush to recycle, no pressure to empty the bins. I'd left my reading glasses on the tray.

"You won't need to hire cleaners," Augie said.

"Really?" Between work and visiting my mother, I thought I'd been neglectful.

"The house is immaculate, but the smell . . ." He shook his head. "Bleach won't sell it."

"Oh. Is it bothering you?"

"No, no. I'm fine." He moved to stand beside me, his shoulder touching mine as he reached to tap on the partition between the kitchen and living room. "You might think about knocking down this wall. Make it all open plan."

How long had it been since I'd felt a man's shoulder against mine? I moved away and walked toward the living room, where Mom's recliner sat in lonely splendour.

Augie followed. "There's still no floor, I see."

It was too early to offer him a drink so I could have one too. I had rules: don't clean after nine p.m. and no alcohol before it. "Yep, the subfloor still."

"Memory of old times."

"You remember when Mom ripped it up?"

"Hard to miss. The carpet was piled up outside on garbage day. My father called to tell Mom about it. Long distance call—it was a big deal."

"Why would he do that?"

"Dad felt responsible for Vivien's situation because Mark had stayed with us. I could hear him yelling on the phone, and I came downstairs, thinking something was wrong. But he was just upset with Mom—not so unusual—and she was telling him it wasn't Mark."

"It had to be."

Augie shrugged. "She didn't think so."

"Too bad there was no DNA testing back then."

"Would it have made a difference?" Augie was looking at me as if he had another question in mind, and I glanced at the ceiling—no spider webs there, not even in the corners. I swept them down regularly.

"Probably not."

He'd moved closer to me again. I liked the scent of his aftershave.

"What should I do about the floor?"

"Broadloom is fast and cheaper, but hardwood is a feature. Your choice. You'll need to get furniture. And curtains."

Without curtains, nothing obscured the light. The sky was pink, the sun just starting to set. There were maple trees in the backyard, two of them planted when my sister and I were born, a third much later, when I graduated from medical school. A robin was nesting in the bare branches of the smallest. It's the female who builds the nest, the male singing while she works.

Next, Augie inspected the three bedrooms. I stood in the hallway while he checked out the ensuite in Mom's room and then the main bathroom. He turned taps. He looked into closets. Hand on my arm, he asked whether I'd move back downtown if the house was sold, and I said, "One step at a time," and wished I smelled of something better than bleach. I thought, *What's wrong with you—it's just Augie.*

We discussed the age of the appliances as we went down to the basement. He checked the operation of the sliding glass doors that opened onto the backyard. Heat moved up from my feet and reddened my face—there's no privacy of feeling in menopause.

He turned to me and said, "The bones of the house are good and the back-split gives you a bright basement, but that's just a start. Buyers react emotionally. They want to see themselves in a home, and it's hard to see yourself in one that looks unfinished. Fix it up as if it's yours. Make it a place you'd want to live, and someone else will too."

What *I'd* want? When did I have the right to want anything? "I don't know how I'm going to find the time."

"You should try. The house will sell faster and you'll get what it's worth. Or, if you really can't manage, I can recommend an interior decorator who specializes in staging houses."

"Let me think about it, Augie."

"Sure. When you're ready, give me a call. Even if you're not—I'm always happy to hear from you."

"Okay, I will. Thanks."

I assumed he was just being polite.

After Augie left, I made myself a cup of tea, taking advantage of Mom's absence to add sugar and milk. (She objected to sugar because it attracted ants, and though she still ate beef, she considered cow secretions unhygienic.) With mug in hand, I stood at the kitchen counter in front of my laptop, reading a review of data on toxicity versus survival in cancer treatments given to patients with a prognosis of six months. By the time I was done, it was well after nine, and I poured myself a shot of whisky. Then I sat in my mother's recliner, tentatively at first—if Mom did return home, she might notice lint from my sweatpants. But after a while, I relaxed. The footrest up and phone in hand, I started browsing

Facebook. The little rush I got every time notifications popped up was unexpected, even embarrassing.

Ping. *Oscar Karlsson and 23 others reacted to your photo.*

Ping. *There have been 10+ new posts since you last visited Knitting for Life*

Ping. *Raoul Delgado commented on your photo "I remember that hippo"*

Vivien's feed: headlines from the *New Internationalist* (a photo of a fire, "How to Avoid Climate Breakdown"); a UNICEF post (in small letters, *Sponsored, Paid for*); a photo of a camping mat crocheted out of plastic bags; a video of a nurse kicking the cap off a bottle; a post about a young gay man severely beaten on the outskirts of the largest city in the northeast of Nigeria, where Grace was based. This was her post, and it was generating heated argument about how to respond, though—unlike my sister's posts—the privacy setting was friends only. I'd had a Nigerian patient once and knew that in some regions of the country, being gay was a crime, punishable by flogging or worse.

Ping. *Grace Musa: What do you think? Organize a protest?*

Though Vivien had never shied away from activism, how could I say, *Yes, put yourself in harm's way?* While I was blinking and blinking at my phone, Grace was waiting for me to respond.

TUE, APR 23, 10:25 PM
Grace: Viv?

I couldn't claim the shaky signal excuse with that green dot in the corner of Vivien's profile picture proclaiming, *I'm here with my phone, gazing at your message.* I tapped the screen, as if I could make the picture go away, and a new page appeared. There, on the screen below something called *Message Requests* was a link to settings that showed how to toggle from active to non-active status. I toggled it off and the green dot disappeared. A temporary fix. I finished my drink and toggled it on again.

> **Vivien:** Your mothers and babies are refugees. They escaped extremists. If you protest and end up in hospital or jail you can't help them
> **Grace:** Most reasonable advice anyone's given

The green dot beside her name disappeared, but I wasn't alarmed by her rapid departure. After all, she'd said *reasonable*. I returned to Message Requests, a column of messages from scammers and desperate people who clearly didn't know Vivien. Scrolling down, I saw that a man named Bruno Edery had sent a message on March 4. It began, like the others, *I saw your profile*. His profile picture was a cartoon dog, and I tapped it, hoping for comic relief.

> I saw your profile, and you're the right age and born in the right place. I think you might be my mother. Are you Vivien Leigh Connor date of birth January 17, 1960? If I'm mistaken, please let me know anyway, and I'll cross you off my list. I'm not looking to intrude on your life. I'm just hoping to get some medical information.

The message had been sent when Vivien was still alive. As I reread it, my eyes blurring, it looked like this: *I think you might be. My mother, are you? Vivien Leigh Connor date of birth January 17, 1960.*

I read it again, and all I saw was: *Are you?*

No. Yes.

Which *you?*

Yes. I tapped send.

CHAPTER 9

After Mom's panic attack, the doctor had prescribed medication. Wrapped in the cotton wool of a tranquilizer, she drifted away whenever I tried to talk to her. At night, adding a sleeping pill to the mix, she was dead to the world. Dad was relieved that she hadn't been in any actual danger, so he kept drinking as if his vow—made under duress—was meaningless. After getting home from work, he'd sit in the basement, drink himself into a stupor and then pass out on the carpet. That's how I came to be the only one awake when Vivien went into labour, twelve days ahead of her due date.

At a minute after midnight on May 1, she said, "Happy birthday, Sis." I was lying beside her, and we were reminiscing: how she used to put Smarties in the cereal because she liked the way I giggled every time I bit into one; how she taught me to lick a red Smartie and then rub it on my lips, pretending it was makeup. I told her that I'd babysit anytime she wanted—I still thought she was keeping the baby.

Then she said, "Picture Mom with a stinky diaper pail."

"She had us. She changed our diapers."

"I hate to tell you, Roo. She doesn't care about us."

"She does."

"She made us think she was dying. For attention."

"A panic attack is real."

"She threw out the *crib*. My baby needs a home."

"So, we could share an apartment. I can get a job after school. It's only a few years until I graduate."

"Just be real for once." Her voice sounded tired, as if we'd been going over this for hours instead of minutes. "I want my baby to have a good home, and if you say *ours*, I'll smack you."

Vivien's contractions began soon after, but because it was still a little early, she thought it was another bout of false labour. I followed her lead as usual. We were kids. Stupid kids. We didn't realize it was the real thing, not even when her water broke, and she said she'd peed in her bed, and I changed the sheets, which smelled nothing like pee. Not until the contractions were fierce and close together, and she was screaming. I ran into my parents' bedroom, but I couldn't rouse Mom—a sleeping pill muffles the brain's response even to a loud noise, like a fire alarm, and she was tranquilized on top of it—so I dashed down the stairs to the basement. Dad woke up, but he didn't seem to understand what I was saying, and Vivien was still screaming. I hurried upstairs and once again dialed 911.

The ambulance didn't get to our house on time.

There was nothing surprising at the birth, and there was everything: my nephew's perfect fingernails, his wrinkly feet, the tongue in the circle of his mouth as he cried for the world, Vivien reaching for him and then changing her mind.

Turning her head. Arms crossed, pressed against her breasts. "Don't you want to hold him?" Silence. I didn't know what to do. On TV, newborns were bathed and weighed, but he was so tiny and he was shivering, and so I hugged him close, staining my pyjama top with the gore of birth until the ambulance arrived and the EMTs stormed our house. One of them went for the adults, the other attended to Vivien. Dad finally stumbled up the stairs, saying, "Is that my grandson?" Vivien shook her head, tears on her cheeks. The medic pried the baby from me as I cried, "Don't take him yet, he doesn't have a name."

I studied Bruno's profile pic: Snoopy in a helmet and scarf, fighting an imaginary air battle from his perch on the roof of a doghouse. Was my nephew an aviator? A fan of old cartoons? Did he look like anyone in our family? Have kids? I pictured three, four, five, eight of them standing in a row from tallest to smallest, my nephew whistling like the captain in *The Sound of Music*, which my mother had loved and watched over and over until the tape wore out, something remarkable in a house where nothing got old except the people in it. I had the same squared-off fingers as Vivien, unlike Mom's, which were long and slender, made for rings or playing the piano. She'd always wished she'd had music lessons. Did Bruno have her fingers? Did his kids? Eight of them in a row with rings on their fingers?

I didn't sleep much the night I opened his message. When the moon rose, it was one in the morning, and afraid I'd been too abrupt, I sent him a question in return: *Is your date of birth May 1, 1977?*

The next morning, birdsong woke me up before sunrise, and I checked for a reply. There was nothing from the man who could be my sister's son. I went off to shower.

Wet hair in a turban of towel and wearing the white bathrobe that matched my mother's, I stood at the counter to eat toast and eggs while I reviewed some patient notes I hadn't gotten to the night before. I heard a ping on my phone. Bruno had replied. *Yes, that's my birth date. Thanks for responding.* I began to tap back, but my thumbs felt as clumsy as an old person's. I turned to my laptop and opened Messenger on a browser. Next to Bruno Edery, a green dot was lit up like an open eye. I clicked. He was somewhere typing; in the pop-up box, smaller black dots were wiggling. I started writing too, so he would see that I was awake and with him.

> **WED, APR 24, 06:21 AM**
> **Vivien:** Are you all right. Has your life been all right?
> **Bruno:** Yes fine
> **Vivien:** It was a shock, finding your message. It was buried away in Message Requests.
> **Bruno:** Sorry to bother you. There was only one other Vivien Leigh Connor. In Ireland
> **Vivien:** Don't be sorry. I'm glad you got in touch

Now, I thought, *tell him that you're not Vivien, that Vivien has died.* Write, *I'm sorry, I've got to let you know.* But the dots were wiggling—I wanted to see what he was going to say.

> **Bruno:** I won't keep you long. I'm just looking for medical history. For my son.

I started to reply with the truth, then deleted it. Vivien's Facebook posts were public. What if he wrote condolences on her timeline? Mom might see it before I had time to take it down. He just wanted information—why complicate things?

Bruno: Are there any illnesses that run in the family?
Vivien: My father was an alcoholic and mother has compulsive spartanism
Bruno: What's that?
Vivien: An obsession with getting rid of things. Also she's fond of cleaning
Bruno: No worries about that in my house
Bruno: Any other medical history? Diabetes? Heart disease? Cancer?
Vivien: Heart disease, yes. Not before age sixty

That was all there was to say. Conversation over. Nephew gone. The stab of regret shook me. I thought, *This is the only chance you'll get. Ask about his life.*

Vivien: So you've only got one child?
Bruno: Two. I also have a stepdaughter

I began typing, *So did I*, but then remembered I was Vivien and backspaced it away. Needing to calm down, I got myself a glass of water and drank it before returning to the laptop.

Bruno: I haven't been able to get any information on my birth father. Could you give me the contact info?

I paused, and he waited. What would my sister have said to a question she didn't want to answer? Nothing. She'd have closed the tab. And my Vivien?

> **Vivien:** I don't have it
> **Bruno:** Then the name
> **Vivien:** It's not mine to give
> **Bruno:** It's mine to know. My right. Not yours to with-hold.

I nearly told him then, *I can't give it to you; I'm just the aunt.* But no—I'd already considered the consequences. I'd have to resort to the truth as I understood it.

> **Vivien:** The birth certificate says Unknown for a reason
> **Bruno:** I don't believe this. What gives you the right to keep that from me?
> **Bruno:** Every other human being knows where they come from. I couldn't even get access to my birth certificate until ten years ago.
> **Bruno:** It's like I'm from Mars

I felt his need, the hole in him, as if it was mine. The missing piece just out of reach. His frustration. His desperation. The intensity of it would have made Vivien angry. I was just acting, trying to give him a feel for her. Wasn't I? My index fingers on the keyboard, jabbing.

> **Vivien:** I was sixteen when I got pregnant. It wasn't my plan to fuck up your life or mine

The snap of keys was ever so satisfying. The last tap—send. I did it without a pause. It took a full half-minute for self-recrimination to smack the back of my head.

Vivien: I'll try to get in touch with him
Bruno: This is intense for me too. Thanks
Vivien: Give me time

Bruno's green dot disappeared.

Was perpetuating the lie so wrong? It couldn't last much longer—just until I gave him what he needed.

Over the next three days, I saw patients, wrote up notes, visited my mother, spoke to her case manager and begged for more time. I uploaded a photo to Facebook of the bone protruding from the leg of the motorcycle-accident patient, with the caption: *Bad breaks in every sense.* (Oscar and Raoul liked it immediately. I wondered about Grace, but figured she must be in a village somewhere, out of touch). There was a message from Oscar about his mother attempting to report him for elder abuse because he'd gone to a conference instead of taking her to her hairdresser. (I sent him a link: *5 Tips for Coping with Aging Parents.*) I put a bowl under the kitchen sink to catch water from a leak, got a plumber in to fix it, and went to my storage locker, where I read my diary from the summer of 1976—which mentioned Mark, but never his last name; if I wanted that I'd have to ask Augie—all the while half-listening for the ping of my phone. On Friday evening, my sister's son, my nephew, finally messaged me again.

FRI, APR 26, 10:37 PM
Bruno: So you're a nurse in the DRC
Vivien: I looked you up too, but all I could find was your Facebook profile with nothing in it

I imagined Mark crossed with my sister. Blond, pointy-nosed, sharp-tongued.

Bruno: Try B.G. Edery
Vivien: Got it. You're a carpenter

He specialized in custom doors—his website showed one carved with a fish leaping from a river, another inlaid with squares depicting celestial bodies—and he lived in Toronto, where he also taught at George Brown College.

Bruno: I like working with my hands
Bruno: Why the DRC?
Vivien: It's a big country and I don't like to stay in one place. I've worked on three continents. Most recently in vaccination outreach
Bruno: I hate needles
Bruno: Why do carpenters make the best witnesses?
Vivien: Why?
Bruno: They saw everything
Vivien: Funny

There was no picture of him in the list of part-time faculty or on his website. I wanted to see my nephew; I wanted to know him. *You're selfish*, I told myself. My self replied, *I lost him too.*

Vivien: Why is your profile pic Snoopy fighting
the Red Baron?
Bruno: I'm a history nerd. Because I never knew
my own
Vivien: I could send you a picture
Bruno: Okay

I chose one of Vivien at an outdoor clinic—bare-armed,
her tattoos visible—and messaged it, hoping he'd respond in
kind. No dots wiggled in reply.

Vivien: Do you look like me?
Bruno: Not really
Bruno: I have a couple of tattoos too
Vivien: I got my first at age 13
Bruno: I waited until I was 25. My parents disapproved.
The Torah forbids it. Leviticus. No making marks in the
skin, dead or alive. You're not Jewish, are you?
Vivien: I'm an atheist
Bruno: So am I. What's that got to do with it? I mean
family background. Any Nazis?
Vivien: No. A few Communists. British Isles
Bruno: That's a relief
Vivien: My father was a bomber pilot in WW2
Bruno: My grandfather was in the Algerian resistance.
The Vichy regime sent his brother to a concentra-
tion camp
Vivien: Edery isn't a Jewish name
Bruno: It is if you're North African. My parents
were forced out because they're Jews. They met
in France

Bruno: Speaking of. Fathers and history. What about mine?
Vivien: Working on it

He was gone again.

I called Augie early the next morning, expecting to leave a message (the script was on my laptop). I was caught off-guard when he picked up, but thought that I managed to be casual enough, asking about the house-stager he'd recommended and dropping in a mention of his stepbrother. "What's he up to these days? By the way, what was his last name? Something common, I remember. Smith? Jones? Johnson?"

It was Cohen. Try looking up Mark Cohen. In Florida. Sixty-two million hits.

SAT, APR 27, 07:44 AM
Augie: I had a weird call with Joan
Vivien: What about
Augie: My stepbrother. I think she's always had a crush on him
Vivien: Great! Give her his email address
Augie: No. Mark's an asshole
Vivien: That's her business
Augie: She's an old friend. I wouldn't do that to her
Vivien: Who are you to tell her what to do, OLD MAN
Augie: Shit. Fine. You don't have to shout

He sent me the email address, but I didn't forward it to Bruno just yet, afraid he'd vanish once he got all the information he wanted. While driving to Valley View that afternoon, I had an idea. It was a terrible idea—*really*, I told myself, *you're going to keep lying?* But chastising Mom as Vivien hadn't led to a lasting change. Maybe telling her about Bruno could galvanize her to co-operate with her treatment plan. All the way to the rehab facility, I debated it. Was I unwilling to go a little further? Just because I'd rather think of myself as a moral person? How could I hide what I knew about her grandson? Was that right? Any guilt over deceiving Bruno had no bearing on what was best for Mom.

The plan seemed all the more feasible because she was in a decent mood when I arrived. Her roommate had been discharged, and her bed was empty, another patient not yet admitted. Mom had used her walker to hobble to the other side of the room to wipe the window ledge clean of dust. She was now lying in bed, worn out, but cheerfully ordering me to swipe the ledge with my finger. I obeyed, glad to turn my back for a moment. Every time I visited, I was startled to see her as a shrunken and sickly old woman.

"No dust, Mom." I pulled the chair closer to her bed and sat. I gave her the Saturday crossword, and she told me about the latest episode of *Our Planet*. Then I said, "So, have you heard from Vivien today?"

"No—why?"

"She asked me to tell you, in case her internet service went down."

"What?" Mom reached for my hand and gripped it.

"It's not bad news. Her son contacted her."

Mom echoed what I'd said, and added, "She told you to tell me that?"

"She did. Mom, are you all right?"

"Yes." She sniffled. I dug a packet of tissues out of my messenger bag and handed it to her. She blew her nose. "Is he . . . How is he?"

"He's good, Mom."

"Do you think I could—would she be mad if I met him?"

It was easy to justify. Who would it hurt? Mom was looking at me, her face open, vulnerable. She needed this. I ignored my qualms. Bruno would benefit from meeting her too. "Just ask Vivien."

"Not me, Joanie. You do it. Ask her for me."

"I would, but . . ." I wondered if Vivien would applaud the cruelty I was about to display. I looked out the window, unable to meet my mother's eyes. "Do you really want him seeing you in a nursing home?"

"I'm not going there!"

"I'm afraid so, Mom. They'll be arranging a transfer mid-week."

"That Martha woman said I could have at least another month here."

"But only if you work with the physiotherapist."

"I will, Joanie. I'm not that tired anymore. I've had a good rest. You tell her that. Please tell her."

"Okay, Mom. And I'll ask Vivien about meeting her son. Just don't expect an answer right away. You know what she's like."

My mother sighed and nodded. Her hands rested in her lap, holding the used tissue as if it was pristine.

First thing on Monday, I called Mom's case manager, but she wasn't available. We managed to connect in the afternoon, just before my appointment with Eddie Wong, and Martha agreed to give Mom another chance. While Eddie was in the washroom, I checked my phone and saw that Bruno had just messaged.

MON, APR 29, 02:30 PM
Bruno: Did you have other children?
Vivien: Only you. Your family?
Bruno: No siblings. Parents are good people, still living.
Wife is also good people. Too good sometimes
Vivien: Like my sister
Bruno: So there's an aunt. Any uncles? Cousins?
Vivien: No. Sorry

I began to write, *There's a grandmother still living. She knows about you.* But Bruno's next message showed up before I tapped send.

Bruno: Did anyone want me?

If I could have reached through the screen to hug him, I would have.

Vivien: I did. Very much. I was just too young.
Vivien: My sister was angry with me for giving you up.
I couldn't stand the look on her face, the accusation.
At least when I ran away, I didn't have to see it

I stared at the words I'd just written—was that the reason Vivien had kept her distance all these years? When Eddie came back to the living room, he looked at me with concern.

"You're pale all of a sudden." I told him I was fine, just tired. He gave me a peppermint candy, like somebody's grandpa, though he was no one's, and I'd never had one either.

Bruno was born as dawn was breaking on the first Sunday in May. By the time the EMTs were loading the stretcher into the back of the ambulance, the sun was fully up. I wanted to go with Vivien and the baby, but though she asked for me, they wouldn't allow it. I sat outside on the front steps, watching the ambulance peel away, and waited for my parents to do something. A robin was hopping in the front yard. Other birds sang their nesting songs. After a while, I went back inside and stripped Vivien's bed. The bundled sheets went straight into the trash with my pyjamas. Then I changed into the one outfit left in my closet: bell-bottom jeans and a peasant blouse, soft from washing.

After Dad roused my mother, they showered and had coffee and called Toronto East General to find out when we could see Vivien. Dad was hungover and Mom was trying to act as if nothing unusual had happened. Dad put on his tie, while she did full face makeup (newly acquired, clearly a priority). He'd lost his licence again, so Mom drove. They were silent on the way, Mom focused on the road and Dad staring straight ahead. Every time I thought of Vivien, I heard the sound of my sleeve ripping as I pulled away from her grip to catch the baby as he slid out, and I shivered, remembering the fear that I'd do something wrong and kill my sister or her child.

The room for newborns was just a few steps from the elevator, a crowd cooing at the large glass windows. We paused, and I pointed at the front row. There he was, with a sign on the bassinet: "Connor Boy." Dad was mesmerized. Mom called him by name a couple of times before she got his attention, then looped her arm through his and marched him forward. She entered Vivien's room as if on a mission, while Dad hovered near the doorway.

Vivien was sitting up in bed, eating pie. She looked weary, dark circles under her eyes. I joined her on the bed, though there was barely space for me beside her.

"How's the pie?" I asked her.

"Good. Apple." She held out a forkful, and I ate it. "They're treating me like a hero because I'm not going to be a burden on society. See—private room. Apparently, most girls are keeping their babies now." Her voice wavered.

Dad remained near the doorway while Mom came to stand at the foot of the bed, hands on her hips. "Of course, you're not a burden. You have a family."

"I've signed the papers," she said. "He's going to be adopted."

"Great," Mom said, as if she still thought she'd gotten her way. "I'll just go and talk to the nurse and we can take you and the baby home. He shouldn't have to be in foster care if he can be with his own family until it's official."

"You don't get it, do you?" Vivien said.

Mom opened her mouth but was interrupted before she could say anything more by a woman who came in, smiling and saying hello to all of us. A name tag was pinned to her knitted vest, which she wore over a turtleneck. The vest, the top, her skirt were all shades of beige. The name tag read, *Beverley Radzinski, social worker.*

"So, this must be Mom, Dad, and Sister. So glad to meet you all." Her tone was calm, disarming. "I've already had a good talk with Vivien. Let's go to my office and let her finish her snack. Don't forget the milk, Vivien!" She nodded at my sister, who nodded back as if they weren't talking about milk at all. "Just follow me, Mom . . . Dad . . ."

"I'll be there in a minute," Dad said.

"Perfect. That will give us ladies a few minutes to ourselves. Room 502," Beverley said.

Once they were gone, Vivien said to Dad, "Everything's in Beverley's file now, so Mom can't lie. There are lots of families that want him. Good families."

"You'd rather give your baby to a stranger?" I'd seen that look on Dad's face only once before. We were at the cottage and he was painting a pilot surrounded by flames.

"Would you even want him? You hate me."

"Don't say that. I was angry—but still. Your child. Of course I want him."

"I don't believe you," Vivien said. "You love drinking. More than us, more than anything. That's what you really want."

Dad made a sound as if all the air had gone out of him. Then he turned on his heel and left the room. I was still lying beside Vivien, pressed against her in order to fit in the single bed, feeling the rise and fall of her rapid breathing. Gradually, it slowed.

"You should have kept the baby," I said, not caring how accusatory I sounded.

"Stop talking about it or go." Vivien pushed. She was too weak to shove me off the bed, but I got up anyway and moved to a chair.

"I'll stay."

Her room was equipped with a TV and a remote—still a novelty then—and I picked it up, avoiding my sister's eyes.

I flicked through the TV channels—it was mostly sports—
until I came to *Scooby-Doo*, which Vivien said we should
watch, though we were both too old for cartoons. We laughed
as the dog bounced off a crocodile and got caught in a vine.
I mumbled, "Sorry," and Vivien mumbled, "S'okay." I moved
the chair closer to her bed. Before anyone else returned, she
said, "Family is so random. We're only sisters because of
chance. Neither of us chose it. Remember that, Roo."

When Mom came back to fetch me, Vivien asked if she
got it now. Mom said she did, that the social worker was very
clear. The last thing she said to Vivien before we left was "I'll
never forgive you."

My sister was discharged the next day. When my parents
went to pick her up, they discovered that she'd already gone.
That evening she called and said she was staying with her
ex-boyfriend, the one with the prison record. Mom phoned
the police, who confirmed what she'd been told: Vivien
couldn't legally drink or vote, but she was entitled to withdraw
from parental control, with no court process and no official
documents required. She could live wherever she chose.
Mom blamed Dad, and he accepted the blame. I assumed he'd
take it to a bar; instead, he went into rehab. By the time he
came out, my sister had left her ex's place, and no one knew
where she was. I remembered what she'd said—that family
was random. Having a sister—having me as her sister—wasn't
enough to make her come back.

I didn't think I'd ever recover. But human beings can
recover from a broken heart. They do it again and again.

CHAPTER 10

A few evenings later, I found myself stalking Bruno on HomeStars, gleaning tidbits about him from happy customers, while he spent hours on Vivien's Facebook page. He reacted to one post with a like and another—about the history of the Congo before it had been colonized, written a year earlier—with a wow face. Every time he reacted, my phone—on the bed beside me—pinged. I shifted position, the laptop warm on my knees. The window was open, and I could hear my neighbour's grandchildren chatting as they smoked on her porch. Across the street, Uncle Jack's house now belonged to a childless couple who were out walking their labradoodles. First, one barked, then the other, joining in on the conversation. As the barking receded, I heard the short whistle of a Messenger notification.

TUE, APR 30, 09:35 PM
Bruno: I have a teenager. Sometimes I worry she might run away for a stupid reason
Vivien: How old?

Bruno: She's fourteen. My son is five
Vivien: What are they like?
Bruno: Dtr a contrarian. Loves to argue. Big reader. Son is sensitive. Thinks Spider-Man has the best mask because it covers his face
Bruno: He did a family tree at school. That's what made me realize I was missing info that might affect his health

I tapped on my phone, *I've got a question for you*, then deleted it. "Vivien" had messaged Mom that she approved of her meeting Bruno, and my mother was now co-operating with her treatment plan. (The Toothy Woman actually gave me a real smile when she popped into Mom's room to update me on her progress.) But I wasn't sure how to introduce the possibility of such a visit to Bruno, much less persuade him to do it.

It was after nine. According to my personal rules, drinking was now permitted and cleaning prohibited. However, I needed to think, and I found that only one of those activities was conducive to it. I stuffed my gloves and supplies into a bucket and carried it to the main bathroom. Much in life is uncertain, but the shine of a well-scrubbed bathtub is indisputable. After that, the sink, the taps, the toilet. By the time I was done, I had a plan: mention Mom to Bruno, point out that she could fill in more family background, see how he replied, and go from there.

I put away my cleaning stuff, picked up my phone and found that Bruno had sent a photograph. The caption said, *My first door*. He was standing beside it, and I spread thumb and forefinger to enlarge the image. Not what I was expecting. He looked exactly like my mother's father if this grandfather had been a light shade of brown. Mark's son? No way this man was the offspring of a sun-burned girl and an Elmer's Paste boy. God, how would this work? Seeing him could trigger both my mother's loathing of her father and her latent racism.

> **Vivien:** I see a family resemblance
> **Bruno:** You've got brown people in your family?
> **Vivien:** The features
> **Bruno:** Right. I've always wondered whether you would have kept me if I was white?

I wished the question shocked me, and for an instant, I thought, *Was that the reason Vivien refused to name the father?* But I also remembered how much she'd wanted to keep her child.

> **Vivien:** That had nothing to do with it. My parents were on self-destruct, and I had no support. That's the only reason
> **Bruno:** So then why didn't you answer my letter?

I had no idea he'd written a letter—Vivien had never told me.

> **Bruno:** Did you think I'd complicate your life? Or were you upset that I waited so long to get on the Adoption Disclosure Register?
> **Bruno:** They told me you registered when I was eighteen

Adoptions from that era were closed, but if both parent and child registered, their contact information would be exchanged by the registry staff. Bruno would have turned eighteen in 1995. My stepdaughter was seven then. I remember Vivien came home for a visit that year. We both went to the school's talent show because Zoe had a magic act and Paul couldn't go. After she performed, we clapped our hands red, grinning at each other. At some point during that visit, Vivien must have contacted the Adoption Disclosure Register, but she'd never said a word.

> **Vivien:** When did you sign up?
> **Bruno:** I was twenty-two. Don't you know?
> **Vivien:** Hang on. Let me think

Minutes passed. I wondered if he was still sitting there, waiting for a reply. I was trying to remember—where was my sister then?

> **Vivien:** I never got your letter. I'd worked in four countries
> by the time you sent it
> **Bruno:** Why didn't you leave your email address with
> the registry office?
> **Vivien:** I didn't have one
> **Bruno:** How could you not have an email address?
> **Vivien:** A lot of people didn't back then. And the refugee
> camps where I worked didn't have enough clean water,
> never mind internet
> **Vivien:** I barely stayed in touch with my sister
> **Bruno:** Then it wasn't me
> **Vivien:** No, it wasn't

And then, being the nicer Vivien, I added:

Vivien: I wish I'd gotten your letter. I'm truly sorry
I didn't
Vivien: You look a lot like my mother's father
Bruno: I never thought about grandparents. Mine died
when I was young. Is your mother still alive?
Vivien: She is, but she's not well
Bruno: Sorry to hear that. Do you think she'd want to
meet me? Answer my questions?

There it was: my plan was unfolding without any effort on my part. Too bad I wasn't sure it was such a good idea anymore. If my sister was watching from the other side, she'd be laughing.

Vivien: Mom brought it up herself. She's at Valley View
for rehab
Bruno: Let me talk to my wife about it
11:51 PM
Bruno: Saturday at 2? We'll both come
Vivien: I'll check with Joan. That's my sister.
11:57 PM
Vivien: It's fine. When you get there, ask for Sheila
Connor's room

WED, MAY 1, 12:01 AM
Vivien: My bf's name was Mark Cohen. His email
address is mjc1960@novaboatreno.com
Vivien: Happy birthday

It was my birthday too. I'd thought of the baby I now knew as Bruno every year.

My sister had kept so much from me, and yet she'd left an imprint of herself for me in the cloud. Why? Was there something she wanted me to find?

I started with Messenger. Whenever I had time, I scrolled back through her conversations with Oscar, Raoul, Grace, and other colleagues who'd commented on Facebook. Many of the messages were short and inconsequential, but even so, added together they were creating a picture. I'd always imagined Vivien dashing from place to place, her relationships short-lived, lasting only until the next crisis pulled her away. But people kept in touch with her, the intensity of their shared experience, however brief, bonding them. I knew she was casual about sex and sometimes hurt men because of it, but Raoul had been her friend both before and after they were a couple. Her confidants were all male, except for Grace. Vivien had been closer to Oscar than I'd have guessed from his recent messages about his research. He'd had a difficult childhood—his father remote and demeaning, his mother a narcissist. My sister expressed sympathy. Sometimes, she shared a memory too: Mom throwing out her records, Dad reacting to fireworks. I suddenly remembered that the five tips I'd sent him included things like *Offer your parent a treat*. Flushing, I sent him a message: *Sorry Oscar, bad joke*. He replied, *Oh. Yes. Good laugh*. I found nothing about the adoption register.

———

When I visited Mom at Valley View, I told her that her grandson's name was Bruno Edery, that he wanted to know more about our family history, and that he and his wife were coming to see her on Saturday. I tried to prepare her, saying that he didn't look like Mark, that he'd been adopted by a Jewish family, and that she needed to be sensitive to the fact that he'd had a life we didn't know anything about. I was talking to a wall. Mom shed a few tears and said, "Blood is thicker than water."

I said, "People can't live without water."

She wasn't listening.

Mom dressed up for Bruno's visit. She wore beige trousers and a white blouse (freshly pressed by me because my mother only wore 100 percent cotton) and lipstick nicely applied, which made me wonder who had helped her with it. The bed was neatly made, covered with a quilt gifted by Mom's previous roommate. She lounged on it like a gracious matriarch. The other bed was still empty, a new roommate not yet assigned.

By five to two, Mom was watching the doorway anxiously, and she kept watching it until Bruno and his wife, Ruth, arrived nineteen minutes late. He carried a backpack and wore jeans, grey sneakers, a black T-shirt. His wife's name was tattooed on his left forearm, and on his right, carpentry tools were inked against a background of trees. Ruth was a petite South Asian woman who wore a spring dress, yellow and flowy, and carried a yellow handbag. In person, Bruno looked even more like my mother's father. I'd met this grandfather just once, at my grandmother's funeral, but he'd made an impression on me: bushy eyebrows, big teeth, long chin, long limbs. A wolf until he smiled and offered me a ride on his shoulders. A shaggy dog then; I'd wanted to pat his thatch of white hair. My mother said, "Not on your life." She and my aunt were outraged that he'd shown up. A few days after the funeral, my aunt returned to Australia, but not before she and my mother cut up all the family pictures that had my grandfather in them.

We all introduced ourselves, then sat in the chairs I'd spaced around Mom's bed. From the backpack at his feet, Bruno withdrew wooden bookends. One of their sides was smooth and into the other he'd carved the figures of a mother and baby. They were simple and stylized, but there was joy in the tilt of the mother's head as she held the baby.

"I thought you might like these."

Bruno handed them to Mom. She took them from him carefully, as if they were made of glass, not wood, and would break if she didn't set them gently on the bedside table.

"I do," Mom said. "So, you're a carpenter. Like Jesus."

I was thinking, *Oh God, she's starting.*

Bruno looked startled, then laughed. His eyes were expressive. He wore a beard as if to minimize how much his face revealed. "And I'm Jewish, also like Jesus." He passed his hand in front of his face. "We both have this Middle Eastern thing going."

"I don't know about that," Mom said, turning to me with a satisfied smile. "Isn't Bruno the spitting image of your father?"

"Something like," I said. (Nothing like.)

"Could we see a picture of him?" Ruth asked. She had a light accent I couldn't immediately place.

"Joan will bring one next time."

"Which one, Mom?" As if there was a cupboard filled with boxes of photos to sift through.

"The one with his father on Remembrance Day, both of them in uniform." I'd never met my paternal grandfather; he'd died before I was born, and I'd never seen that photograph either. "Hugh fought in the Second World War," Mom continued, "and his father in the first. After that, he was shattered until he started working on engines. The father, not Hugh."

"Dad too," I said. "The war scarred him."

"Were any of your adoptive relatives in the service?" Mom emphasized *adoptive*, and Bruno shifted his legs, crossing one over the other.

"My grandfather was in the resistance," he said, putting extra weight on *my* and *grandfather*, with a slight pause between to emphasize that excluded *adoptive*.

"Mine was in the British Army." Ruth put a hand on Bruno's, her eyes soft, concerned, his wary. She was tiny next to him, her hair up in a messy bun.

"You don't sound British," Mom said.

"The British Indian Army," she amended.

"But that's not an Indian accent, is it?"

"No. Because I'm Israeli."

"Oh. You don't look Jewish." Mom was the one who said it, but I'd been thinking it too, now embarrassed by my assumptions.

"I get that a lot. But I am."

Mom smiled. "I had a Jewish lawyer," she said. "If you want a good lawyer, go for a Jew. Is your adoptive father a lawyer, Bruno?"

His shoulders tensed, but when I rolled my eyes and mouthed, *Sorry*, the corners of his mouth lifted. "My dad's retired now. He was a teacher in French Immersion."

"And what do you do, Ruth?" Mom asked.

"I'm an urban planner." She took her phone out of her purse. Its case was yellow, like her dress and her purse, and I wondered if she had a different case and purse for every outfit. "Would you like to see pictures of our kids, Sheila?"

"Very much," Mom said.

Ruth tapped her phone and held it out. "That's Noah and Sarah."

Mom made appreciative noises, then asked, "So what do you want to know, Bruno?"

"Was my birth normal?"

"It was fast," Mom said, as if she'd been awake for it.

"Do you mind if we record this?" Ruth asked.

Bruno put his hand over his wife's phone. "It's not an interrogation."

She moved the phone away from him. "You won't remember everything, and then it'll drive you nuts."

Bruno shook his head, pulling on each of his fingers, cracking the knuckles.

"Aha!" Mom said. "My husband did that all the time. He was double-jointed."

"So is Bruno. Fingers and elbows."

"Hugh could bend his arms backward. It was freaky."

"I know!" Ruth said. They smiled at each other while Bruno took a notebook and pen from his pocket.

"I'd rather use a notebook, anyway," he said.

"Bruno worries about solar flares erasing the cloud," Ruth explained.

He scratched his beard with his pen. "Just because you can't see it, doesn't mean it's not happening. We've had a few C-class flares already. And last year, we had a bunch of X-class—they're a hundred times stronger."

Anything to do with astronomy fascinated Mom, and as she drew him out with enthusiastic questions, Bruno told her everything he knew about the effects of solar flares on world history, which, in a digital era, could also wipe out the historical record. "That's why paper is best," he said.

So, we had that in common, the need for documentation, the anxiety of losing it and having no record of our existence. The difference was that I knew solar flares were much less likely than family to do damage.

"I shouldn't go on like that," Bruno said. "It's boring."

"Not to me," Mom said. "I haven't been this entertained since I went into the hospital. But we can't let you leave without getting what you came for."

"Maybe you could start with your family—where they're from, what they were like," Ruth said.

"My mother's people didn't approve of my father, and they had nothing to do with us even after my parents got divorced."

I looked over at Mom. "I didn't know that."

"My mother always said it wasn't worth thinking about."

"I hate it when things are kept from me," Bruno said.

"As it turned out, my mother's parents were right," Mom said. "He wasn't a nice man, but that had nothing to do with the kind of work he did. Hugh's family was working-class and they were fine people."

"So were Uncle Jack's," I said.

"How is he related?" Bruno had been drawing spokes

from a central hub, himself, his pen poised to add names and dates.

"Jack Rosenstein was my father's best friend. A war buddy. You were born in a bed he gave us."

"That isn't so," my mother said. "Jack gave away nothing but hangovers."

"Nevertheless, he did give us the bed."

Mom paused, her silence cut by the sound of Bruno's pen on the page. I heard laughter from the nurses out in the hallway.

"Oh, yes, now I remember," Mom said. "You girls came home with lice and I had to get rid of everything."

"Sure," I said, going along with her excuse. "Go on, Mom. Your father."

"His full name?" Bruno asked. "And where was he born?"

"Felix Grimshaw. In Toronto. His father came from Manchester, but his mother's family were Scottish fur traders back in the day. There's a Cree ancestor somewhere in there. From around Hudson Bay."

"Do you know his date of birth?"

"I think it was 1905 maybe? I'm not sure. He worked in a factory and there was an accident. Or maybe a fight. They never said exactly how he ended up in the hospital. But what matters is that he did, and he was a handsome man. My mother was a volunteer, bringing good cheer and tea."

My mother had never talked about this either. All I'd known was that her parents had divorced at a time when divorce was shameful; her father had been violent, her mother subservient until the day she found the nerve to throw him out.

"My mother had wanted to be a nurse . . . like Vivien."
She glanced at me. And I pictured Vivien, here, uncomfortable with the tenderness she would feel, meeting her son.
She'd say something about his nose. Call it a honker. Blunt
honesty was her cover.

"But girls from good families were supposed to stay
home until they married. My father wasn't like anyone she'd
known, and he was the first man to chase after her. She
didn't understand what drinking did to him."

"Bruno's pretty funny when he's drunk," Ruth said.

Mom sat up straighter. "My father always said you've got
to drink with your buddies. Then he'd come home and smack
my mother around."

Bruno looked aghast. His pen stilled.

"So," Mom asked, age making her as blunt as Vivien, "are
you an angry drunk?"

"No!" Ruth answered for her husband. "Never!"

Mom relaxed back against the pillows. "Good. You take
after Hugh, then. Even dead drunk, he was gentle."

"Thanks," Bruno said. "I think."

"My father would get quiet and then explode," Mom
said. "When I was fifteen, I would try to get between my
parents. Laura—that's my sister—was six years older than
me, and she'd moved out. The first time, I just got bruised,
but the second time, he broke my collarbone instead of my
mother's, and that's when she threw him out. I swore I'd
never marry a man like him, and I didn't."

I reached for her hand. "I'm sorry you went through
that, Mom."

"Through what?" she asked.

"The abuse."

Mom pulled her hand away. "I wasn't abused. My mother was. I just got in the way."

"Of course," Ruth said. She patted Mom's shoulder and poured water into her glass.

Bruno crossed and recrossed his legs, until Mom said, "Can we have a hug, Bruno?"

He got up, leaned over the bed and wrapped his long arms around her. When he let go, Mom smiled at him. Then she yawned, clearly exhausted.

The visit had gone reasonably well. Relieved, late that afternoon, I turned Mom's recliner to face the window, my phone on the seat beside me, as I stared out into the backyard. I saw that the robin's eggs had hatched, and the open beaks of hungry fledglings poked out of their nest. Squirrels chased each other down the trunk of the other maple. Watching it all through new binoculars—impractical, unnecessary, purchased by and for myself on the spur of the moment after I'd given Bruno and Ruth a ride home—I felt daring, as if the spring air was loaded with pheromones. Whenever my phone pinged, I glanced at the notifications, but my nephew didn't message Vivien until after I'd had dinner.

SAT, MAY 4, 08:07 PM
Bruno: So I met your family
Vivien: My crazy family
Bruno: I liked Joan
Bruno: Your mother is brave. She's been through a lot but doesn't make a big deal of it. Like my parents

Vivien: Really? The word I'd use is limited
Bruno: That too
09:39 PM
Bruno: It would be easier to talk than type. Could we do that on Messenger? Video call?

Me panicking. Getting up, going to the kitchen. I took the bottle of Scotch down from the cupboard. I poured a shot.

10:11 PM
Vivien: I was with a patient so just saw this. Text message is better. My connection is slow and keeps cutting out
Bruno: What about phone call?
Vivien: No bars. As soon as I'm back at a clinic that has stable internet I'll let you know
10:48 PM
Bruno: Ruth thinks our children should meet my bio family. Would you come?

Shit. Shit. Shit. I made myself take a breath. Vivien could handle this.

Vivien: Don't wait for me. There's a travel restriction in my area
Bruno: Why?
Vivien: Ebola
Bruno: Oh shit. And I just found you
Vivien: Same. But this is my life

For a few moments, nothing but wiggling dots. Through

the binoculars, I saw a woodpecker digging out a hollow in my sister's tree.

> **Bruno:** Your mother wants me to see her again for
> more family background. Unchaperoned. Her word
> **Vivien:** Let me know how it goes. Just don't blame me
> for anything she says

Bruno went offline, and I retreated to the backyard with my glass and the bottle. Somewhere, an owl hooted. Sitting on the grass, back to my sister's maple tree, I fixed my eyes on the lights of the city to the south. Vivien could have crossed paths with Bruno's letter, on a plane passing through clouds above the ocean on its way to Africa while she was on a plane coming home. She'd visited in 1999, the year Bruno put his name on the Adoption Disclosure Register and wrote her a letter. She'd stayed just long enough to see my father die.

CHAPTER 11

Sober Dad wasn't an easy man to live with. I expected him to start watching *Laverne & Shirley* with me, help with homework, stand with us in the crowd waiting for a glimpse of Prime Minister Trudeau and the Queen as she came through Toronto, imagining that the Queen would stop because my father had flown in her air force, and he would bow to her. But when Dad wasn't at work, he was at his meetings and doing steps. He didn't even come to the science fair where I took first place. I'd forgiven such absences when he was passed out in the basement, but couldn't understand them when he was clear-headed and vertical.

What I didn't realize was that alcohol had put a gloss on Dad's present and suppressed everything painful in his past. Without booze, the world was grey and his memory unbearably clear. Sober Dad boiled over with resentment, especially for enduring all this for a daughter who was still missing.

He went looking for her. He got Steve—who was the same age as Vivien—to stand with him outside the high school and point out her friends. Most of them simply made fun of Dad. The two boys willing to help gave him leads that were dead ends. Dad called a women's shelter, the first in the city, and they told him—coldly—that their location and the identities of everyone in the shelter were confidential. All the while, he kept working the steps diligently, sourly, and Mom cleaned, muttering to herself, "She's fine, she's fine." I floated like a thread on water, trying not to make a ripple.

Vivien called home just after we turned the clocks back at the end of October. She got no further than saying where she was when Mom slammed the receiver into its cradle. Mom immediately called the operator and asked her to dial the number that had just called our house, but it was a pay phone, and nobody answered. When Dad got home from his AA meeting, Mom told him about it. He was furious, and she attacked him (*you weren't home; you're never home; I was in shock*). At last, she broke down and cried, which he could never resist, wrapping his arms around her protectively. I was in my room, studying for a math test, and I covered my ears.

The next Saturday, the first in November, the house was cold with all the windows open because Mom was repainting the ceilings and the smell of the paint bothered her. Dad was on the phone in the kitchen, pacing like a dog on a chain. After he hung up, he told me to get my coat, saying that Uncle Jack was taking us to the museum.

I was soon in Uncle Jack's car, writing in my journal while we waited for Augie. *November 5th, Is Vivien cold? I hope so. I hope she's freezing.* Then I crossed it out. Uncle Jack was still driving a station wagon with wood panelling on the side. Dad's easel, as well as Uncle Jack's fishing gear from the last trip to the cottage, was in the back. Snowflakes drifted

and melted in wet patches. Steve was away somewhere with
his hockey team.

Finally, Augie came clomping down the front steps.
I shoved the journal in my shoulder bag, and he slid into the
back seat beside me and buried himself in a book. Something
sci-fi with an orange cover and strange ruins on it. I was shy
with him, aware of exactly how much seat there was between
us. I wore a duffle coat and fiddled with the wooden toggles.
I soon noticed that we weren't heading toward the museum.

I said, "Uncle Jack, that's the wrong way."

"It isn't."

"We're not going to the museum," Dad said. "I just didn't
want Mom getting her hopes up. We're looking for Vivien."
His voice grew tight. "She told Mom she was at Church and
Isabella."

As we approached the corner, Uncle Jack slowed down,
and I suddenly realized what Dad thought my sister was
doing. The intersection had a reputation, even in our quiet
suburb. Would there be needle marks on her arms? Didn't all
streetwalkers take heroin? I sank lower in the seat. The
shabby neighbourhood frightened me. Though I wanted
Vivien to come home with us—of course I did—I was reluctant to see her, oddly so, it seemed to me then.

"Pull over," Dad said. "That's her, Joanie. Go talk to her."

I peered at a figure in the distance. How did Dad recognize her from so far? "You go. I don't know what to say."

"I can't," Dad said.

"She won't listen to me." I didn't tell him what I really
feared: that she'd be pathetic, like the child prostitute in *Taxi
Driver*, and that I'd see a stranger looking back at me, not the
sister who'd hidden with me in the ravine, or made my

breakfast out of cereal and candy-covered chocolate, or shown me the pictures in *Our Bodies, Ourselves*, or screamed at me for getting ketchup on the blouse I stole from her closet because we were supposed to wear a white one for the class picture and I didn't have any.

"She didn't run away from you," Dad said, turning around to grip my arm. "You're the one she'll talk to. Hurry up!"

"All right. Just let go of me."

I got out of the car and crossed the street, veering away from the pink-haired woman in a miniskirt and furry jacket, opened to show off her breasts. A car stopped. The window rolled down and the woman bent toward it. By the time I reached the opposite sidewalk, she was in the car and it was driving off. Vivien was standing in front of a convenience store, where a dog was lifting a leg to relieve itself on a lamppost. The dog was one of a pair of toy poodles on leashes that Vivien had wrapped around her wrist. She wasn't wearing a short skirt, but she looked cold in a raincoat too light for the weather. Her hair was up in a ponytail. Her face was bare of makeup. Her lips were chapped. I hoped her face would light up when she saw me. I don't remember if it did. I think I was too scared to look and so I squatted to pat the dog that wasn't peeing.

"Hi," I said.

"Hi."

"What you doing?"

"Walking dogs."

"Are the dogs yours?"

"No." The dog's business done, Vivien started walking and I followed, hands in my pockets because I'd forgotten mitts. She pulled the dogs away from sniffing at a grey-faced man sleeping on the sidewalk. One of his shoes had fallen off. It had no laces. He smelled of marinated sweat and urine and I pinched my nose. Everything was grey on this November street except for my sister's yellow slicker and the matching rain hat with the elastic under her chin, like an air raid warden's helmet.

"Whose dogs are they?"

"Maxine's. She just left."

"The woman who got in the car?"

"Yes. She pays me pretty good, too."

"Oh." I flushed, ashamed that I'd assumed there was only one thing a girl in this neighbourhood could do for money.

I asked Vivien what else she did, and she told me that she also ran errands for Maxine and her friends and had a job washing dishes in a diner at Bloor and Walmer, which I guessed paid enough for room and board but not enough for a winter coat.

"Come home," I said.

We passed a panhandler with a cardboard sign: *Homeless. A quarter for food, a dollar for weed.*

"Did Mom ask you to find me?"

"Dad."

A few doors down, another panhandler held out a cup. When I dropped in a coin, she smiled—she had no teeth—and said, "God bless."

"Uncle Jack drove us. They're waiting for us. Everybody misses you."

"Then why did Mom hang up on me?"

"She didn't mean to. She was surprised to hear your voice."

Vivien shook her head. "It doesn't matter. I'm fine. I've got everything I need."

"Why didn't you call before?"

"I wanted to send you a postcard."

"But you didn't."

"No." She linked her arm with mine then, pulling me in like she did when she'd walked me to school. "I've got a place in a rooming house on Walmer."

"At least come to the car and get warm," I said.

"No."

"Dad stopped drinking."

"Good for him."

"Why don't you come home?"

"I can't. I'll go crazy."

"It's not that bad. Or at least it wouldn't be if you were there with me."

She looked away. Her wrists were red from the cold.

"Have my jacket," I said.

"You'll be cold."

I unbuttoned it. "Here."

"Okay." Vivien unzipped her raincoat, moving the leashes from hand to hand as she struggled out of it and into my jacket. She kept the rain hat. "I don't have a phone, but I'll give you my address if you promise not to tell."

"I promise."

"Swear."

"I swear."

She let me walk her to the end of the block, where I said that I'd come visit her very soon. She nodded and then said I should get back to the car before Dad decided he'd had enough of sobriety and went off to find a bar. As I turned away, she gave me a little shove.

My father was livid that I returned alone. He made Uncle Jack drive around the block over and over, but Vivien had disappeared. When we couldn't find her, Dad hit his own head with his fist until I cried, and Uncle Jack said that he'd have to get out and take the bus home if he didn't stop. Through it all, Augie kept steadily turning the pages.

"Daddy," I finally said, "I know where she lives."

"Where? Why didn't you say?"

"Vivien made me swear not to."

"Is she on drugs? She must be on drugs. Or . . . she's not hooking, is she?"

"Dad!"

"Is she?"

"No!" I shouted as if I hadn't thought the same thing myself. "She's a dog walker."

"Okay, okay, okay. Just give me the address." The words were ordinary, but my father's face was terrifying in its agony. And so I did. Vivien might never talk to me again, but at least we'd get her home and she'd be safe.

Uncle Jack drove to the address and parked across from it. The rooming house was large and Victorian, with a turret. I wondered if Vivien had a round room. Some of the windows were cracked and the cracks covered with peeling tape. There were cracks in the sky too, where blue showed through dark clouds. On the street, the bare branches of old maple trees extended overhead, dry leaves blowing from the yards onto the road. Uncle Jack let the car idle so we wouldn't get cold. Even with the windows closed, I could smell the exhaust. Dad kept fuming, now about landlords taking advantage of minors and why didn't they call the parents, and he was going in there to punch his lights out, until Uncle Jack said, "Settle down, Hugh. I doubt the landlord lives in his own slum." He turned off the ignition. "Let me see if anyone's in there I can talk to."

"I'm coming with you," Dad said, opening the car door.

"No, you're not." Uncle Jack reached over to pull it shut.

"Who the hell do you think you are?"

"Fuck off, Hugh. There's nothing worse than a dry drunk."

Uncle Jack got out of the car and crossed the street. We could see him pressing the buttons beside the door. Dad rolled down the window and lit a cigarette, blowing the smoke outside. When Uncle Jack disappeared inside the house, Dad jumped out of the car but remained near us, smoking and stamping his feet as if he needed to dispel the energy somehow. That's when Augie put down the book and reached for my hand. When Uncle Jack returned, we let go, not wanting our fathers to see.

As soon as they were both back inside the car, Uncle Jack said, "There's a janitor living in the basement. He told me that Vivien left a couple of days ago. She missed rent and skipped out without paying."

Defeated, Dad let Uncle Jack drive us home.

After that, I tried to find her on my own. Every few days, I told my mother that I had science club or choir and took transit downtown after school. This was before a Starbucks or a Tim Hortons was on every corner. The only shelter at Church and Isabella was a twenty-four-hour doughnut shop that catered to the ill-washed. With a textbook in front of me, I sat at the counter, pretending to do homework while I looked out the smudged window, hoping to catch sight of my sister. One time, I was approached by a pimp in a flashy suit, but the owner told him to lay off.

Finally, I spotted my sister, without the dogs but with a

shopping bag. I ran out of the doughnut shop, calling out to her, leaving my math book on the counter. She stopped and let me catch up. She looked tired and smelled of weed and worse—like one of the regulars in the doughnut shop. She hung back for a moment as if she was embarrassed about it, then lunged forward, pecked me on the cheek and thanked me for giving her the duffle coat. But she still wouldn't come home. Alone and in despair, I went back to retrieve my textbook.

A couple of weeks later, a cold spell did what I couldn't. Vivien came back. At first, we were all on tenterhooks, afraid she'd take off again, but gradually my parents relaxed, rejoicing at every new sign of normalcy. They were proud of Vivien for going to school every morning, for returning home, for wearing jeans and T-shirts and sneakers, for brushing her teeth, for showing me how to wrap my hair around an empty Coke can to straighten it like the other girls and going so far as to do it herself—practically preparatory to winning the Nobel Prize—and using up my Love's Fresh Lemon cologne as if smelling like a good girl would make it believable.

One night, I woke up anxious and went to stand in her doorway to reassure myself that she was still there. Her room was furnished again with a bed and dresser and desk, various sized rectangles in the moonlight. A person-shaped hump was sitting up in bed.

"Can't sleep?" I asked.

"I had a bad dream."

"About what?"

"Usual. Can't leave the party."

"That doesn't sound so bad."

"It is when you want to leave." She scooted over to make room, and I got in beside her. She was shaking, and I supposed she was cold because the window was open. She always kept the window open at night. If Mom closed it, she'd jump out of bed to lift the sash again.

"Why did you wait so long to come home?"

"I had your coat and a sleeping bag. That kept me warm until there was snow on the ground."

"So, if I hadn't given you my coat, you'd have come back sooner?"

"Probably." She yawned.

"I just didn't want you to be cold."

"You're a good kid."

But she'd have come home. So I wasn't good. "Do you miss the baby?"

She shrugged. "I don't know him enough to miss him, do I?"

"Why are you doing this? Acting like someone else."

"If you're a model inmate in prison, you're released quicker, right? And then you get away as far as you can."

"But this isn't a prison," I said.

"That's your problem, Roo. You're so good, you don't even see the bars."

Vivien had enrolled in an alternative school that encouraged students to go at their own pace. That usually meant slowly, but Vivien sped along, using a ruler to help her focus on each line in her textbooks and dictating her notes into a cassette recorder, replaying the tapes in the bathroom, on her way to school, all evening in her room. After she graduated from high school, she did the same thing in nursing school, taking courses through the summer so she could finish sooner. My parents' pride filled the house; my mother only skimmed surfaces to clear away stuff, and my father took up handball, his outbursts of temper becoming sporadic.

I knew my sister's model behaviour was temporary, conditional—she'd warned me. As soon as she had her nursing diploma, she slept for a week. Then she left for Afghanistan, where the Russians had just invaded and Doctors Without Borders were treating casualties. I remember seeing hospitals bombarded on the news, worried that she was in one of them. That was followed by Sri Lanka (civil war), a break in the UK for additional training in trauma surgery, then Nigeria (meningitis vaccination, too tame for her), Cambodia (AIDS crisis), Albania (refugee camps), Nigeria again (better this time—trauma surgery), and the DRC (livened up by the ever-present threat of bandits and marauding soldiers).

But that night, sitting on her bed, I put my hands out, one of them palm up, the other palm down. Her hands met mine in reverse. We slapped hands and turned them to slap again as if we were in a schoolyard at recess, an endless recess where girls in short dresses and braids taught each other one hand-clapping game after another, and we sang in a whisper because sober Dad was wakeful.

> *Tulips together, tie them together*
> *Bring back my love to me*
> *What is the mean-ean-ing*
> *Of all the flow-ow-ers,*
> *They tell the stor-or-ry*
> *The story of love*
> *From me to you-ou-ou-ou*

Years later, when Dad was at the park with us one afternoon, pushing Zoe in a swing, he told me that he'd heard us giggling, and it had made him weep, silently so he wouldn't disturb Mom, who'd cut down on her sleeping pills.

Dad was sober for nineteen years. When my sister went overseas, I worried that he'd start drinking again. If anything, it bolstered his sobriety. She was a nurse; she devoted herself to the least fortunate; she was courageous—all proof that he hadn't failed. Mom's anxiety, kept in check by medication and a calm home life, petered out until her compulsion was barely distinguishable from a redecorating hobby. My parents became content just sharing a life: Dad working, Mom cooking, going to the theatre together, trying new restaurants, joining a curling club, joining a book club.

It gave me permission to have a life. I graduated from medical school, met Paul, became a stepmother. I chose emergency medicine because I was well-suited to its requirements—a combination of patience and thinking on your feet—and every shift included problems I could fix. Vivien visited every few years, never staying long.

When Dad was seventy-three, he retired. The business sold, he and Uncle Jack had more time to go up to the cottage. However, Captain Edwin—older than they were by a decade—soon decided to move into a retirement home. Then Uncle Jack ended up in long-term care. He'd already had a mild stroke, but now a serious bleed in his brain stem left him with locked-in syndrome: he was conscious but unable to move any muscle except for his eyes. He couldn't talk, couldn't swallow, was incontinent, and communicated laboriously by blinking, but often just closed his eyes, giving up the attempt.

Dad became as surly as he'd been in the early days of his sobriety. His nightmares returned with a twist. Mom told me he dreamt he was in a POW camp, locked in a small concrete box for an unknown infraction, unable to move, his own voice echoing back at him. Dad visited Uncle Jack every day. After one of those visits, Dad stopped at a liquor store on his way home. I urged him to return to AA, but he wasn't interested. Eventually, the damage to his liver destroyed him.

Dad was in a coma for five weeks. I spent as much time as I could with him. Sometimes, I rubbed lotion on his dry feet or talked—telling him about Zoe wanting to get her ears pierced, and how happy Paul was to finally have joint custody. Mom would come by from time to time, kiss Dad on the forehead, then leave, saying she couldn't bear to see him like this. I searched used bookstores for titles that had been in his bookcase when I was young, and in the hospital room, I read them aloud to him.

Work was a slog. Budget cuts meant more patients and fewer options for them. I had outputs to meet as if it was factory work, pushing the sick and injured along the assembly line. Every time I sent a patient home, I'd wonder if they were going to come back. Sometimes, they had a horrible death at my hands. One day, I sat in the chair next to Dad's bed, head bowed, and told him about an elderly patient whose family insisted on heroic measures. I'd had to apply compressions to his fragile chest. I broke his bones. I heard them crack. I smelled his bowels evacuate from distress. He died painfully. With strangers hurting him. "No one better do that to you, Dad," I said.

When I left his room, I ran into Larry Klieger in the corridor, wheeling along the hallway after visiting a patient. His yarmulke dropped off his head, and I picked it up and handed it to him. That's how we met. After he introduced himself, he mentioned having seen me coming out of ER, looking dejected. He invited me to have coffee with him in the cafeteria. We talked about his practice. He told me palliative care is about helping patients have a good life and then a good death. No more *clock is ticking, shove the patient out the door*. His appointments with patients lasted as long as they needed. I asked myself whether I'd become a physician to cure or to heal. The answer had been to cure—but was it still?

I'd been trying to reach Vivien to tell her about Dad, but the phone number I had for her was out of service. Those were the early days of the internet—before Facebook—and the places Vivien worked had no access. I resorted to snail mail. Luckily, an intern at her last place of work saw the envelope and happened to know that Vivien had left for a mountain enclave of refugees. He sent the letter with the next supply truck.

She got home in time to say goodbye to Dad. As if he knew she was back, sitting with him, my father let go of his life on May 19, 1999, while I was working my last shift in ER, unable to be there to hold his hand.

CHAPTER 12

Galvanized by meeting her grandson, Mom worked hard with her physiotherapist. As soon as she was strong enough to spend a few hours at home, she invited Bruno and his family for Sunday dinner. Did she remember that this particular Sunday was the twentieth anniversary of my father's death? I wasn't sure and decided not to mention it.

That morning, I went shopping for a pair of jeans, so I'd have something to wear besides work clothes and sweats. I ended up with a silky shirt, a camisole and the jeans, and was just leaving the mall when my pager went off. I was soon in the car, headed for the home of a patient who was in her final hours.

She wasn't much older than me and had pancreatic cancer. Her initial prognosis was only six months, but subsequent genetic testing had indicated she was a candidate for a new treatment, which had extended her life by another year. She'd worked for Costco and enjoyed karaoke and movies. The extra time had meant she'd held her first grandchild.

Her husband let me in. I checked her vitals: blood pressure low, oxygen saturation low, patient unresponsive, respiration slow and gurgling, jaw dropping with each breath. She was in the final stage of dying. I administered medications to make her comfortable: a low dose of antipsychotic, opioid for pain, and glycopyrrolate—not so much for her as the family, because the sound of wet breathing disturbs people. Her son had made a Spotify list of her favourite songs, which played softly from a Bluetooth speaker. Her father, her sister, her husband, her son and her daughter-in-law sat on either side of the hospital bed, which had been delivered to the house just in time for her to die in it. Her husband told me that during the night, my patient had whispered his name and moved her hand to cover his.

At the edge of life, everything petty melts away. That morning, in that house, love took up all the air space, and I stayed in the background, breathing it in. My patient's father stroked the dandelion puffs of hair on her head. The sound of her breathing changed; there were now long pauses between each ragged inhalation. When she died, the room lightened and quickly dimmed in a mist of tears. I took out my stethoscope and listened to the stillness in her chest, then filled out the death certificate.

After I left, alone in my car, I wondered who would sit with me when I died. Who had been with Vivien?

On the way home, I stopped in at Metro to pick up some flowers, along with cold cuts, salad and juice for dinner. Mom had ordered me to "make the house nice," giving me her blessing to acquire as many things and spend as much of my money as needed. I'd spent several evenings after work making sure I had dinner plates and glasses and cutlery, a table to hold them up, and chairs to sit on. (Rush delivery extra.)

After I put the flowers in a newly purchased vase and put away the food, I picked up my phone. Look at all the notifications—Facebook still loved Vivien—and there was even a message from Grace. She'd remembered the anniversary and sent an e-card with the image of a dove and a cross and added text: *Be at peace, luv.* I replied, *Thank you, heart emoji*—writing it out as Vivien sometimes did. What could be wrong with that?

And then Augie's chat head popped up.

SUN, MAY 19, 01:32 PM

Augie: How's Raoul?

Vivien: Gone. How's your love life?

Augie: My finger is sore from swiping right but it avails me naught

Vivien: The problem with dating apps is that men swipe above their pay grade. Every male thinks he deserves a twenty-year-old model studying neurosurgery

Augie: Who will give it up because he's all she really needs

Vivien: Him and his basement apartment with the sock smell

Augie: My apartment is high up and it doesn't stink

Vivien: So you say

Augie: I'll send you a pic

Vivien: How do I know you didn't steal it off the internet?

Augie: A selfie

Vivien: Could be someone else's place

Augie: What if Joan verifies? She could attest to the smell too

Vivien: You can always depend on Joan

At four, I changed into my new clothes and went to fetch Mom. She'd achieved a perfection of pallor: her hair puffed and sprayed, her skin like bleached sugar, her dress—more of a robe—long and loose with white lilies embroidered on creamy cotton. She didn't look ill to me, just ethereal, reminding me of how she'd floated through my childhood nights. As we came in through the front door, she stopped in the hallway. The pail and rag for cleaning shoes was gone, and in its place, there was a shoe tray. Mom looked at me, then at the tray.

I waited for her to snipe, but all she said was "Help me take off my shoes."

I did, and then she insisted on a tour of the house, gamely pushing her walker. She checked out her bedroom first. To save time, I'd bought entire room displays, and her suite was called High Gloss Nepal. White, clean lines. I had no idea what this had to do with the Himalayan mountains. The bed faced the door, the dresser was against the wall to the left, and her recliner was in the corner to the right.

"There wasn't time to paint," I said.

"White walls go with everything." She hung on to her walker with one hand and with the other pulled open a dresser drawer. "But why is this empty?"

"What was I supposed to put in it?"

"I don't know." She looked distressed, but then her expression cleared. "It's all right. I'll get everything when I come home."

We proceeded to my room—which had a grey suite—and Vivien's old bedroom, set up as a den in lighter grey, then the living room, which was called Athena Beige. There, the new flooring was engineered wood that looked like oak. I'd hung sheer curtains over the windows and on the wall an abstract print on canvas. The dining room table was set up at the end of the living room closest to the kitchen. Around it were six white vinyl chairs. Last, we came to the kitchen. Remembering Augie's comment about the bleach, I'd used a lemon-scented cleanser. Mom sniffed, and I felt ridiculous for tensing as if I was still a kid, but she said, "Citrus is fresh. I like it." She had trouble reaching up to open a cabinet, so I did it for her, and brought down one of the new plates—square and also white.

"It's all so nice. Thank you," Mom said. Letting go of her walker, she faltered and caught herself, then reached out to hug me. I hung on tight, feeling my mother's bones, remembering how much Dad loved to dance with her.

The Ederys arrived in a burst of colour, like spring flowers encroaching on the slushy palette of winter. Bruno wore a red T-shirt and jeans, Ruth a turquoise dress, her purse the same colour. Hanging on to her walker, Mom greeted them at the door, and they all took off their shoes without being asked. Noah, his face concealed by a Spider-Man mask, hid behind his mother until I asked if he really was an Avenger.

He peeked around her and said, "Yes. Do you like Spider-Man?"

I told him I did, immensely. Though he wouldn't let his mother remove the face mask, he allowed his sister, Sarah, to hold his hand and take him into the living room, where she deposited him in a chair at the dining table. Sarah looked like her mother but sounded like neither parent. She was growing out bangs, kept off her face by a glittery hair clip. The rest of her hair was in a long braid, which she used as a weapon, flicking it at her brother to keep him in line. Even though Sarah wasn't related to my sister, something about her reminded me of Vivien—a spikiness in her energy and the way she took charge of her little brother.

Bruno and Ruth had brought Tupperware containers of food, which they carried to the kitchen. It turned out they were vegetarians and had brought their own supper because they didn't like to impose. I surreptitiously shoved the cold cuts to the back of the fridge.

I set the table while Ruth put her food in serving bowls. Bruno took a seat opposite Mom and beside his son, who was restless until Bruno gave him his phone in exchange for the mask. On Mom's side of the table, Sarah chose a seat facing an empty chair, leaving another between her and Mom, as if—forced to come—she was making a point that all this had nothing to do with her. When she took out her own phone, Bruno told her to put it away. Sarah pointed at her brother, engrossed in a game. Bruno then tried to take his phone away from Noah, who scratched Bruno's hand trying to get it back and then started to cry because he'd hurt his father. Bruno gave his son the phone again, and Sarah returned to hers with a smirk.

"Can Noah read?" Mom asked.

Noah looked up and shook his head.

"You will," Bruno said to his son, then told Mom that he'd been a reluctant reader himself until he discovered comic books. He was using them now to teach Noah. "Letters still jump around for me. Placing a ruler under each line helps."

"Vivien did that too." I put a plate in front of Mom. Then I asked, as if I didn't know, "Did she mention it?" Bruno shook his head. "She took notes with a tape recorder. I think she had"—should I have said *has*?—"undiagnosed learning disabilities."

"No, Vivien is very smart," Mom said, as if one precluded the other. I looked at Bruno and rolled my eyes.

"That's my new grandma," Noah piped up. "I'm smart too."

"She isn't mine," Sarah muttered.

Back in the kitchen, I filled a pitcher with water, fetching ice and juice from the fridge. Ruth put a serving spoon in a bowl of tabbouleh. The scent of herbs and spices was making me hungry.

"How long have you been with Bruno?" I asked.

"Since Sarah was three. I used to be married to a Goldberg, and whenever someone was expecting a Ruth Goldberg, they'd look over my shoulder for a white woman. Bruno and I have talked about that, people's expectations when you're a minority within a minority. His parents aren't white, but he was nervous about how they'd react to me. Being divorced and having a child and everything. Luckily, they were just happy I was Jewish. My ex is still in Toronto, though he doesn't see Sarah much. Bruno's the one who holds her head when she throws up. He may not be her father, but he's her dad."

"Family is what you make it," I said. "How did you meet?"

"Through a friend. I thought he was too easygoing at first—that maybe he didn't really care. My ex cared about everything—how to make a bed, bag garbage, do my hair, nurse my baby."

"What made you leave?"

"When Sarah was two, he started in on her. *She's too old to be in diapers, she holds her spoon funny.* He made fun of her lisp. I said, 'She's two!' And then he said, 'Is she even my kid? She's too dark to be mine.' That was it. He only had to say it once. I left that night. I was afraid he'd come after me. Men do. But he just dumped us."

"My ex moved to the other side of the country. It was a long time ago, but I still miss my stepdaughter."

"Maybe God will bring you together." She said it casually, as if living with an atheist didn't require her to keep her beliefs to herself. "You know what's funny? Bruno goes to synagogue to keep his father company, even though he thinks it's all bullshit. I never go, but I talk to God whenever I'm upset."

"I believe sometimes, though never on a Sunday."

She laughed. "I can finish up here. Go on and sit down."

"Not till you do."

Mom was telling Bruno a story about my father, whose first girlfriend broke up with him for a boy with a better car. Bruno told her about failing his first driving test. Once Ruth had brought the tabbouleh, lentils and rice, spicy eggplant, cucumber and tomato salad to the table, she sat next to Noah while I took the last empty chair, between Mom and Sarah.

"Is there chicken in any of this?" Mom asked.

"No, Mom," I said. "They're vegetarians."

"Or cheese?"

"Just a little feta in the tabbouleh," Ruth said. "Being vegetarians makes it easier to keep kosher for my in-laws. We don't have to deal with all the rules about meat."

Mom gave me an odd look—some kind of warning I didn't understand.

Bruno was now telling her about Ruth's family, who were Cochin Jews. Her ancestors had settled in southern India over two thousand years ago, around the same time as his parents' ancestors had arrived in Algeria. Much later, European Jews expelled from Spain found refuge in both Africa and India. The newcomers thought that brown Jews weren't real Jews—the human capacity to splinter into opposing groups being endless. During decolonization, Bruno's family, feeling insecure as minorities, had gone to France, while Ruth's had emigrated to Israel.

"I wanted Sarah to learn Hebrew," Ruth said.

The girl glanced up from her phone. "I'm not interested in the language of colonizers."

Ruth just shook her head, but Bruno said, "Then you're done speaking English?"

He and Sarah proceeded to argue about the Middle East, Sarah getting hot under the collar, her dad retaliating with a joke that made her scowl. I tried to picture Bruno growing up in our house and talking with my father like that. Our family arguments were never about issues, but about stuff— misusing it or losing it—as if we were all in survival mode and there was little space for ideas or ideals.

Ruth spoke over her husband and daughter, interrupting them to ask me about my work. I began to talk about palliative care and why it was the most satisfying work I'd ever done, but I didn't get far.

Mom had been poking at her food and now set down her fork. Head down, she murmured, "I need the washroom."

I'd ordered a raised toilet seat and a bar for the shower, but there had been a shipping delay, and Mom would need my assistance. Getting to my feet, I said we'd be right back.

Once inside the washroom, I locked the door, and Mom pulled down her underwear, then held on to my arms while lowering herself to the toilet. I turned my back to give her privacy. A minute later, she asked me to help her up, and I did, wishing I could say something to dispel the sad look on her face.

"We could have had years of this," she said, leaning heavily on the edge of the sink as she washed her hands.

"Of what?"

"Family meals."

"I wish we'd met him sooner too." *If only Vivien had gotten his letter*, I thought.

"Dad wanted a son. He should have been ours. I still don't understand why Vivien gave him to strangers."

I kept my voice gentle. "Bruno has other parents, but he's letting you be a part of his life now. We don't want to push him away."

Mom's eyes welled up as she nodded. "I want a picture."

"Let's ask them."

She dabbed her eyes with a towel, then followed me out, keeping a tight grip on her walker. When we were settled again at the dining table, I suggested we take a group picture. Everyone gathered around Mom, huddling close, and Ruth held her phone at arm's length to snap a selfie. "I'll share it to both of you."

Conversation resumed when we were back in our seats. Mom interrogated Bruno about carpentry until Noah— bored by long replies—was bouncing in his chair. Then Mom said, "I have something in my purse. Go have a look, Noah. It's in my room, on top of the dresser."

"Candy?"

"Maybe. Bring back my phone too so I can see the picture your mom just took."

Noah looked at his mother, and she nodded. He scrambled off his chair and tore down the corridor. He soon returned with the phone and the bag of candy Mom had bought in the hospital's gift shop. He dug into the bag and pulled out a Tootsie Pop for himself and one for Sarah, who smiled and cuffed him, then took it.

"You remind me of Vivien," I said to Sarah quietly, almost without meaning to, while her parents were turned toward my mother, who was recalling the popular candy of her youth.

"How?"

"She was her own person."

Sarah smiled.

"Annoying."

Sarah's smile broadened.

But it was my stepdaughter I was thinking of, wondering what she looked like now. The last time I saw her, she was a preteen, ears newly pierced with small gold hoops, and she was yelling, "You're not my mother!"

When we were done eating, Bruno and Ruth began to clear the table, but I told them I'd do it later. Mom was fading, and I needed to get her back to Valley View. As soon as they left, I got her into the car, and she fell sleep, snoring lightly. When we reached the facility, I parked and then woke her up. I was concerned she'd be disoriented, but she asked for my water bottle and, after she drank, said, "I wish your father could have been there today."

"I miss him too."

"Family is everything. I can meet my maker now," Mom said.

I kept a hand on her arm in the elevator, and once in her room, I helped her change into pyjamas. She lay down on the bed and curled onto her side; I tucked her in. It was the Victoria Day weekend, and in the park next to Valley View, fireworks were going off in celebration of a random monarch's birthday, giving people an excuse to frighten dogs and surprise the night with fountains of shattering colour.

CHAPTER 13

T en days after the Ederys came for dinner, my mother was discharged from Valley View. She was elated to come home. The fridge I'd filled had nothing disgusting in it. There was no bit of lint on the couch or crumb on the counter to indicate I'd grown sloppy with the cleaning.

Unfortunately, her elation didn't extend to the caregiver I'd hired. Mom immediately fired her because she couldn't stand having a stranger in her house. One of our retired neighbours then offered to check in while I was at work, and whenever Mom had an appointment, I booked time off to accompany her.

"Vivien" had been messaging Bruno every couple of days—short messages, sometimes with one of her photos of the clinic. He replied with a picture of a door or a joke and sent Vivien a Facebook friend request, which I accepted. Now that I had access to Bruno's "friends only" posts, I was able to see photos of his children. Noah in a snowsuit, with the caption: *Noah says Santa Claus is real. Santa doesn't come to our house because he knows we're Jewish.* Sarah as the tooth fairy on Halloween, dressed in black and carrying a bag of ceramic teeth. Noah feeding ducks. Sarah mimicking chimpanzees at the zoo.

Whenever I had trouble sleeping, there was always somebody on Facebook lit up with the green dot. Just knowing my—Vivien's—friends were up too comforted me. The dutiful day receded and my constricted self took a breath. I could like, heart, wow and bitch. I didn't have to take time to deliberate or worry over the wording to make sure I said the right thing, the helpful thing. This person I was online— mischievous, free, wanted and missed—I liked her. When I felt a prickle of guilt over deceiving Bruno, I pushed it aside, focusing instead on what I had to get done. In addition to dealing with work and Mom, I was still making my way through Vivien's emails and chats, hoping for a sign from her, something to explain why she'd left them for me.

My mother was mobile but barely. When she had her cardiology appointment, I was able to park in the medical building's garage. Even so, between the car and the elevator, she walked with her head down as if it was too hard to move the walker and stay fully erect, her glasses sliding so far down her nose, they fell off, landing in the walker's basket. I picked them out, and my mother put them on. We walked a few more steps, and the glasses fell again, this time hitting the pavement. If they hadn't been the extra durable plastic kind, they surely would have shattered. Mom joked she wouldn't mind if they had so she could get a new pair, less durable and more attractive. Her doctor was pleased with the improvement in her oxygen intake, and Mom was pleased with the new decor in his waiting room, which she chatted about with the receptionist. Clean lines, like our house, she said.

After her appointment, we went home and watched Netflix together until she fell asleep. Then I reviewed patient notes and went to bed myself. I had insomnia, but didn't dig into why. Hearing Mom snore in the next room, I just propped up my pillows against the grey headboard, put my laptop on my knees, and opened Facebook. Soon, I had several conversations going at once.

In one chat box, I was asking Augie why he hadn't asked Joan to see his place yet. In another, I flirted with Raoul. When I typed, *I'm not wearing anything at all*, in Augie's box by mistake, he replied with an umbrella emoji, and I wrote back, *Not for you*. He sent a sad face and a good-night sticker. By then, it was nearly one a.m. Oscar came online—it was morning in Stockholm—and we chatted about alternatives to expensive medical equipment.

I posted a challenge: *Thinking about my most interesting employers: I'll go first. Prostitutes. I walked their dogs. Yours?*

Ping, a like. Ping, open-mouthed emoji. Ping, *Jesus hates abortionists*, link to the Church of Pure Believers. I changed the privacy setting from Public to Friends. Ping, ping, ping, *Amazon reviewer; mattress tester; snake milker; cat walker; crime scene cleaner; cemetery greeter; sex toy courier; chicken sexer* (You had sex with chickens? *No, I determined their sex, it's harder than you think.* Why does anyone need to know? *Males aren't productive, no eggs, most of them are terminated. Is there a lesson in that?*)

And then I posted this: *Stuffing sneakers with newspapers does not keep your feet dry. Chilblains. Are. Real.*

I linked to an image of toes with crusty nails and swollen red patches, the skin beneath shiny and stretched with edema. It was greeted with numerous sad faces. And comments:

Oscar: How old were you?
Vivien: Seventeen. My sister gave me her coat but forgot boots
Raoul: You expect too much from people
Vivien: She expects too much from herself

Mom's snoring stopped, but it was followed by coughing, and I got up to check on her. She thought she was still at Valley View and wondered what I was doing there. I brought her a glass of water, and it took a while to settle her down. When she was asleep again, I returned to my bed and picked up my laptop. Another chat box had opened. Grace was messaging, *Hello.*

TUE, JUN 4, 02:45 AM
Vivien: Hi! Haven't heard from you in a while
Grace: I've been busy. I met someone

I was happy for her, as much as if I was my sister and she was my old friend. Like Vivien, I teased her.

Vivien: Good excuse. I hope he's worth it
Grace: He??

Not he? She wasn't straight? Had I missed something in her profile? I checked, and I hadn't. But there wouldn't be anything to indicate that she was gay—it was too dangerous where she lived. Surely there would have been some reference in an email or a message. But I hadn't had time to sift through them all.

Vivien: Typo
Grace: Funny typo.

Had I scared her? Was she worried I'd blackmail her over her sexual orientation? Had I done that to my sister's friend?

Grace: Why aren't you in the WhatsApp chat?

WhatsApp wasn't even on the list of apps and passwords my sister had sent me.

Vivien: No WiFi
Grace: That's what I thought when you didn't show up in the last couple. But you've got WiFi now
Grace: And you sound different
Vivien: How?
Grace: Just different. You told me not to get involved with the protest. You didn't roll your eyes at the e-card with the cross on it
Grace: I think you're someone who's taken over this account

My hands were cold—how could that be when I was hot with humiliation? A muscle in my belly started twitching. I could see it flutter my pyjama top.

Vivien: That's crazy
Grace: Then tell me something only Vivien would know
Vivien: We worked together in Port Harcourt
Grace: In my profile

There was no time to search through her conversations with my sister. The green dots were wiggling again.

Vivien: How do I know you're really Grace?
Grace: I was adopted in the UK. We met in a support group there for birth moms and adoptees

Vivien had gone to the UK for trauma training twenty-five years ago. And they were friends all the way back then, but I'd never even heard of Grace? My sister had kept so much from me.

Vivien: What city?
Grace: Manchester. Your turn
Vivien: I have a son
Grace: More
Vivien: His birth date is May 1, 1977. I put my name on the adoption disclosure register in 1995
Grace: I got you to do it. But if you were really Vivien you'd know that
Grace: Maybe you're a sick person who works at the registry

I responded quickly, fingers pounding the keyboard.

Vivien: My little sister delivered the baby. My first tattoo was a V. I got it after my mother made me give away the cat I brought home because I needed something to love. Enough?
Grace: Enough. But why are you being so odd?
Vivien: My son contacted me recently

Grace: And you didn't tell me!

Vivien: It shook me up. I haven't been able to tell anyone

Grace: Send a picture

Vivien: I will

Grace: Gtg. Shift starting.

Vivien: Be careful with your someone

Grace: Always am. See you in the next chat if not sooner

And if she didn't? *Liar, liar.*

I needed to get into my sister's phone.

On the weekend, while Mom was having an afternoon nap, I unlocked Dad's liquor cabinet and pulled out Vivien's box. I sat cross-legged on the shag carpet, the box in front of me. A bottom corner had been squashed during shipping. I pushed back the flaps and picked items out one at a time.

Vivien's hairbrush. It had a wooden handle. The bristles were white. There were strands of her henna-red hair entangled in them.

An old issue of *Alert*, the magazine published by Doctors Without Borders.

A clipboard, a flashlight, her sun hat.

A pair of water shoes, mud-encrusted.

A 1960 penny with a hole in it strung on a leather cord.

Knitting needles with a half-finished baby blanket on it.

The Practical Guide to Humanitarian Law.

Several T-shirts, washed and folded, free of any lingering scent.

A canvas backpack. Inside it, there was a zippered compartment that held a wallet, a key, and a crumpled tissue. There was some foreign currency in the wallet, a driver's licence, an International Driving Permit, her Canadian social insurance number card, an American Express card and a BCDC Mastercard. Her phone was in a side pocket. I'd have to charge it before seeing if I could get into it. I felt around at the bottom of the pack and touched something papery. I pulled out an envelope containing a pair of tickets to Spain—one in my sister's name, the other in mine—departing July 1, returning a week later. Non-refundable. She'd taken a chance on me.

After putting everything but the phone back in the box, I found a charger, plugged it in, and then went back upstairs to check on Mom. Her eyes were closed, her hand on her phone. I sat on the bed, my hip touching her legs. That touch doesn't age. I'd known it all my life. It was me in a bathing suit sitting on Mom's lap at the pool before a swim lesson, legs dangling between hers; head against her chest at the doctor's office, my arm bared for a shot; gliding down her stretched-out legs on a bench at the park, not ready for the big slide—how old could I have been? Two? Rare moments when my mother was calm, the world calm.

Her eyes opened, and she sat up to tell me about a conversation she'd just had with Noah. He'd used his father's phone to Skype with her and asked her to get an iPhone so they could FaceTime. Could she do that? The mall wouldn't close until eight, and it was only three thirty.

Since she'd come home, Mom's eyes often shone with gratitude, just like my patients' did as they neared the end. For instance, cancer. A patient gets sicker and crankier,

struggling for life, but when the realization hits that illness
has a deep hold, something changes. An uptick in kindness. In compassion. Selflessness. If the patient undergoes
chemo and the disease is knocked back, they become selfish again. At the last, sometimes there's another surge of
kindness as if the soul has overtaken ego, preparing to
leave it behind with the stuff of life. I knew now that my
mother's hourglass was nearly empty.

I didn't think she was strong enough to make it down the
front steps to the driveway, never mind into the car and then
a mall. But Mom insisted we try, telling me there were eleva-
tors in Yorkdale and that the mall also had scooters for the
elderly. So, we went. She managed, slowly and hanging on
to me, and she acquired an iPhone. By evening, she was
FaceTiming with her great-grandson. After the call was over,
I came in and perched on her bed.

"Mom, we've never talked about the future."

"Yes, we have." She had her crossword puzzle on her lap,
but she wasn't filling in any of the squares. "You know I don't
want to go to a nursing home."

"I do know that."

"Good." She picked up the paper. Discussion over.

Not over. "I mean what kind of procedures you would
want or not want. If you have to go to the hospital again."

She dropped her pen, and it rolled onto the floor. I picked
it up. "Do we have to talk about this now?"

"I see families having to make decisions when they
aren't sure what their mother would have wanted. It's ago-
nizing for them."

"Vivien knows what to do."

"You're very confident."

"Because I told her."

"When? How?"

"When I found out I had congestive heart failure. We talked about it."

"Mom, I'll be the one here, and I don't want you to suffer. Please tell me."

"It's simple. If I can come home, do everything. If I can't, nothing."

"It's not that simple. What if there's a procedure that carries with it the risk of a stroke? Or you go on a ventilator, but you can't come off it again? What is too much for you, Mom?"

She looked away from me, toward the window. It was open, and I could smell the perfume of a locust tree blooming next door. Nesting birds were singing down the sun. "I like the colours in the living room," she said. "White and beige look so nice together. I should have done it ages ago."

If my mother was my patient, I'd have kept trying. But she wasn't, so I acted as if home decorating was a fascinating subject, telling her about the different samples of flooring I'd looked at. Then I asked her, "Why didn't you ever take care of it?"

She said, "What?"

"A new floor in the living room. All that time. You never had company over. You always went to a friend's house or out to a movie."

"We didn't have a lot of friends."

"I'm not asking about the number of friends you had, but why you didn't do anything about the floor."

She said, "I was waiting."

"For what?"

"For Vivien to go shopping with me."

The next day, I decided to approach my sister's email system-atically, searching for a clue to her phone's password or something about Grace that would allay her suspicions if I couldn't get into the chat. First page: "1-50 of 4,987" emails. I scrolled through pages of emails with subject headers like *Red Tag Sale* or *Action Required* or *Updates From*. Finally, just as I was thinking, *Pointless, you're obsessing, stop it*, I acciden-tally clicked on something that reversed the order of emails, showing the oldest first.

> Grace Musa   Thursday, April 30, 2009
> To: Vivien Connor
> Subject: Birthday
> Hello luv. Are you settled in? I know tomorrow is a tough day and you'll be thinking of your son. I wish you were still here and I could make you tea. For you I would even bake muffins.
> BFF
> Grace

> Grace, dear, don't worry about me. I'm not going to get depressed again. I've come to a place of accep-tance. If my son had wanted to contact me, he would have done it a long time ago. Don't start with me. I did as you asked and sent the adoption registry my email

address, but he's going to be 32. I'm not expecting anything.

That email was followed by another on May 1, 2009, Vivien wishing me a happy birthday. I replied, *Thanks*. Neither of us mentioned her son. In all the years we'd both been thinking about him, I'd never brought him up because I was afraid it would push her further away. Now I could barely breathe—she'd wanted to connect with her son. She'd tried and tried again. What went wrong?

I had to wait until the next business day to call the adoption registry. The young woman who answered the phone was kind and apologetic as she asked questions to verify my (Vivien's) identity. (Date of birth, last address, place of baby's birth, social insurance number—which I got from Vivien's wallet.) I was on hold while she searched the database.

"Your email address was pending," she said. "It was never verified."

"What email address did you have?" I asked.

"Connorviv960@gmail.com."

I imagined my sister, nervous, hopeful, typing quickly. Her address was connorviv1960@gmail.com, but she'd left out the 1.

Because of that, she'd never met her son.

Late that evening, after taking care of Mom and updating my patient files, I huddled in a corner of the new couch with my phone, a glass of Scotch within reach.

There was a message from Grace: *Next WhatsApp chat Aug 11 usual time*. I replied with a thumbs-up and set a reminder on my phone for August 10: *Disaster tomorrow*. I checked my pulse. Normal. I drank and scrolled through Facebook.

One of Vivien's friends was biking around the world, another was vlogging about a refugee crisis. I uploaded a photo of a group of smiling mothers with infants Vivien had delivered and then reposted it to Instagram (#catchingbabies #feedthechildren). Raoul was back in Spain and had posted a beach picture. I hearted it, then wrote a saucy comment about the size of his swimsuit.

I was on my third drink when my phone rang. My finger swiped up, accepting the call a moment faster than my brain could process the caller's name and realize it was coming via Messenger. This call was for Vivien.

"Hi. It's Bruno."

"Hi." I got up and walked to the kitchen, wanting to get farther from Mom, forgetting that even if she woke up, she wouldn't be able to hear me.

"You answered."

"I did." If I spoke in short sentences, maybe he wouldn't recognize my voice. I stepped out into the backyard.

"Noah talked to Sheila today." He sounded nervous, maybe tipsy himself. "It just seemed like I should call you."

"That's good." I sat on the back steps. The trees were shapes in the darkness, nesting birds asleep.

"Do I sound like you imagined?"

"Much older." I laughed, then stopped myself, afraid it would sound familiar. Then I remembered I had never laughed in his presence, so all I had to do was never laugh again as me and it would be fine, which made me laugh harder.

Bruno laughed too.

"People say I sound a lot like Joan on the phone."

"Not really."

"Oh?"

"She's more reserved. Flatter."

"Living with Mom will do that."

"Mark hasn't replied to my email."

"Asshole." My growl was a pretty good imitation of Vivien's.

"I don't know what else I can do."

Nothing would have been the simple answer. But I owed him; I owed Vivien. "I'm friends with Mark's stepbrother. I'll talk to him."

"Appreciate it. Did you see the picture of us at your house?"

"You have a nice family."

"They're your grandkids."

"I know." My voice cracked.

"They'd like to meet you too."

"You're breaking up." I tried not to cry. How did I let the lie get so big?

He repeated himself, then added, "By the way, I like metal too. Have you heard A Pale Horse Named Death?"

"I'll check it out. Have to run. Working."

"Okay. Talk to you again?"

"Sorry, I'm losing the connection. Take care of yourself and your sweet kids."

Tap the icon. End call.

Deception has a life of its own. The only choice, it seemed, was to keep it going.

═══

I went inside and down to the basement.

To get into Vivien's phone, I'd already tried the obvious—her birthday, mine, my parents', Bruno's. This time, I attempted it with the year Vivien graduated from nursing school, the year she'd put her name on the Adoption Disclosure Register, and house numbers—ours, Uncle Jack's, even my old condo's. Nothing worked.

I opened her box to rifle through it again. I put her wallet in my back pocket, threw on one of her T-shirts and walked to the laundry room, where I stood in front of the sink, looking at myself in the mirror. The light was too bright. I flicked the switch off and tapped the flashlight on my phone. Now in the mirror—a reasonable facsimile of my sister.

"Yes," I whispered. "I'll meet you in Spain."

I messaged Augie: *My son contacted me. Mark not responding. Can you speak to him?*

CHAPTER 14

WED, JUN 12, 01:22 AM

Augie: What are you doing up so early?

Vivien: On shift

Augie: I finally got through to Mark. So I guess I'm an uncle

Vivien: Not biologically. Stepbrother's kid

Augie: And possibly not even that?

Vivien: Meaning?

Augie: Mark wants a paternity test and as usual he expects someone else to deal with it

Vivien: Asshole

Augie: Schmuck

Augie: You can give Bruno my email address. I'll arrange it. For a favour

Vivien: How big a favour?

Augie: Not much. Just thinking of asking Joan out. Tell me what she likes. Movie? Concert?

Vivien: Feed her. Nobody ever takes care of her

Vivien: But there's no way for her to get the time. Not with Mom

Augie: Too bad

JUN 12, 01:24 AM

Bruno: What are you doing up so late?

Vivien: It's not late for me, it's morning. You?

Bruno: Noah threw up

Bruno: He's lying on the couch and I'm keeping him company

Bruno: Ruth has to get up for work tomorrow

Vivien: Speaking of Mark

Bruno: We weren't

Vivien: I was, with his stepbrother. He said Mark wants a paternity test

Bruno: That's fine

(It would buy a little time—until he found out Mark wasn't his father.)

Vivien: Work out the logistics with Augie. The stepbrother. Augie.Rosenstein@augiesellshouses.com

Bruno: Why not Mark?

Vivien: If he could get someone else to shit for him he would

Bruno: Lol. What do you call a lazy kangaroo?

Vivien: What

Bruno: A pouch potato

The next day, I woke up with a headache and regretted staying up so late—it was becoming a bad habit. I dragged myself through the day until I got to my last appointment, which was with Eddie Wong. He'd gained a bit of weight. His cheeks were rounder, his eyes alert and thoughtful. I could see something of the man in his wedding picture, broad-shouldered and proud, shorter than his wife.

Chemo had knocked Eddie's cancer back enough to reduce his fatigue, and radiotherapy had shrunk the tumours in his abdomen so that he could stand and walk more easily. Because there's a waiting list for home care, as long as patients are well enough to ride in a car or take transit, they're expected to make use of the palliative outpatient clinic at the hospital. The improvement in Eddie's strength and mobility meant that his symptoms would be managed by the doctors there until his cancer resurged. This would be our last appointment for a while, and he reminded me of our agreement.

"You understand that I can't even draw," I said.

"Didn't you ever paint with your father?"

"No—he didn't believe in encouraging kids just for the sake of building up their egos. He was serious about art."

"Good man."

I nodded.

"So, you're coming next week?"

"I thought you understood, Eddie. You'll be going to the palliative care clinic at the hospital now."

"No, no. I mean to paint with me. To honour your father's memory."

So, a week later, on the day before the summer solstice, I headed for Eddie's apartment after I was done with my other patients. There were still hours of light ahead of us, his living room as bright as noon on a sunny winter's day. His dining room table was set up with tubes of acrylic paint, a pair of palettes, a jar of brushes, another of water to dilute paint or clean a brush, and the table easel. For me, there was a floor easel between the couch and stereo cabinet, where I could stand with the light behind me, facing the table. Eddie had a stack of different-sized canvases. When I picked up a small one, he shook his head and pointed at the large canvas he'd placed on my easel. He liked to paint to music and asked whether I'd rather have *Pictures at an Exhibition*, appropriate to the endeavour, or *The Rough Guide to the Music of China*, which was already on the stereo, playing a mournful song from the 1920s that his parents had admired. By the time I said, "Let's keep this one," the needle had moved to the next track, contemporary punk, and I found myself nodding along as I loaded up my palette with colours. I wished I could paint the lake—a rough heap of waves the grey-blue of my sister's eyes—but that was beyond me. It was all beyond me, but I doggedly took a large brush to match the large canvas and coated the bristles with paint. The first thick slick of purple down the middle of the canvas made me remember.

One weekend, while Dad and Vivien were up at the cottage, I was helping Mom paint the house. We stood in the living room, considering the walls, or at least Mom was considering and I was imitating her, hands on my hips, head tilted, eyes narrowed, both of us in aprons to protect our clothes. The aprons were red and white plaid, like tablecloths. Maybe they were tablecloths—I remember a safety pin at my waist. I said, "I wish we didn't have art at school. I hate it."

Mom said, "Mmm."

I said, "I'm no good at it."

Mom said, "Mmm."

I said, "Vivien's good."

Mom said, "I used to paint."

"When?"

"When I was dating your father." She scooped up her blond hair and wrapped a rubber band around it. The ponytail bounced. "We went to art galleries and talked about art, and he invited me up to the cottage to paint *en plein air*."

"What's that?"

"Painting the outdoors as you observe it, like the Group of Seven did. Dad and Captain Edwin were good at it, but I wasn't, so I gave up. Besides, it creates so much mess. Why don't we both paint something on the walls?"

I couldn't believe that Mom would let me do that. "With what?"

"We'll use the paint samples."

She'd bought a couple dozen of them in all kinds of colours, though in the end, she always went with Cloud White. And she had an array of brushes too, so she could get around corners and into small spaces. I always thought it would be okay if I missed a spot because the ceiling and walls were the same colour of nothing, but Mom could see flaws even in white on white.

"I'll take this wall," she said, "and you do whatever you want on that one. We won't look at each other's painting until we both yell, 'Done.' Then we'll cover it all with the wall paint, so no one but us will ever see it. That way, it doesn't matter if it's any good. Right?"

I nodded and set out to paint a horse on my wall. It ended up looking more like a cow or a pig and got worse when I tried to fix it, resembling no creature that ever existed. Frustrated,

I started slapping on paint to cover it up, and now I remembered how good that felt, the sound of the slap, the thickness of the paint, choosing different-shaped brushes to pull the paint in lines, to press bristles against the wall, to swoosh with a flick of my wrist. I glanced at Mom though we'd agreed not to peek until we were done. Her back was very straight, and without turning, she said, "Keep at it!"

When I'd turned my wall into an explosion of colour, I yelled, "Done," and Mom yelled, "Done," too. We looked at each other's walls. Mom's painting was small and delicate, something fairy-ish or angel-like but more interesting than either, with strings of colour emanating from the central figure. My wall pleased me so much, I was reluctant to roll Cloud White over it. Nowadays, I'd take a picture with my phone so it would last forever in the cloud, but Mom didn't have a camera, and if she had, the album of photos would have been tossed with the others when she was getting rid of "junk." I remember how bright and beautiful her face was as she looked from wall to wall. We admired the paintings until the walls dried. Then she poured Cloud White into a tray and picked up a roller, saying, "It'll always be perfect in your mind."

But it wasn't. I'd forgotten all about it until I was standing in an old man's apartment, looking out over a Great Lake. What if Eddie had never asked me to paint with him? What if I wasn't compelled to keep a promise made in passing? Memory is sadistic; so much of what we remember haunts us, and so much of what we forget could be a comfort. I chose another brush, picked red this time, and moved my arm in large, slow semicircles as I painted my regrets—betraying Paul, losing my stepdaughter, lashing out at my sister when she most needed me.

"Is this relaxing?" Eddie asked.

"It depends on what you mean," I said.

"On the beach, under an umbrella. You have a drink. You have a nap."

"Not exactly. It reminds me of something that I'm glad to remember and other things that make me sad."

"Ah," he said. "Yes."

"Does painting bring back memories for you too?"

"Maybe I don't need to remember something I forgot."

"What does it do, then?"

"Have a look."

He turned the easel to give me a full view unobstructed by his shoulder. He'd painted me, more or less. It was a quick sketch, but recognizable. Eddie had given me a wild look.

"That's you painting," he said.

"Huh. I wouldn't have guessed."

He laughed.

"I'm going to miss talking to you, Eddie."

"I'll be seeing you again," he said. "You told me I could. When I have to go back into home care."

"You're still my patient," I said, and then my phone rang. It was my mother's neighbour from next door, Mrs. Rossi. She was sorry, so sorry, she said, but my mother was in an ambulance on its way to St. Mike's because the closest ER was full. "She's alive," Mrs. Rossi said. "Or at least she was still breathing when she left."

What a thing it is. To have consciousness. Why are we designed this way? What evolutionary advantage does it confer? To be aware of what's coming. That it's happening to a me and a you. Standing astride the tracks in a dark tunnel, unable to jump away from the oncoming train, unable to pull your mother away from it.

By the time I got to the hospital, my mother had been admitted to the ICU. She was in cardiogenic shock—her heart wasn't pumping enough blood. Her pulse was rapid, blood pressure dangerously low. Her hand was cold, and I held it between both of mine to warm it up. A nurse came and checked her IV drip and her blood pressure. I know the cardiologist discussed her EKG with me, but I don't remember what she said. Sometimes I picture the doctor with red hair, sometimes with black. I have no idea. Mom dozed and then woke, smiled and told me that there was the most beautiful bed among the stars waiting for her. Then she frowned and said her legs hurt and mumbled something incomprehensible. It sounded like, *Dude get the road wiped.* She dozed again.

An hour or so later, she opened her eyes, and I said, "How do you feel?"

She blinked and said, "I need my passport."

She slept some more, and I watched the liquid in the IV bag drip down the tube. I wished every one of my patients a good death, but not my mother, because mothers must be immortal and take any option offered that will extend their lives. When she next woke up, her legs were still bothering her, but she wasn't having trouble breathing. She asked where Vivien was, and when I said she was in the DRC, Mom shook her head and assured me Vivien was on her way.

The sun set in the west as it does every day, though you never know about tomorrow. Smog made for a pretty sunset.

Around the time the sun was setting, there was a shift change. New nurse, new doctor. I recognized this cardiologist, a youngish man named Dennis Kim, who'd done a palliative care rotation with me during his medical training. He was concerned. Though the medications had increased my mother's comfort, she was still not getting enough blood to her organs. He took her vitals and adjusted her treatment; the IV bag was changed. I was hungry and thirsty but afraid to leave her side. The nurse brought me a glass of water. I thought that was excessively kind and got teary over it.

In the dark of night, the ICU was tranquil, the background hum of machines soothing. Nurses floated along the corridor, their shoes skimming the floor with a whispering sound. I looked out the window at city lights like stars and hoped that my mother was stabilizing, her organs flushed with blood. Though it would only mean another few months of going in and out of the hospital, enduring crisis after crisis, emerging weaker and more diminished each time, I wanted her to live. I was selfish in the human way, aware of my own aching self, even with everything I knew. I wasn't a physician in my dying mother's presence— just a person among the machines with their beeps and hisses, like any other person torn to the bone. I stroked Mom's forehead.

At around one in the morning, Dennis came back and pulled over a chair to sit beside me. I was glad to see that he'd learned something from me and also wary. When there are decisions to be made, I'd advised, don't stand over the patient and relatives. Come to their level so they know you're not a remote god beyond approach or reproach, just a guy with a stethoscope on their team.

He told me that the first line of treatment wasn't working. The next step would involve inserting a large line through my mother's groin so that he could administer dopamine. He said he needed consent because it would be uncomfortable. Mom's ears were working fine just then. She snapped, "You mean painful."

He didn't deny it but replied to her by explaining her situation.

She turned her head to look at me. "What?"

Dying is life magnified. It's majestic. Also grotesque, tender, ridiculous. I bent to my mother's ear. I wanted to shout, *Do it*, but I was dutiful, and in a raised voice, only said, "You aren't stabilizing. He wants to try dopamine. He says that with the big line, you've got a 30 percent chance. Without it, death will occur in twenty-four to forty-eight hours."

"But will I go home?"

I thought she might not have noticed Dennis shaking his head, so I said, "I don't know."

It wasn't a lie. I didn't know for sure, not absolutely 100 percent for sure, only 99.99.

Mom did. With a frail hand, she covered the ear I was speaking into. She said, "That's not a life. My legs hurt. No."

I gently pulled her hand away and spoke into her ear some more. I wanted to be sure she understood what was at stake.

She said, "I'm tired. No more. I don't want it."

I said, "You're leaving me alone."

"There's Vivien."

Did she mean I still had my sister, or that she saw Vivien in the room, waiting to accompany her?

"I'll give you privacy," Dennis said, and left us.

I tried to rub Mom's legs, but my touch made her groan, so I went back to holding her hand. I wondered whether to call Bruno. It was late and I didn't want to disturb him, but this was his grandmother, even if newly discovered and unrelated to his life. When I asked her whether she wanted to see him, she mustered her dwindling energy to nod emphatically.

Bruno and Ruth left Sarah in charge and were at the hospital in half an hour. I was surprised at how relieved I was to see them walk in. Ruth immediately took Mom's other hand as Bruno hovered uncertainly nearby.

"Come closer," Ruth said to him.

He knelt beside the bed and my mother turned her head to see him. "I'm glad I found you," he said.

"Me too," she replied.

We stayed with her that way, the women holding her hands, the grandson kneeling. I kissed my mother's forehead, stroked it, told her that I loved her. When she fell asleep, Bruno brought in an extra chair so he could sit too. We spoke quietly of ordinary things, keeping vigil.

My mother stirred. It was just after three a.m. Summer solstice. I thought I smelled my sister's perfume, musk and moss and forest. Mom's feet stuck out from under the sheet. She said, "There's something I have to do."

"What, Mom?"

"Before I finish packing. I have to talk to Vivien."

"She's at her clinic," I said.

"I want to call her."

I panicked, thinking she can't find out now, it'll kill her. "She won't have service," I said.

"I'll leave a message. Dial her for me, Joanie."

I couldn't use my phone to call myself, so I let go of my mother's hand to get her bag from the side table. It was large, black and shiny, empty except for a credit card and the new iPhone, which I removed and unlocked. I tapped on my sister's icon, then held the phone to Mom's ear, and she spoke clearly, using up her remaining strength. "I'm sorry I couldn't wait for you to come home. I tried, but I can't. I love you. I love you."

After I replaced the phone in her bag, I said, "Is there anything else, Mom?"

"So tired," she said. "The flight's delayed." Having given twice to the absent child, she had nothing left for me.

We all settled in for a long wait. But about twenty minutes later, my mother shot out of her body. Her back arched, she convulsed briefly and took her last breath. Dennis came in to listen to her stilled heart and pronounce time of death. The nurse turned off the machines. As he touched her wrist to remove the line, I put a hand on his arm. He looked at me and nodded and said, "Mrs. Connor, I'm removing the line now."

Bruno was the only one who cried. Personally, I didn't believe it had happened.

I announced my mother's death on Vivien's Facebook page at four in the morning. Then I gave myself up to its luminescence as condolences poured in. Bruno must have written as soon as he and Ruth got home. Oscar sent a long message about the complicated feelings he'd had after the death of his narcissistic mother. Grace posted a GIF with praying hands and a flickering candle and, in purple script, *I'm here for you always*. Vivien replied graciously and gratefully.

As for me, I couldn't grasp that anyone was gone, not my sister (she was alive; I was her) and not my mother (she was asleep in the room across from mine; any minute I'd hear her snoring).

Eventually, I showered and got ready for the morning check-in call, but then my phone rang, and it was Augie. He'd seen Vivien's post. "How are you doing? How are you doing really?"

As we spoke, I remembered him at my father's memorial. Dad had died, my partner had left me, my stepdaughter was off limits, my condo was listed for sale, and I was holding my mother up, literally—she couldn't walk without leaning on me. Augie took her other arm as if I couldn't manage, which was annoying, but I didn't stop him because it was such a relief to feel anything at all. He told us that he didn't know how his father would be able to bear his trapped life without Dad's visits. Months later, I cried buckets at Uncle Jack's funeral. I cried so hard, my nose bled.

Now Augie kept me on the phone, ignoring me when I said I should go. He told me that he'd been in touch with Bruno and Mark, who'd received their DNA kits and had mailed their samples to the lab. I said that Vivien was getting tested too (I'd used hennaed strands from her hairbrush). I said that I expected to sell the house—for real this time. Augie offered to help. I told him to make up with his mother before she died.

After we hung up, I realized I'd lost track of time and called the office to explain that I'd missed the morning meeting because my mother had died.

Later that morning, a fruit basket arrived from my work and I brought it to Mrs. Rossi. The next day, I saw patients, but I couldn't eat, and every time I'd come close to sleeping, I'd fall awake as if I'd landed on cement. I could have had a colleague prescribe a sedative, but I thought I'd manage, as I'd often managed, even if I couldn't sleep. All I had to do was fill a glass and sip Scotch while I read my sister's email.

Bruno Edery   Friday, June 21, 10:11 PM (1 day ago)
To me
Dear Vivien,
Honestly I don't know what to say. Ruth told me to start with I'm sorry. So, yes, I'm sorry for your loss. Your mother was a dignified and self-possessed woman who was generous with her stories and answered everything I asked. I'm sorry I won't get to know her better. My condolences. That's also something people say.

What I really want you to know is that when I was a kid, I didn't think about being adopted. Not until I was eight and went to France. I have a lot of cousins there. They were great and I fit right in. Then an older cousin, I think he was about fourteen, told me that our grandfather was sorry for my parents because they couldn't have their own kids. My cousin said not to worry about it, my parents were lucky. I'd be a better basketball player than any kid they could have had on their own, seeing as how I was tall and they were not. That was high praise since my cousin was obsessed with basketball. But until then I'd taken it for granted that Mom and Dad loved me, were proud of me, thought I was the best kid on the playground. They had to because they were my parents. But because of what this cousin said, I realized they could have picked another kid or had another kid picked for them. I wasn't sure how it all worked and didn't want to ask them, but the point was that I could have ended up somewhere else. They could have had a different son. The shadow of that other, better son followed me. He got better marks. He told better jokes. He had ears that didn't stick out. He was a great reader and got a PhD.

This has to do with your mother. I had a long talk with her on my own one day, and it made me see things in a different light. That's what I want you to know. She got to be a grandma.

Xo

Bruno

CHAPTER 15

When I arrived at McClure's funeral home on Monday morning, Bruno was sitting on the steps outside, waiting for me. I'd chosen McClure's because it was downtown, allowing me to make arrangements between seeing patients. I hadn't realized that it was around the corner from Church and Isabella, where my sister had walked the prostitute's dogs some forty years ago.

Wearing a blue button-down shirt, pressed pants, and dark leather shoes, Bruno was holding a couple of grande cappuccinos from Starbucks. As he handed one of them to me, I saw what my mother must have, a hint of Dad in his fingers and those cup-handle ears, revealed by a recent haircut.

"Thanks for coming," I said, joining him on the steps.

"It was Ruth's idea."

"Thanks anyway."

"No problem."

"You do look a bit like my father. He used to say the Prince of Wales had his ears."

"Noah liked to hang on to them when he was a baby."

I laughed. My first laugh.

We sat for a bit, sipping coffee, because I wasn't ready to go in. Bruno had never been inside a funeral home and said he hoped it would be interesting, which made me smile and ask what else he found interesting. The list was long. It included: abandoned buildings, Cold War spies, deep-sea creatures, heavy metal bands, the origins of the universe, and ancient construction methods. Did I know that the old Romans had a recipe for concrete superior to ours, sadly lost? I did not.

My coffee was done and so was his. "I'm ready now," I said.

Bruno pulled on the door handle, but it was locked. I pressed the button on the intercom. After buzzing us in, Harold Preston, the Respectful Remembrance Planning Professional, apologized for the locked door. It was a precaution taken after a recent break-in in which computers and coffins had been stolen.

I'd been to funeral services and memorials in churches, synagogues, mosques, gardens, funeral homes, a psychiatric hospital, the beach, a dog park where the dogs were the main mourners. I was at ease in all of them, even feeling a bit superior because of my familiarity with death's habits. I thought I was prepared for this.

Harold ushered us into the McClure library, offering condolences in the manner of a police officer talking down a jumper. Tone calmly monotonous. Face neutral. No smiling. Not even his eyebrows moved. How did he manage that?

His sales pitch was practised but decorous. He spoke slowly enough; I got every other word, I think. He took notes on a yellow steno pad, using a cheap stick pen. I suppose that—unlike investment advisers, whose attire and premises emphasize their success—he was playing down the profit-ability of the death business. A basic funeral and burial plot began at seventeen thousand dollars. Not much less for cremation and a niche. I wondered if Mom would mind joining Dad in my storage locker. His urn was a matte black vessel with gold trim, which I'd stashed on a shelving unit until Mom made up her mind what to do with it. She never did.

"Did your mother have a religious affiliation?" Harold asked.

"Not really," I said.

"We have a non-denominational chapel. You can have anyone conduct a service, or one of our funeral directors can assist."

"She wanted to be cremated," I said, trying to maintain my composure.

He flipped to another page in the brochure. "Here's the package I'd recommend."

There were no books in this library, just a display case with urns and framed photographs of dignified elderly men and women with unnaturally white teeth. The frames, which came with an embedded thumbprint taken from the dear departed, were only $275 each, Harold pointed out.

Nothing was real here. My mother dead? Absurd. After all, this was a funeral *home*. It had multiple living rooms. The decor: blue and beige, crystal chandeliers, faux fireplaces, gilded paintings of weeping willows. Stately, unlike death. Nothing rotting in this place. Certainly not the body I'd spied through an open door, head on a pillow as if asleep. Good makeup job. Lifelike, but not life. Everyone in this home could be replaced by robots, and I'd fit right in. Pre-programmed to help.

"I can't do this," I said. "My mother in an urn, and me having to shake everyone's hand. I can't." I leaned against Bruno as if he was my own son, young and sturdy, then straightened up because he wasn't.

"Do you want to put it off?" Bruno asked.

"Yes! No. I can't leave her."

"How about just doing the cremation?" He turned to Harold. "Does my aunt have to choose an urn?"

"Usually, people do, because the ashes come to us in a plain black box."

"Great. What if you just take the box, Joan? Forget the niche. We'll deal with the memorial later."

His aunt. *We.* I liked that. It made me sigh with relief. "Yes."

After the forms were filled out and the charge put on my credit card, I meant to give Bruno a ride home, but as soon as we got into the car, for some reason my foot trembled on the brake and I couldn't turn on the ignition, only cry and cry until Bruno found tissues in my glove compartment and handed me one. We changed places. He took the wheel to drive me to my next appointment. The sun was shining on one side of the street and rain sprinkled on the other. We arrived at the patient's building a few minutes early, and Bruno sat with me in the car, the window rolled down, his arm resting on the frame and his elbow sticking out.

"Ruth is better at this than me," he said. "She always knows what to say."

"I'll be fine." I blew my nose. "I'm just afraid to go home."

"It's a weird place. As if it's nobody's. Like a hotel."

"I got it furnished in a hurry because Mom wanted it nice for you." That nearly undid me again.

"Sorry. Told you I'm no good at this."

"No, you're right. It's worse than when it was empty."

"Then come to our place," Bruno said. "Stay awhile."

"I don't want to impose."

"I'm not being nice. We have a basement apartment and just had to evict the tenants," he said. "They still owe us four months' rent and the place is a disaster. All I can offer is a key. You'll have to bring a camping bed or something."

"I've got an air mattress. But you've got to let me repay you somehow."

"If you'd give us a hand in fixing up the basement, it would be a big help. I've patched the holes in the wall, but that's it."

"I'll bring my own cleaning supplies."

"Great."

I got the address from Bruno, and we got out of the car. I thought, *When I buy my next car, it's not going to be a practical colour.*

I saw as many patients as I could handle that afternoon—a total of one—and called Larry Klieger. He gave me a week off to mourn whether I wanted it or not. I protested, but he didn't relent, and then he had to go because he was on his way to the airport.

I made a fast trip to the house to pick up toiletries, clothes and cleaning supplies—everything else I would need was already in the trunk of the car. On my way to Bruno's, I stopped at a liquor store to pick up a bottle of Scotch. His house was on a tree-lined street north of Bloor near Christie. Toronto is a city of neighbourhoods, and Bruno's was an urban one. At its heart was an old quarry converted into a bowl-shaped park with baseball diamonds, playgrounds and a swimming pool. Horses used to drink at the equine fountains on every corner. Houses stood close together, alleys running behind them. People still sat on porches, knocked on neighbours' doors, stopped in the street to talk. Bruno and Ruth's place was a new build sandwiched between century-old semis, next to the park. Their front yard was mostly taken up by a linden tree in bloom. Its perfume followed me up the steps to the porch. I rang the bell.

"Why are you Great-Aunt?" Noah asked as he let me in, his voice a bit muffled by the Spider-Man mask. "You're younger than Great-Grandma. Your hair isn't white, and your face isn't pleated."

"I'm your dad's aunt. So that makes me your great-aunt."

"And Great-Grandma is your mommy?"

"That's right."

"When are we going to visit her again?"

Bruno appeared and placed a large hand on his son's masked head. He said, "You know, Great-Grandma died."

"Uh-huh. Mommy told me she went to be with God. Is Great-Grandma playing with Libby?"

"Who's Libby?" I asked.

"Our cat," Noah said. "She's visiting God too."

Over the boy's head, Bruno rolled his eyes.

"All right," I said. Then, "Isn't it uncomfortable to breathe through that mask?"

"Yes." Noah took it off. He had a spot of jam near the corner of his mouth. I took a tissue from my pocket.

He said, "You have to put it near my mouth so I can spit on it."

I obeyed, he spit and I wiped away the jam.

Ruth was out, meeting an old friend for coffee. Sarah was having a shower in the upstairs bathroom. Bruno said, "Let me help you with all that stuff. I forgot to tell you that you can park on the pad behind the house. I keep my truck in the workshop. Come, I'll show you around."

The house was furnished with Bruno's experiments and mistakes, brought over from his workshop in the double garage he rented in the alley that ran perpendicular to his backyard. At one point, he'd thought about getting into upholstery, but never went further than the couch in his living room. The dining room chairs were Bruno's only foray into using willow trees purpose-grown in bent shapes. An oak door he'd cut a few millimetres too short for a customer made a workable tabletop. Ruth loved to read as much as her daughter, and bookcases—one with hanging dividers for comics—occupied every space that wasn't required for something nearly as essential, say a refrigerator. The smell of old books mingling with playdough, paint and spices.

Noah provided running commentary. "That's the kitchen. That's the backyard. That's my tomato plant."

"Are you hungry?" Bruno said at last, and I might have eaten something, though all I remember is sitting at the table while Noah had a bowl of post-dinner cereal. Then I gathered my corn broom, Dustbuster, dusting cloths, micro-fibre cleaning cloths, sponges, steel-wool pads, bleach, bathroom cleanser, toilet cleanser, hardwood cleaner, window cleaner, spray bottle with vinegar and water, oven cleaner, Magic Erasers, toilet bowl brush, several pairs of rubber gloves, squeegee, bucket, two kinds of mops—Swiffer and string. Also, a butter knife. I carried it all from the car to the basement myself, waving away help.

The apartment had a kitchen-living room. An octopus splatter on the wall could only have been created by someone flinging a plate of spaghetti at it. There was also a small bedroom, and a bathroom with a tub. Natural light came through a window in the front and also a side window at ground level. At the back, a doorway led to a small, shared laundry room and a staircase to the main house.

I could see where the holes in walls and ceilings had been plastered. Abandoned possessions had been boxed for pickup by Got Your Junk. The door still needed to be replaced. Bathtub—rusty and crusty. Toilet bowl. I wondered if I should scrape off a specimen. Wearing latex gloves, I sprayed the bowl with cleanser, scoured and flushed. Repeat twice. The bathroom was small. I could touch the walls from anywhere I stood. The size suited me, as if I was hiding in a cardboard box with the flaps closed.

When I was done scrubbing the bathtub, I dried it with a towel and lay down in it. Eyes closed, I pictured Mom telling me she wanted to message Vivien, the peace on her face when she did. It was safe now to tell everyone that Vivien had died. I'd kept my promise and Mom had had a good death. All I needed to do now was to go on Vivien's social media as myself and announce that Vivien was gone too. Then the lie would be over.

When Dad passed away, Vivien didn't stay for the service, but caught the next flight out. NATO was bombing Serbia and nurses were desperately needed. Anyway, Dad was dead, she said, and a funeral was an empty ritual. Surely, as a doctor, I could understand that.

What I understood was that she'd left me on my own to deal with the rest. Death might be a sacred process, but after-death is all about the paperwork.

My father's filing cabinet in the basement was empty. Mom had taken the contents to a recycling depot in the third week of his coma and couldn't remember the name of the lawyer who'd drafted the will. Even as Dad's next of kin, she needed a marriage certificate or a tax return to prove it.

She told me she was afraid to sleep in the house alone, and I replied that I'd come stay until she got used to things. While Mom stood on a stepladder, attempting to remove track lighting from the living room ceiling, I worked on tracking down the necessary documents. No luck. Finally, I asked Augie—who had just divorced and had also returned to his childhood home for a while—whether I could check their attic. With Augie right behind me, I clambered up and looked around. I found some of Dad's paintings, one of Vivien's drawings, the photo of us playing Candy Land, and the original marriage certificate, on the back of which was a sketch of a young woman sitting on the railing at Niagara Falls. It was my mother, but I'd never seen her like that—simply happy—and I didn't again until she met my sister's son.

Once Dad's estate was settled, I took Mom to my lawyer, Gary Lyons, to get her own affairs in order. His office made her uncomfortable and that gave me pleasure, I'm ashamed to say: Mom sitting at the front of her seat to minimize contact between herself and the chair, which wasn't that clean but not that dirty either. Hands folded in her lap, feet crossed primly at the ankles, she was barely in her mid-sixties, wearing a cream-coloured suit and beige loafers with fringes.

Gary had left a Bay Street practice to work from home. He lived in a Victorian house on a side street between the hospital and the office for the palliative care practice, which I'd just joined. In the hallway near his front door, there was newspaper on the floor to protect it from one of his cats, who was elderly and incontinent. Mom made herself thinner— even her feet seemed narrower—as she pushed away an edge of the newspaper with the toe of a shoe. The house didn't smell at all, not to me, not of cats at least. Gary only had four, and he changed the litter boxes and newspaper regularly. I'll admit it did have a library archive kind of odour, which shouldn't have made Mom's nostrils flare and then pinch. Gary didn't hang on to last year's newspapers, like a patient of mine did, but he did keep client files. Boxes of them were piled up in towering cliffs, forming a narrow corridor that had to be traversed from the front door and up the stairs to his office on the second floor, and from the office door to his desk below the window, with side corridors to the printer, fax machine and filing cabinets.

He drafted a power of attorney and Mom's will: *My estate is to be shared equally between my children, Vivien Leigh Connor and Joan Connor. If either of them predeceases me and has left issue, her children shall share her share in equal shares per stirpes.*

When I was taking Mom home, she said she would have a heart attack if I ever made her step into a place like that again. But while we'd been at Gary's, except for the awkward way she perched, Mom didn't show her disgust. She made conversation as easily as she did with anyone, discovering that Gary had a twin who suffered from schizophrenia and that he'd only stopped waiting for his own psychotic break when he turned fifty. Gary was charmed.

Without my mother, life was simple. Sterile. Empty. As empty as a gutted house.

I couldn't go home yet. That's what I realized, lying in the dry bathtub in Bruno's basement. I couldn't just rip out the lie—it had become a necessary part of me. *Dear God, please give me a little longer until I go back to that life.*

CHAPTER 16

For the next several days, I scrubbed walls, counters, closets and cupboards—inside and out. I dug into grime on the stove and in the oven, and I scraped away unidentifiable goo in the refrigerator and freezer. Cleaning kept me sane, and Facebook consoled me. I ate cereal out of the box. At some point, Ruth brought me a bag of groceries and Bruno installed a new door.

One afternoon, Noah came down to the basement, curious about what I was doing. He had an action figure with him, and when I asked about it, he told me a long story about Spider-Man and the Black Cat, who started out as a bad guy but then became a good guy who was a girl. I must have expressed enough interest, because he visited again, this time with a comic book, which he pretended to read to me. When Sarah came down to get him, I told her he wasn't bothering me, and so she stayed for a while, asking me more about her dad's mother. Standing on a stepladder to clean the ceiling with a long-handled brush, I told her about Vivien bringing home the stray cat and getting the tattoo. Noah wanted to know if the cat was black.

Then their mother called them home, and I was alone
again. As long as I cleaned, my grief wasn't overwhelming,
and I kept going until I was so tired, I fell onto my air
mattress. By late Thursday evening, I was done. The apartment gleamed. My muscles ached. I looked around, thinking of all that I'd lost and all that I'd done to mess up my
life, and then I fetched a glass, the bottle of Scotch and
my phone. I'm not sure how much I'd drunk before I messaged Augie.

THU, JUNE 27, 11:42 PM

Vivien: Why didn't you ever sleep with me?

Augie: I did, you forget?

Vivien: The list is long

Augie: Don't blame you. It was a mercy fuck. But you
did relieve me of my virginity. So thanks.

Vivien: Hey don't be mad, you're a good friend

Augie: It's okay. I'm not really your type

Vivien: And what would that be?

Augie: Idk dangerous weird forbidden

Vivien: You're forbidden

Augie: Why?

Vivien: Joan *likes* you

Augie: I don't think so

Vivien: Whatever you say

Vivien: Hey. No time like the present to refresh my
memory

Augie: I'm not into sexting. Too detached

Vivien: There's video

Augie: Maybe

Vivien: Got something better to do?

Augie: Not really. Turn on the webcam
Vivien: How's that?

What can I say? I was lonely and intoxicated, and in low light, I really did look like my sister. The next morning, I hoped the whole thing had been a dream. Then I saw that Augie had messaged Vivien: *Thanks for the refresher. Don't tell Joan.* I wanted to drop the phone in the toilet and flush it away.

On Friday, Ruth and Bruno insisted I come for dinner. I agreed, provided I could bring dessert, which kept me occupied all day despite a hangover: shopping for bowls, baking pan, utensils and ingredients, and baking the chocolate cake— absorbed in the sensations of whisking, stirring, pouring. While the cake was in the oven, I cleaned up.

I went upstairs at seven, with the cake in the pan because I hadn't thought of buying a plate. Bruno was still cooking, and the kitchen was a mess. Olive oil, spices, yogurt, lemons and limes, and random vegetables cooked and raw crowded on the counter, minced onion and garlic dropped here and there, used pots and pans stashed wherever there was space. I shoved aside a pot to make room for the cake while Bruno told me that Ruth had called to say she was running a bit late. On the way home from work, she was picking up Sarah from her friend's house.

"Should I come back?"

Bruno shook his head. "Stay and keep me company."

Through the glass door, I could see Noah in the back-yard, setting up action figures in a scenario he was creating with rocks, blocks and sponges. I remembered being a kid in June, the long days with my sister in the ravine, shooed away from the house by Mom. Vivien would pretend to be Cinderella and I'd be the wicked stepmother. As the younger sister, I had to be the villain if I wanted her to play with me. When we were a bit older, she was Captain Kirk and I was a deceitful Romulan. The part fit, so it now seemed.

As Bruno sliced eggplant, he asked why I became a doctor, and I told him about my father's books, my sense of purpose, the excitement of working in the ER and eventually my disillusionment with it. By then, he'd spiced and fried the eggplant, the fragrance filling the kitchen. Bruno moved on to chopping tomatoes and then cucumbers for a salad.

"Thanks for making things easier for me," I said. "I've booked a hotel room as of tomorrow night. Hopefully, I can find an apartment close to work once I sell the house."

"Don't go to a hotel. Ruth and I talked. Stay here until you've got a place."

"It could take a month or more."

"Having you downstairs is a lot better than our last tenant."

"Then let me pay rent." We went back and forth on that, but in the end, he conceded.

I asked if there was anything I could do to help with dinner.

"Get the salad bowl?" He pointed to a cupboard. In it was an assortment of stuff, including a blender and a bottle of whisky. Dalwhinnie, single malt. Dad's brand.

Wondering how often Bruno told his funny jokes while drinking, I handed him the salad bowl.

He tossed the vegetables into it. The hammer and saw tattooed on his forearm were outlined in black, the trees coloured green. I heard the front door swing open and Sarah calling, "Are Gra-mere and Papi here yet?"

I hadn't realized that it was a Sabbath meal and that Bruno's parents would be here too. Having guests for Sabbath made it more festive, Ruth explained, and sharing food was a tradition. They'd also invited Augie to thank him for coordinating the paternity tests.

A few minutes later, Bruno's parents arrived. His mother held a platter covered in tinfoil. She was plump, her husband equally so, though he'd been a svelte young man bearing an uncanny resemblance to Bruno, as I shortly discovered in a family photo—among many—that hung in the dining room. His mother was younger than mine by a decade. Her hair was dyed dark, she wore a red dress, and she smiled at everyone, not defensively in the way some people fend off aggression, but as if she found you, personally, endlessly entertaining. Nothing seemed to amuse Bruno's father. He regarded everything with the profoundest consideration, uncomfortable in his roundness as if it trivialized his preoccupations by giving him too jolly a look. He kissed his son on both cheeks, then his daughter-in-law and grandson.

"Mom, Dad, this is Joan," Bruno said, an arm around his mother's shoulders. Her smile faltered as she looked at me. "My parents, George and Denise."

George said he was sorry for my loss. Denise echoed him and added that she wished she'd had a chance to meet—she hesitated, then gathered herself to say—Bruno's biological grandmother. But at least she could get to know his aunt by . . . Bruno nudged his mother, and she refrained from adding *birth*.

"*Great*-Aunt Joan, Gra-mere," Noah said. Then he pulled his grandfather away to see the tableau of action figures in the backyard, and Denise bustled off to the kitchen.

When Augie rang the doorbell, I was hiding out in the bathroom. What had possessed me to come for dinner? I felt like an intruder, as well as an imposter, and nervous about seeing Augie—having just seen more of him than I cared to remember. But I couldn't stay in the bathroom forever.

As soon as he saw me enter the dining room, he came in for a hug. Why not? We were old friends who'd supported each other through our fathers' funerals. But all I could think of was Augie's face when he came. Oddly, that made me want to giggle, and I hugged him back tightly to suppress the sound, which I think he took for a small sob. I inhaled his just-showered, hair-still-wet, soapy smell, and when I pulled away, the dining room seemed too bright.

My mother would have been impressed by the gleam of silver: the candlesticks, the goblet, even the tray on which they stood on the sideboard. The white tablecloth was so pristine as to be practically silver. Crystal wineglasses glittered in the light from tall candles aflame under Ruth's waving hands while she blessed them. There was another pair of candles in stubby clay holders Noah had made in kindergarten, which she lit and blessed with equal enthusiasm. Bruno's father told Noah to put on a kippah. He picked a blue one—printed with dancing Snoopys—out of a basket near a vase of flowers Ruth had placed beside the tray.

"You don't call it a yarmulke?" I asked.

"We don't have chicken soup and matzo balls either. Everyone thinks Ashkenazim are the only Jews," George said. "Polish. Russian. Cold places. They never heard of cumin."

"Not everyone," Ruth said. "Not in Israel or Ethiopia, say."

"Details." George's accent became more pronounced. "Don't pick nits with me." He bent down and lifted his kippah so that Noah could rub the top of his bald head. Sarah sauntered in, wearing a semi-transparent top and was sent back to her room to change.

When she came back, in her usual T-shirt this time, George opened a small prayer book with metal hinges and a cover decorated with four turquoise stones and embossed with the Ark of the Covenant. The pages were so thin, they were almost translucent. He said he'd bought the prayer book when the adoption papers were final, with the hope that it would be used by his son and grandson in turn. George didn't need to look at the words to sing the Sabbath prayer. Bruno stood beside his father, his face showing no hint of cynicism. We all drank wine. Another blessing over braided bread. No knife to cut it because the Sabbath is a day of peace and cutting is an act of violence. Instead, we each tore off a chunk.

After we were seated around the dining table, Denise went to the kitchen and returned with a platter of fish.

Bruno said, "Mom, you know we're vegetarians. We've been vegetarians since we were married."

His mother said, "Fish is vegetarian, it's *parev*." She turned to me. "That means it's kosher with any kind of meal, meat or dairy." She turned back to Bruno. "How can you have Sabbath without fish?"

Ruth, carrying in a tureen of lentil soup, said, "You have it, you and Dad."

"Can't I have just a little?" Noah asked.

Ruth sighed. "I've never met another five-year-old who likes spicy fish, but fine."

Sarah, sitting next to me, leaned in to say, "We have this argument every Friday."

Augie was on my other side. He and George were soon trading songs. George's North African tunes made me picture camel caravans and women in tents, reclining on colourful rugs, while Augie's melodies reminded me of old men and the smell of pickled herring. Augie's parents hadn't been especially religious, going to synagogue only on the High Holy Days, his father even giving up that as soon as Augie's mother—the only one of his wives who was Jewish—was out of the picture. By the time his father died, Augie had forgotten any prayers he'd learned for his bar mitzvah. Nevertheless, after his first stroke, Uncle Jack had told Augie that he hoped, when he died, his sons would sit shiva for the full week and say the mourner's prayer at synagogue for the traditional year. After the funeral, I went for a long walk with Augie, while Steve sat in their living room, now occupied by religious men conducting the necessary prayers. They'd made my Uncle Jack's house strange to me.

This house, my nephew's, was strange to me too, but now the sensation was somehow comforting. The whole world was strange to me, this world without my mother. I barely existed in it. My sister was more real—for one thing, she was having sex.

It didn't take much wine for me to lose my place in the conversation. When I heard raised voices, my awareness turned back to the dining table as if I was watching reality TV—The Ederys at Dinner, with guest Augie Rosenstein.

Sarah: "Why shouldn't I eat bacon? Papi keeps kosher but he drives on Shabbat."

George: "We wouldn't drive if you lived closer."

Ruth: "Do you want bacon?"

Sarah: "Whether I want it or not isn't the point. I'm talking about whether I *could*."

George: "The point is the Torah says no pig."

Sarah: "Does your God say you can drive, Papi?"

George: "He isn't *my* God; He's God. *Melekh Ha-Olam*."

Bruno (calmer): "Or she."

George (louder): "She? She? You don't even believe in God."

Bruno: "The god I don't believe in doesn't have a gender."

Sarah: "Does God let you drive or not, Papi?"

Denise: "My God wants me to see my grandchildren."

Augie: "My mother blamed God for the Holocaust. But she didn't come to my wedding because my ex-wife was a shiksa."

Sarah: "People are so hypocritical."

Ruth: "Ready for dessert?"

Sarah: "Don't try to shut us down, Mom! You always shut things down."

Ruth: "I just want to enjoy the cake Gra-mere baked."

Denise: "It's your favourite, *mon petit chou*. Orange cardamom."

Noah (yawning): "I'm not tired."

Sarah: "Can I have some wine?"

Bruno and Ruth: "No!"

Denise: "More fish, Joan?"

Me: "Oh. I don't know."

Denise: "She doesn't know because she's exhausted. Cleaning? Is that a way to treat a guest? Someone in mourning?"

There's nobody standing between me and death.

That's what I had been thinking. Maybe I said it out loud, because a silence fell and the circle of sympathetic eyes got my back up. I didn't know what to do with their sympathy. So, I concentrated on my plate until I heard the scrape of a chair being pushed back. I looked up, thinking someone was taking away plates and I should help. But it was just Noah, who came over to hug me, rolling his *r*s like a tiny Tony the Tiger: "Grrreat-Auntie, don't be sad." He pushed something onto my lap. One of his Spider-Man action figures. "See how the arms and legs bend and Spidey shoots out a web to catch the bad guys." He told me it was his second favourite. He told me to keep it. And then, in a small, worried voice, he added that I could keep it as long as I was at their house.

I said, "Of course. A superhero needs his secret hideout."

At the end of the evening, I took the action figure downstairs and stood him on my windowsill, like a guardian angel.

CHAPTER 17

After darkness fell on Canada Day, I sat outside on the porch with Bruno and his family, eating popcorn as we watched fiery comets and fountains shoot into the sky from the bowl of the park near their house. It was a warm night, the sky clear enough to see a few stars, even here in the centre of the city. After the last of the fireworks, I said good night and retreated to the basement. I was brushing my teeth when the phone rang. I spit into the sink and picked it up, but the screen was blank. The ringing kept up and I followed it to my closet and the backpack hanging on a hook. I removed Vivien's phone. On the screen: *Private Caller*. I couldn't ignore it any more than if it was Vivien herself reaching down from heaven—I had to know who was calling my sister. I tapped *Answer* and held the phone to my ear.

"Hello?"

A man replied with a Spanish accent, "Where the hell are you, Vivien?"

"Raoul?" I was standing in the middle of the room, facing my father's small painting, which I'd hung on the wall above the air mattress. Two little black-haired girls, nearly identical except for height, playing on the bank of a creek.

"Of course, it's Raoul. Are you expecting the devil? I was at the airport all night because your flight was delayed. When you didn't show, I waited for the next plane too."

I'd forgotten the tickets Vivien had bought for us. I froze, not knowing how to respond, but then he continued. "What happened? Why didn't you message? My cousin cleaned the apartment for you and your sister. Where the hell are you? My mother prepared a feast."

"My mother died," I said.

"No! This is terrible. I'm very much sorry." His voice contrite now. "When?"

"Ten days ago. I posted."

"It wasn't in my feed. Stupid algorithm. This isn't the first time I missed something important. Why didn't you call me?"

"I didn't call anyone. I was trying to get home. That's all I could think of."

"So, you're in Toronto?"

"Yes." I stumbled over the word, ending on an uptick as if it was questionable.

"How is it, seeing your sister again?"

"It would be better on a beach."

He laughed. I laughed. He said something I didn't hear because I was thinking about Facebook. I'd just backed myself into a corner—Raoul would expect Vivien to post about Toronto, and I needed her back in the DRC.

"I meant to say it will be better on the beach when we get there. I wasn't able to book a flight home."

"What? You said you're in Toronto. I'm confused. No,

wait. *You're* confused. I recognize that tone . . . You're hiding something. Are you high, Vivien?"

"You got me," I mumbled.

"This is not all right." I breathed a sigh of relief as he continued to scold me. "You should know better than self-medicating with weed. Because your mother died or is it the nightmares?"

Nightmares still? My brave and wild sister? "I can't talk right now."

"I told you before. You need to take a break. See a professional."

"I will. Later." It was the kind of thing Vivien would say when I asked her to come home for a visit.

"You always say later."

"There should be a memorial for Mom."

"Which is when?"

I picked a date out of the air, off in the distant future. "Mid-September."

"I'm going to be in Chicago for my brother's wedding then. I'll stop over in Toronto on my way."

"You didn't mention that." Now I'd backed myself into a new corner. (How many corners does a single lie have?)

"It didn't come up. We haven't seen each other for too long, *mi amor.*"

"Phone dying." *End call.*

The next day, on my way to an appointment with my lawyer, I nearly ran a red light because I thought I saw Vivien. When the woman turned around, I realized she looked nothing like my sister. The odd thing, I realized, was that she hadn't reminded me of Vivien as I'd last seen her, nearing sixty, but of her as a much younger woman, having a tickle fight with three-year-old Zoe, both of them laughing at each other adoringly.

Gary greeted me with condolences at the door. He was semi-retired and, at seventy-five, indecently healthy despite a diet of baked potatoes and sour cream. File boxes still formed cliffs, but as I walked through the corridor between them, I also had to step over crates of dishes and other sundries. Gary told me he had just bought a summer cabin in a Newfoundland outport. He was about to drive there on his own, accompanied by all his cats and a cellphone, which he never remembered to turn on but was a gift imposed on him by his son.

When I sat, he put a kitten in my lap, offered me tea from a silver tea service, used tongs to drop sugar cubes in my cup, and poured milk from a pitcher. The kitten, named Snowball, was black and white and grey and it kneaded my bare knees with tiny claws. We were meeting in the dining room, since Gary had recently turned his office into a home theatre.

He handed me a form. I signed it. He handed me another. "The will isn't in effect until it goes through probate," he said. "That'll take at least six weeks, and you can't do anything as the executor until then, but once probate is complete, you can sell off the assets and split the proceeds with your sister."

"Okay." I drank more tea. "Just curious—if someone gives up a baby for adoption, would that baby share in the biological parent's estate?"

Gary tapped his pen. "They'd have to specify that in the will. Just saying issue or offspring won't do it—adopted children as such don't have any rights to a share in the estates of biological relatives." He peered at me as if expecting a confession.

"Why?"

"Putting up a child for adoption terminates the biological parents' rights and responsibilities, which are then transferred to the adoptive parents."

"Good to know."

But Mom considered Bruno family. If she'd known Vivien was gone, she could have changed her will. It was only our lie—mine and Vivien's—that had prevented her from doing so. So, when the house sold, I'd give him a cheque for half and explain that it was his by rights, even if not legally required. (And in my fantasy, he would be touched; it would soften telling him about the lie itself.)

"Are you thinking about drafting your own will, Joan?"

"Not today." Afraid he'd press, I asked him how his other cats were. The oldest, who'd been a kitten when he'd drafted my mother's will, was still alive but ailing, he said. He had four others besides Snowball. Ever since the kitten had arrived, the elderly tabby had begun to punish Gary by using the hall rug as a litter box. He seemed amused by his old cat's defiance.

He watched me for a moment as I stroked the ears of the purring kitten, then asked if I'd take Snowball with me. He didn't think he could stand the drive to Newfoundland with the tabby hissing and pissing in protest all over the back of the car. I texted Ruth and asked if she'd mind just one cat in the basement, and she replied that she was fine with it.

That night, while I slept on the cold air mattress, Snowball lay across my neck like a scarf.

Natural deadlines for coming clean about my lie loomed: Bruno's paternity results, the WhatsApp chat, Raoul expecting to meet up with Vivien. I couldn't get through all of those, could I? And even if I did, Mom's will would go through probate, her house would sell, and I had her wishes to fulfill.

The Saturday after I met with Gary was a sultry day, and I didn't want to leave the cool basement. Mom's passing had put a pause on digging through Vivien's communications, but now, sitting on a folding chair with my laptop, feet on the air mattress, I got back to it. Trying a different approach, I searched around significant dates in her email—birthdays, anniversaries, holidays. I found a number of bland emails I'd sent and Vivien's neutral replies. Every year on Christmas Eve, Grace sent a picture of the tree in her clinic, and Vivien sent one of hers. I was starting to think that holidays were the worst time for anything meaningful, when I came across an exchange she had with Oscar about a month after her last visit home. He'd sent season's greetings, she'd replied with a question about how it *really* was for him, and he'd written at length about the tensions in his family. He asked, *What was your worst Christmas?*

> To: Oscar Karlsson   December 24, 2015
> When I was pregnant, Mom got her best tree ever. It
> was loaded with decorations and lights. Big. It touched
> the ceiling. Like something you'd see in a magazine

with the perfect family sitting around it. I don't know
what set me off, maybe it was the tree. All I remember
is that we were all in the kitchen and Dad had just got
home, stinking of booze. I called him a drunk. He
slapped me so hard, it bruised. Then he called me a
tramp, and I slapped him back.

Mom was standing right there, mopping the
kitchen floor, and just kept on mopping. All she said
was "Move your feet." Joan's usual M.O. when things
got tense was to run away to hide out with a book in
the basement. But after I slapped Dad, and he raised
his hand again, she grabbed his arm and yelled at him,
"How do I know you're my father? You got proof? I bet
you aren't. My father wouldn't hit a girl."

What did I remember about that Christmas? She was
sixteen, gaining weight and unhappy about it. I'd helped
Mom choose that big tree. Most of the presents were
for Vivien's baby. The crib had a big red bow taped to the
box. She'd wanted a camera and didn't get one. The email
continued:

I wish I could talk to my sister. Just once have a real
conversation. But in my family there's no such thing.
Don't mention the unmentionable. Every time I go
home, I'm sixteen again. As soon as I fall asleep, I'm
getting passed around at a party and I don't care
because I'm high and it's so fun. And then I dream
about Mom cleaning, she's spraying me with Lysol, and
I can't breathe. I wake up and I still can't breathe.

My sister high, being passed around. What did that mean? Real or a dream? Had she been assaulted? There had been a lot of parties the summer she got pregnant. I knew she'd had bad dreams about them. The night I'd come to her room and asked why she was still awake, she hadn't stopped shaking until I got into bed with her. Raoul said she was still having nightmares.

The email ended with Vivien thanking Oscar for his openness and wishing him a not-terrible day. I sat for a moment, then closed the laptop. Unable to stay still, I slipped out of the house as quietly as I could. I got into my car and drove to the storage locker.

As soon as I got there, I opened the filing cabinet where I kept my old journals and pulled out 1976. I flipped to December. I'd written something every day, but not on December 24 or 25. The next entry mentioned that I'd gotten books for Christmas: *Ordinary People* and *The Dark Side of the Sun*. And that I didn't like the greasiness of lipstick. There was nothing about my father hitting Vivien. I didn't remember it. I tried—nothing. Mom often said he'd never touched anyone when he was drunk, and I'd agreed. I couldn't even remember defending my sister. So, if I'd blocked out her reality to that extent, was it any wonder she couldn't talk to me?

But I'd written this, on December 31: *It's been a good year and a horrible year. Augie was nice and then he ignored me. I got to talk to Dad, but he's turned into an ogre. Mom is nicer now and it's freaky. Vivien isn't herself. It's like she's acting the part of being Vivien. Coming home late cuz that's a Vivien thing but her eyes aren't her eyes. There's no shine in them. Sometimes she treats me like a human being. It makes me sad, and I wish I could put the shine back in her eyes. I hope her baby has the shine.*

I was in the laundry room Wednesday evening when my phone vibrated just as I was about to take a load of wash out of the dryer. I read the message from Bruno: *Paternity test result came. Mark isn't my father.* My mind went blank. All the thinking I'd done about this moment evaporated. I replied, *Ah*, then put the phone back in my pocket. If this was the time to tell him, I had no idea what to say.

From upstairs, I could hear Sarah call out. "Dad! Can I use your Sharpies?"

"What are you doing in there, Sarah?"

"I needed the big table to spread out the protest signs."

"What are you protesting?"

"The principal scheduled a field trip during Pride week."

"It's July—school's over."

"So?"

"Take the Sharpies. I've got a call to make."

Her footsteps receded. I retrieved the clothes from the dryer, hurried into the basement apartment and shut the door quietly. I'd made notes in my journal—pros and cons of when and how to disclose the truth. Useless now. I dumped the laundry basket in my room and grabbed the Scotch. No need for a glass—I took a swig right from the bottle. Then I moved to the bathroom just in time to answer the Messenger call. Sitting on the bath mat, squeezed between tub and toilet, so I wouldn't be overheard if anyone came down to the laundry room, I pressed *Accept*.

"Hey." I spoke hoarsely, my voice just above a whisper.

"Do you have a cold?" Bruno asked.

"I'm fine. Patients sleeping."

Silence. A cough. "Why did you lie to me?"

"Mark was my boyfriend. It was possible."

"Augie sent me a picture of him. You must have known I wasn't his." His voice was slurred. I imagined him upstairs, the bottle of Dalwhinnie to hand. "I feel like an idiot for contacting him. Why did you put us in touch for no reason?"

"Because I don't know who the others were."

"Seriously? How can you not know?"

"I was high and partying and there was a lot of sex that wasn't always of my choosing."

"You were raped? I'm the product of a rape?"

"I don't know—it's more complicated." I pictured my sister at sixteen. Even with my flawed memory, I now understood more. There had to be some truth I could offer her son. "I felt closed in. Partying was a release. I liked the danger. I got myself into risky situations. Sometimes it was fun. Sometimes it was a nightmare. But if you were the result, that's the best part of it. I shouldn't have misled you. I know you deserve better. That's why I gave you up." I started crying, which Vivien would never do—she'd have hung up first. But it made Bruno cry too, and for a few minutes, there was just the sound of us crying.

When Bruno could speak, he said he was sorry it had been so awful, and I thanked him. Then he told me that the first human death he'd witnessed had been my mother's. When she'd convulsed and died, he said, she'd looked a lot like Libby, the Persian cat they'd owned, who'd died the year before. It wasn't a good look. He was afraid of dying like that and freaking out his kids. He was afraid of dying, period. Not the actual death part, but the almost-dead, facing obliteration bit. And even that would be bearable as long as he went first. Before Ruth.

"What's worse is having no one to live on after you," I said.

"You've got Joan. And us."

"For how long?" I whispered.

"What?"

"Patients, have to go."

I hung up.

CHAPTER 18

After I told Augie that I now needed a pet-friendly apartment, he went through all the rental listings he managed. Not satisfied by any of them, he called around. A friend of his had a cousin who was leaving the country for an unexpected job offer overseas and hadn't yet put his condo on the market because he wasn't sure he wanted to sell. The Saturday after Bruno got his paternity results, Augie picked me up and we drove up to see the apartment, which was on the fourth floor of a low-rise building overlooking the Rosedale ravine. The view was peaceful and the condo was only a half-hour walk from my nephew's. I offered to rent it until Augie's friend's cousin made up his mind.

We were back in Augie's car, the windows down to cool it off after baking in the sun. (His car was black, not a practical colour.) The interior smelled of the basket of strawberries on the back seat, which he'd bought earlier that day at a farmers' market. I couldn't remember the last time my mother had permitted produce that didn't come shrink-wrapped. I was wearing a second pair of jeans I'd recently

purchased, black this time. Also sandals—my toes felt airy—
and a sleeveless blouse that was red with black buttons.

"Thanks, Augie," I said.

"Least I can do."

"I have to head up to Mom's." To keep the insurance in
good standing, I had to check it weekly.

"I'll drive you there," Augie said.

"It's too much trouble. Just drop me at my car."

Augie turned on the ignition. "No trouble. You can come
back to my place after. I'll feed you."

I found myself nodding. "It would be nice to be fed."

Augie had just moved into a loft in a converted industrial
building on Wellington, which he'd done up like a show-
room, everything slim and sleek as if the furniture was on a
diet. In the kitchen, the counters were granite, all the appliances were recessed, and the cupboards had no knobs. White
leather on the dining room chairs, black leather for the living
room couch.

We sat on the couch, drinking wine. He'd set out plates
of finger foods on the coffee table: small sandwiches that
he'd prepared himself, cherry tomatoes, baby carrots, cauli-
flower florets, dips, the strawberries. For the first time since
Mom died, I was hungry, and while we talked, I ate. Most of
a wall opposite the couch was taken up by a flat-screen TV
that doubled as a digital frame that displayed a slideshow of
prize-winning nature photographs from a cloud service. The
only Augie-ness I recognized in this place was the guitar in
the corner. That and Augie himself, in his sports jacket and
jeans. He was looking at me as if he liked what he saw.

We'd known each other as far back as I could remember. When Augie had started first grade, he was skinny, short, asthmatic and already familiar with Dad's after-poker zigzag gait, so I wasn't too intimidated to have him play at our house. Also, he wasn't allowed to play anywhere else because his mother worried about his health. Aunt Dora didn't much like Mom, and the feeling was mutual, but she respected my mother's passion for bleach, believing it would kill anything harmful to her son. (In fact, it wasn't good for Augie's respiratory issues, but he was just happy to have somewhere to go and never told his mother that the smell of bleach made him cough.)

Dora was a Holocaust survivor. She'd been a kid when the war started and was the only one in her family who was still alive at the end of it. As far as I was concerned, she was maternal enough because she made us orange-juice ice pops and gave me ginger ale when I was carsick. But to her kids, she was a paradox—anxious about their well-being but emotionally withholding, as if she was afraid of losing everything and caring about it would intensify the loss. I knew the feeling. One day, you'd have a teddy; the next day, it would be in the garbage can. Maybe that's why I was drawn to her.

She'd married Uncle Jack because he was Jewish and a liberator, which awed her, and then she had the two boys, who surprised and disappointed her when nothing they did compensated for the loss of her entire family, a whole people and the world they'd inhabited. Eventually, she got over her awe and realized that Uncle Jack was an ordinary man, despite his war record. After the divorce, she went to Florida to get warm, and there she broke a tooth. Mark's father was the dentist who fixed it. They had lunch. Mr. Cohen offered to cap all her teeth at a discount. He thought she was the real deal, an authentic suffering Jew. In their wedding pictures, she had a beautiful smile. No one could tell that she'd been starved from the age of nine to fifteen. From babyhood on, Augie had never stopped trying to get her approval.

The desert scene on the flat-screen slid away, replaced by a tropical waterfall with a double rainbow. Outside on the road, a truck honked. I was going to say, *Nice place*. I was thinking that he must have had an interior decorator, maybe the one he'd wanted me to use at my mother's house. But what I said instead was, "All this—it's for your mother?"

"What do you mean?"

"To impress her."

"She never visits."

"Did you send her pictures?"

"Maybe."

"And my mother's house gives you the creeps? God, you're just like me."

"That's hilarious—I left home when I was eighteen. You'd still be living with your mother if she wasn't dead."

"You still want yours to come back. This . . ." I waved my hand in a circle ". . . isn't you."

"How do you know what's me?"

"I know everything."

"Like what?"

"Like my sister was your first."

He sneezed.

"Bless you. I'm just wondering when."

"She told you?"

"Yes."

"She said she never would."

"Never is a long time."

He pointed his phone at what I thought was a modern painting but was actually a built-in speaker system. As music wafted over us like a soundtrack, he began to talk. It was that summer when the Montreal Olympics was on TV every night, the week after he gave me the piggyback ride on our way to get pizza.

Had I told Vivien? Had I said that if he'd tried to kiss me, I wouldn't have kicked him?

The night of the closing ceremony, she came over to his house to wait for Mark because they were supposed to go to a concert. But Mark didn't get home until after two. My sister didn't exit through the window of Augie's room and climb down a tree like in a movie. While Uncle Jack was yelling at Mark in the front hall, she just got dressed, walked down the stairs, said, "Hi, Mark," and crossed the street.

"Wait. What? So, you could have been . . . ," I said.

"I didn't know if I should say anything, but I figured since Vivien thought it was Mark, she'd know. When he wasn't, I hoped . . ."

"You hoped what?"

"Maybe that I was." He shrugged. "It would've been messy. And if I was his father and you were the aunt, that would be quasi-incestuous."

"Quasi."

"Well, it could be off-putting if we ever . . ."

We already had, sort of, even if he didn't know it, which made it seem like less of a leap, and I wondered if his lips were soft.

"What makes you think I want my sister's hand-me-downs?"

"It was only once. When we were kids." He looked

amused, his eyes crinkling at the corners. I've always liked brown eyes. "I don't think that counts."

We were sitting close, and the scent of his aftershave was pleasant, so I leaned in.

The next morning, the sun woke me up, the room alight with it. The curtains were open, and so was the window, but no one could see in—his apartment was on the floor below the penthouse, and the building was higher than anything around it. Augie yawned and stretched, then smiled as if he was pleased to see me still there and said, "Good morning."

I got up to pee, and I didn't care that I was naked, because he'd seen it all. I was almost at the door when I heard him say, "Oh fuck." I turned around. The expression on his face. I should have kept going. My clothes were in the living room. I could have picked them up and got out of there.

Instead, I said, "What?"

"You look so much like Vivien."

"Is that why you slept with me?"

"I don't know how I missed it. How could you do that? Pretend to be her?"

"What are you going on about?"

"The webcam. It was you—no tattoos."

"You're not the injured party here. You thought you were having sex with Vivien, and then you do the sister. What do you call that?"

"Don't put it on me. Vivien and I were just having fun. We weren't even touching. She knew I was interested in you."

"Oh, oh. Is that what you say every time you cheat?"

"I don't know why you're . . . Wait . . . You're twisting this around. I didn't do that with Vivien, did I? It was you. Jesus. Whose idea was it? Were you two making fun of me?"

I could have said yes. I could have said that we got him good or something like that. But this was Augie.

"It wasn't that, not at all," I said.

"Did she watch the video?"

"No." I came back and sat on the bed.

"I don't believe you."

"She couldn't watch anything, Augie. She's gone. She's left us all." The curtains plumped out with a gust of wind, brushing against something on Augie's nightstand that rattled. When I was done crying and had thrown out the pile of tissues I'd used and was in a bathrobe Augie had given me, I explained it all to him—how my sister had made me promise, for my mother's sake, to pretend to be her if something happened so that Mom wouldn't be sad for her last few months, and it had worked, but there had been complications. Bruno wasn't part of the plan, but I had to keep up the charade for my mother's sake. It wasn't like I got a kick out of it. Well, maybe I did. But not at first. And then Mom died, and I ended up living in Bruno's basement. While I was talking, I couldn't look at him, and then I did, flapping the bathrobe because all that truth had made me hot.

Augie's eyes had teared up, and he said, "I'm sorry about Vivien."

"Me too."

"She was something, your sister."

"I know."

He shook his head. "I'd never have thought you had it in you."

"I'm full of surprises."

"But you have to tell them, Joanie."

"I will. At the right time."

"I don't want to be in the middle of this."

"Your part in this is over."

"But I know them now. I ate with them. They called me for advice on screening tenants. George said I should get a seat at his synagogue for the High Holy Days."

"But you're not religious."

"So what? It's once a year. I've been thinking I'd like to hear their tunes."

"You only did your bar mitzvah because you wanted the presents."

"Don't change the subject."

I wasn't changing it. That was the point—the subject was my Augie. Who was this?

"You have to tell them."

"Yes, of course."

"It's worse if you wait."

He didn't know anything. I went to shower, wishing I had a change of underwear with me.

When you're a kid, summer hangs on as if time has stopped. That's all I wanted.

When I got back to the basement apartment, I immediately posted on Facebook: *Going on a relief mission, will be out of contact. See you on my return, folks!* Then I messaged Grace that I wouldn't have WiFi for the next WhatsApp chat, and she told me to come back in one piece. I thought I should quit Facebook cold turkey, like Dad quit drinking, and I uninstalled the app from my phone, but there was still my laptop, and sometimes, when I couldn't sleep, I scrolled through the timeline, wishing I could be someone else. When Augie texted (me, not Vivien)—*Are we good? Still friends?*—I said, *Yes. All good.* But it wasn't, not really. And when he reached out again, I told him I couldn't see him. I had a lot on my plate at work, I said.

In early August, I moved into the apartment that overlooked the ravine but was nervous about furnishing it in case everything had to be removed for reasons unforeseen though inevitable. That's how the mind works: you think the old familiar crisis is sure to come again. Not the one that's looming.

I brought things out of my storage locker one at a time: the photograph of me and my sister playing Candy Land; a larger painting of the ravine where we used to run around; the armchair rocker. I remembered sitting in it with Zoe on my lap when she was five and had bad dreams, soothing her with the motion. I wondered what my sister had done when she woke up from a nightmare all those years away from me.

At first, I slept on the air mattress, but it was uncomfortable in the long term, so I gave in and bought a bed. Snowball grew bigger until he was too heavy to sleep on my neck. When I uploaded patient notes, he curled up in my lap, kneading my thighs with his claws. I trimmed them. I ordered a rug and a coffee table. Sarah and Noah visited and discovered that they could play games they couldn't play at home because my internet speed was so much faster. (Ruth and Bruno had kept their home connection slow, hoping it would discourage their kids from life in front of a screen.) They became regular visitors, Sarah bringing her own laptop, and Noah using an old one of mine. I bought a large pot and made popcorn for them in it. Then I got a kitchen table and chairs for them to sit on. An Xbox and a TV. An L-shaped couch. In mid-August, Sarah had her fifteenth birthday and Noah his sixth. I got them both video games.

I was expected at Bruno's for Friday dinners and I went, bringing my chocolate cake, the recipe modified with loads of chocolate chips, icing and sprinkles. When I arrived, Noah—who'd decided Spider-Man was for little kids and his favourite colour was now blue—always hugged me. His sister had started going out with a boy nearly as tall as her father, and they were usually in her room, the door partially open as required by Ruth, who periodically checked to ensure it was. After dinner, I helped clean up. While the other adults bustled around, George sat like a king, and I teased him about it. He got me right back: "Joan runs to the kitchen like I'm going to bite, but I am a good doggie, I stay in the dining room." It was as if I was part of the family. I *felt* like part of the family. Also not. Since it was all based on a lie.

The poignancy of George's affection, of all their affection, made me cry when I was at home. I'd stand on the balcony of my new apartment with tears rolling off my chin, falling on the ravine below. Some evenings, I was surprised to look from the darkening sky to the clock and notice the days getting shorter.

Patients died; I took care of others. A new patient assigned to me had no jaw, and I steeled myself for meeting him by watching an interview with Roger Ebert, the movie critic who'd had the same surgery and ended up looking like a ventriloquist's dummy. It wasn't as shocking as I'd feared.

My patient was still himself. He couldn't preach sermons anymore or fly-fish, but when I arrived, he was engrossed in a mystery featuring a fly-fisherman-ex-priest.

Toward the end of August, my lawyer returned from his Newfoundland cabin. When I was walking through the ravine at dusk, he called to tell me that probate had been granted, so I could now execute the will's provisions. I looked up at the purple sky, at the wisps of green at the edge of the rising moon.

Augie and I met at Mom's house. It was awkward, but we were both polite, keeping the conversation focused on business. I wanted to sell the house with all its contents rather than deal with storing things that meant nothing to me. He listed it for what I thought was an outrageous amount, and I was relieved, believing the sale would take ages. So, there was no rush to talk to Bruno about his inheritance, and I still had some time to figure out how to deal with Raoul. Augie left in his car; I left in mine.

The first weekend in September, there was a bidding war on Mom's house. Apparently, the price wasn't outrageous enough, since it sold by Monday. The buyers were eager to move in right away. The funds landed in my bank account and I wrote out a cheque for Bruno, which I put in my wallet, the edge poking above the bill pocket. Whenever I opened my wallet, it reminded me that I had to deal with this soon.

I planned where and how I'd tell him—in a coffee shop, at the library, on his porch, on the moon, at my lawyer's. I'd tell Gary about Vivien then too and kill one bird with two stones. Or was it the other way around? Dead birds were involved anyway. I thought having someone there to mediate would make it more civilized.

The next Friday—it was the thirteenth, but Ruth said Jews didn't consider the date bad luck—I noticed she didn't eat dessert. Ruth loved sweets. I'd baked a lemon cake and it had turned out all right. Everyone else liked it, but Ruth said she wasn't hungry. She hadn't eaten much dinner, either, and her colour was off, unnaturally greyish like smoked oak. I knew she'd had a bit of blood in her urine from a bladder infection, for which she'd had a course of antibiotics, and was still experiencing pain in her abdomen. She told me that she was taking probiotics and would be fine in a few days. While the rest of us ate dessert, she excused herself and went to bed.

After the dishes were dried and everything put away, I asked Bruno, "Okay if I just go upstairs to say goodbye to Ruth?"

He said, "Of course. She'd like that."

She was still awake, and I sat on her bed. Had the clinic taken a urine sample to culture? She thought so. Had they called with the results? No. I asked her to call them and inquire. Could I examine her? She nodded. I remember the feeling of her thin wrist under my fingers. The bedroom was at the front of the house; waves of sound and odour rolled off the street and floated through the open window: wood burning in someone's fireplace, a bundle buggy or stroller rattling by, someone crying, someone calling, cigarettes—tobacco first and a few minutes later weed. Where I grew up in the suburbs, you didn't hear or smell your neighbours; that was the point of it.

Ruth's pulse was a bit fast but not worrisome. Then I laid my hands on Ruth's abdomen and quickly removed them. She asked me why, and I mumbled something about cold hands because the truth was ridiculous: for a moment, I'd felt what I can only describe as worms wriggling under my palms. I rubbed my hands together and then placed them again on Ruth's belly, keeping them there by force of will as I palpated. I felt nothing hard and her organs were where they should be. I asked her to let me know what she found out when she called the clinic.

That night, I wrote in my journal, *I need to get more sleep.*

The next morning, I took my car in for an oil change. I was sitting in the waiting room of the garage when Raoul messaged Vivien: *I'm here!*

For an instant, I thought he'd gone back to the DRC. Then I remembered. He was here, in Toronto, for the supposed memorial for Mom. Mid-September had seemed so far in the future when we'd talked, I'd put it out of my mind. My heart didn't race—there was no excitement in fooling anyone now. It just had to be done.

> **SAT, SEP 14, 09:32 AM**
> **Vivien:** Where are you now?
> **Raoul:** The airport. Terminal 1
> **Vivien:** Why didn't you send me your flight info?
> **Raoul:** I told you I'd stop over on the way to Chicago
> **Vivien:** But I didn't go home. We decided not to have a memorial service
> **Raoul:** Oh no! And I booked such a nice hotel. What do I do now?
> **Vivien:** Change your flight

About half an hour later, my car was ready, and just as I was getting into the driver's seat, Raoul messaged that the earliest flight he could get to Chicago was at five thirty. He had nothing to do (sad face, sad face).

I sat for a moment, thinking, then replied, *Joan can pick you up. Wait at the taxi drop-off.*

I needed to meet someone who'd known my sister better than I had in these last years—to see his face, hear his voice, with no screen between us. When I got to Arrivals, I saw him standing near the curb, recognizable from the photos I'd studied: brushed-back hair, impish smile, button eyes.

Behind me a taxi was honking. I unlocked the car door and leaned over to open it. "Raoul! Get in."

He slid into the front seat, threw a bag into the back and quickly closed the door. "Thank you, Joan. You still look the same."

"As what?" I pulled away from the curb.

"The picture pinned up in Vivien's office. You were watching a video with your stepdaughter."

"That's an old one."

"She said that was the only one she had that showed how beautiful you are."

We were at a stoplight. I turned to look at him. "Vivien didn't say that."

"No, she did. First, she said that for once in a photo you didn't look like you smelled something bad. Then she said you are beautiful."

I was astounded: that she'd kept the picture, that she thought of me as beautiful. For a few minutes, I couldn't speak. Then I got myself together and offered to show Raoul around Toronto, but he wasn't interested. He only had a couple of hours before he had to be back at the airport, so we settled on lunch in Kensington Market. All the way there, Raoul talked about setting up a gym in his Madrid apartment, and I didn't interrupt. When we got to College Street, I parked. It was a short walk to Wanda's Pie in the Sky. At the counter, we ordered salad and dessert, then took our seats at a table.

"It's good to see someone who knows Vivien," Raoul said at last.

"For me too. You must have cared for her a lot."

He toyed with his fork. "I wanted her to come live with me in Spain."

"She stayed with you longer than anyone else."

His face brightened, then fell. "She broke up with me when her nightmares started. She just said she needed a change. Maybe if I understood, I could—I don't know—persuade her."

"I've always thought the same thing. I could make her come back. Did she ever tell you about her baby?"

He nodded. "When I told her I didn't want kids because it doesn't go with my work, too much travel, too much risk. She didn't say very much, only that she'd had a baby she gave up for adoption. Does that have something to do with the nightmares?" He was leaning forward eagerly, as if I was the one who could relieve him of his confusion, his pain, and not the other way around.

I said, "She never told me, but I can guess."

"Do you think she was assaulted? If I came up behind her, she went crazy on me."

I nodded. "That's part of it. The summer she got pregnant, her boyfriend cheated on her, and she cheated on him. They also went to a lot of parties. Got high. Sometimes, she was out of control. That didn't give anyone the right."

He murmured his agreement.

"It was all good until it wasn't. I don't know if she was too high to say no, or if she thought she was getting into one thing and it turned into something else, or if she was physically restrained. It could have been all of the above, and on multiple occasions. Whatever happened, it was frightening, and she didn't feel like she could get away."

"*I can't leave the party.* She said that when she woke up from the nightmares."

"I remember."

"She is a puzzle, your sister. Do you think that's why we love her?"

"Maybe everyone's a puzzle," I said. "She just didn't pretend otherwise."

At the airport, we parted as friends. He kissed me on the cheek before he got out of the car. As he retrieved his bag from the back seat, he said, "She's not coming back, is she?"

I didn't hide my tears from him. "No. Never."

CHAPTER 19

For a couple of days, I was on autopilot. Sunday was laundry day. On Monday, I rode my bike to see patients. The next day, after school, Sarah showed up at my place to work on a media project that she couldn't do at home because of their slow internet. I ordered pizza for her. While she ate, I settled on the other side of the dining table with my laptop. She asked if I was working, and I told her no, I was writing about the day, as I always did, which led to me telling her about the journals I'd kept since I wasn't much older than her brother.

"What have you said about us?" she asked.

"Let's see." I searched for the first appearance of her name and read aloud to her what I thought were the best bits. She made a sound in her throat, like an unarticulated snort, and when I glanced up at her, she was looking at me skeptically.

"It was just my first impression," I said.

"But everyone is paper white."

"I never said that."

"You sort of did. If you don't say what anyone is, that's what people think. White is the default."

I explained that I write in my journal to figure out how to deal with life and loss, and that death doesn't perceive colour, and she replied that she hadn't thought I was one of *those* white people. My heart sank at disappointing her.

"And?" I said.

"And if you say you're colour-blind, you're erasing my experience. You're taking away who I am."

"What would *you* say?"

She slipped into the chair beside mine, and I pushed my laptop toward her. Tapping quickly on the keyboard, she typed the names of everyone in her family and their mix of backgrounds: South Asian and Jewish and North African and European. She hesitated, glanced at me, and beside Bruno's name added, *and unknown*. By then it was dark, and she needed to get home. I insisted on walking with her, even though she said she'd be fine. Before we left, I grabbed my bag.

It was the third Tuesday in September. A warm front had displaced the onset of autumn, and the fragrance wafting from the ravine reminded me of my sister's perfume. I took off my sweater and tied the arms around my waist. We walked downhill toward Sarah's house, and on the way, stopped in at Loblaws because I'd run out of coffee. While we were there, Sarah browsed the toiletries section and picked up some expensive face cream. In self-checkout, I scanned it along with the coffee and, opening my wallet, saw the edge of the cheque. After paying, I put the coffee in my bag, and she took the cream.

"Thanks, Aunt Joan," she said.

"No problem. Just one question."

"Okay."

"What happened to rejecting the propaganda of the beauty industry?"

She shrugged. "I'm over it."

"How come?"

"They're all witches."

"Who?" We left the store and crossed the street.

"The feminists."

"I thought they were socialists."

"Same. Those white girls at my school, they're always in your face, shouting. And they're mean."

"What do they say?"

"I don't remember. Different things."

"I'm sorry they're mean."

"It's okay."

"It isn't."

Then, bitterly, "They think they're better than everyone. They know everything."

I paused, remembering high school. The world after it is both different and not. I said, "I've had colleagues like that."

"What do you do?"

"Envy them."

"Why?"

"That confidence. Being so sure you've got it right."

"I'd rather be in the wrong."

"Then you'll always have me for company."

She smiled at me as if I was really her auntie.

I said, not as casually as I intended, "Remember, Sarah. You can text me anytime. No matter what. You've got my number."

We'd arrived at her house, and I would have turned around to go home if Bruno hadn't been sitting on the porch.

"Come have a glass of wine," he called, and I followed Sarah up the walkway.

"Did Ruth call the clinic about the urine culture?" I asked as I climbed the stairs.

"She did, and it was negative."

No bacteria, no infection—then what was causing the symptoms? "I should talk to her."

"I'll tell her to call you. She went to bed early again."

I seated myself on a patio chair, the bag at my feet, while Bruno went inside to get me a glass. He returned with Noah, who was wearing his PJs and wanted to say good night to me. He plopped a kiss on my cheek, then padded back into the house. On the small porch, there was barely an arm's length between my chair and Bruno's. In the bubble of night, his voice was soothing. While he talked about a new course he was teaching in wood carving—his first for continuing education, Monday nights at a local high school—I watched a gaggle of teenagers flirting under the street lamp. My wineglass had a sunset streak where a drop of wine had spilled over the rim. I wiped it with my finger. The wind was picking up, the temperature dropping, and I put my sweater on.

"Do you remember being like those kids?" I asked, interrupting him.

"I was too shy to ever be like them."

"When we first met, I didn't think you were shy at all."

"It was awkward. I didn't know what to expect."

"I had to bite my tongue when Mom said you look like my father."

"You mean I don't?" he asked.

"Maybe your ears," I said, and he laughed.

It went on like that—friendly, both of us at ease. He said, "I was nervous going up in the elevator to see her at the hospital. I was afraid Sheila would gush."

"She's not the gushing type."

"I didn't know that. I was already feeling like I was in a bad TV movie."

He put his empty wineglass on the railing and cracked his knuckles. "On the way over, Ruth said being embarrassed isn't fatal. I hated she could tell I was embarrassed and that made me angry. I felt bad about that—I mean it's Ruth; she's my wife."

I said, "I was tense too."

"Ruth told me not to get upset if you were standoffish."

"I just felt torn. How do you know what to do? What's the right thing for everyone? It's so complicated. And when I saw you, it threw me off because I didn't know what to do about the whole who's the father thing. Also, Mom's stories. Not that she made it all up, but the way she distorted things."

"Like what?"

"Like acting as if she was there when you were born."

"Wasn't she?"

"Technically. She was in the house. Zoned out on pills."

"What really happened?" he asked.

So, I told him. How my father was passed out drunk. There was a heat wave. We didn't have air conditioning. Sweat stung my eyes. I called 911 late—neither Vivien nor I knew anything about labour. The dispatcher stayed on the line until the ambulance got there, but the phone was in the living room and I couldn't move my sister, so I was running back and forth. She thought she was going to die. She told me where she'd hidden things so I could have them. Running back from the phone, I tripped and landed on my face. My nose bled on the floor. I worried about the stain and getting yelled at for it. And then I was back in Vivien's room, and it was happening. I saw the top of his head.

I paused, looking at Bruno to see how he was taking the fact of his teenage mother giving birth with only her little sister to help. His eyes were wide, appalled, and he murmured, "Go on."

I told him how I caught him and, as the dispatcher had instructed, sawed through the umbilical cord with my sister's penknife. I was terrified he'd die of cold because movies about people giving birth always involved boiling water, so I wrapped him—still gooey—in a sweatshirt. Vivien refused to hold him. At the time, I was angry, but later I realized it was too painful for her, knowing she was giving him up. By the time the ambulance arrived, Vivien was delivering the placenta. It needed to be examined to ensure it was complete. The medics asked for a container, and I got my mother's cookie jar to put it in. The jar was big but not big enough, and the afterbirth flowed over the top. They'd had difficulty shaking Mom awake, and Dad was incoherent. They took my sister to the hospital, alone.

Bruno's eyes filled with pity. He murmured, "Poor kid." I told him that Vivien had hoped she could raise him with my mother's help, but it was clear then, if it hadn't been before, that no child could grow up safe and well in our house. In the hospital, she told the social worker everything. Mom was furious about that, but Vivien had made the decision to give him the best life she could, though it drove her onto the street.

"And then she came back so she could go to school. She put everything she had into making a difference in the world," I said.

"Have you heard from her?" Bruno asked, his voice heavy with emotion.

And that was it. I couldn't keep the secret anymore. "I've got bad news, Bruno."

"Should I bring out the rest of the bottle?"

"It's not all bad." I dug into my bag, found my wallet, opened it, and took out the cheque. "This is for you."

"What is it?"

I unfolded the cheque and handed it to him. "Take it."

He glanced at it, then looked more carefully. "What?"

"It's your half of Mom's house."

"I don't understand."

"My mom's will left half to me and half to Vivien, and in the event one of us predeceased her, to our issue. Her issue. That was her wish, so this is yours."

"What are you saying?"

"I didn't know how to tell you." My eyes were dry, my eyelids sandpaper. I said, "Vivien died."

"No."

"Yes."

Bruno said, "That's impossible. She sent me a message this morning. See?" He pulled out his phone and read it aloud. "*Not able to reply properly right now. Explain later.*"

"That was me," I said. "Before it happened, she asked me . . . She told me to contact people if . . ."

"Shit. No."

"Yes."

He looked stricken. "How?"

I explained it to him: The remoteness of the area. The epidemic. The restrictions on movement in or out.

"When did you find out?" he asked.

I could have lied and said, *Yesterday*. But I felt compelled to tell him the truth, as if my sister was making me. "Last March. Before Mom died."

"Six months ago?" Bruno asked.

I nodded. "So much was going on, with Mom, and then you. It was non-stop. Also—"

"Wait," Bruno said.

"My mother was very sick and when I was Skyping with Vivien, it was her idea, and neither of us expected—"

"But I talked to her," Bruno said. "We spoke. I heard her voice."

"You heard *me*," I said. "I had her account. The first time we spoke, I was at Mom's house, the other time in the basement."

"In my basement, you mean." He looked at me as if I'd turned into a gigantic centipede or a cockroach. "You would do that? To me? To us. All this time," Bruno said.

"Let me explain."

"I invited you into my house. I trusted my children with you," Bruno said, a look of growing horror on his face. "Are you even a doctor?"

I flinched. "Of course, I am."

"How do we know? Do I know anything about you?"

"You can call the College of Physicians and Surgeons to verify that I'm a member."

"Is Vivien even my mother? Are you her sister?"

"Yes. Of course, I am."

"Maybe you're faking that too."

"You don't know what it's been like."

"I don't care." He held out the cheque. "I don't know what this is, but I don't want it."

"I'm just doing what they'd have wished. Please, Bruno. It's yours. Vivien and Mom—"

He tore the cheque in half and dropped the pieces on my lap.

"Please hear me out. Mom was very sick—"

"Stop." He hit the railing with his open palm. My wine-glass tipped over into the yard.

"Vivien asked me to do it. I promised her—"

"Get off my porch. I don't ever want to see you again. I don't want you to talk to me or my wife or anyone in my family." Bruno didn't shout. He sounded like no one in my family.

"Can't I say goodbye to Sarah and Noah?" I asked.

"You're unbelievable." He stood up. "If I see you on my property again, I'll call the police." He pushed past me to the front door.

I said to his back, "You stole my sister from me. She got pregnant and it wrecked her life."

The problem, I thought, was that Bruno had kept interrupting me. If he was made aware of everything that had led to my impersonating Vivien, he'd understand. After I got home, I took my time writing out an explanation, adding, revising, as if I hadn't seen my nephew's disgust or heard his contempt. I finished the message with capital letters: *LOVE TO ALL*. Shouting into the ether.

I was ready to copy it into Messenger. All I had to do was click on the chat with Bruno.

It wasn't there.

Maybe something was wrong with my computer. I opened the app on my phone. The conversation was gone from there too. Confused, I opened Facebook and scrolled through the list of Vivien's friends: Bruno and Ruth weren't among them. They weren't anywhere. I thought of writing a note and putting it in their mailbox, but Bruno would surely shred it like the cheque, without even opening it.

I decided to call, praying I got voice mail so Bruno wouldn't hang up on me, and then I'd read the message aloud. I crossed my fingers, holding the phone with one hand. The line only rang once. Then an automated voice responded, "The person you are calling is no longer available." I tried Ruth's number. "The person you are calling is no longer available." It's easy to block a number—you just tap on the contact, then *block*. I pictured Bruno going inside, telling Ruth that I'd been posing as my sister for months, both of them with their phones, eradicating me. What would they tell their kids?

It made me dizzy; I had to sit. Then I texted Augie.

Tuesday, Sept 17, 11:02 PM
Joan: I did it. I told Bruno. He hates me
Augie: Should I come over?
Joan: No I can't face you
Augie: Is that why you've been avoiding me?
Joan: Yes. It's too humiliating
Augie: We've known each other forever. Let me be there for you
Joan: I can't. Not now

In the days that followed, I told myself that I didn't mind being alone. I didn't wish that Bruno had never sent the Facebook message. He'd brought my mother joy. It would have been selfish to regret getting involved with him and his family just because I missed them now. Was I selfish? No. And I wasn't lonely. How could I be? I was surrounded by people—patients, their many relatives, my colleagues, hospital staff—so much negotiating with humanity that it was a pleasure—yes it was—to come home to my quiet apartment with nothing more demanding than a black and white cat whose claws needed trimming again. I didn't cry while shoving the Xbox into a closet—the children weren't mine to cry over—and the big-screen TV wasn't a waste, either. It was great for watching movies at three a.m. while I was struggling to write my sister's obituary.

> *Vivien Connor was a brave woman, who gave her life to save others and was always true to herself.*
>
> *She was a consolation to her elderly mother and a mentor to her sister.*
>
> *She was honest to a fault. Also, she got her sister to lie for her, which must have given God a good laugh.*
>
> *If there is a God, why did the better sister die?*

Every time I came home, I felt like I was walking into a stranger's apartment. This place belonged to someone else, the person who'd made popcorn for young relatives and was welcomed for Sabbath dinners. Cleaning was no relief. But Mom had taught me what to do when you're on the verge of falling into a bottomless pit—redecorate. The next weekend, I stopped in at the closest hardware store for brushes, trays, plastic sheeting, and purple paint to match my armchair rocker.

It turned out to be a different shade, and the mismatch hurt my eyes. *Fine. Fine.* My new favourite word. I'd get rid of the chair. Less clutter. With some struggle, I carried it to the elevator and down to the curb. Purple was all wrong anyway. I got more paint, this time a neutral white. Perfect. First primer to cover the purple. Then I slapped on the white. The smell of acrylic took me back to my childhood, but I still wasn't a neat painter like my mother. When I poured, paint splashed around the tray. I got it on my hands and touched my hair with it, aging me.

But at last, I achieved an immaculate wall, the cadaverous purple gone. I stood back to evaluate, and it was a clean look all right: cold, blank, institutional without mercy, the wall of an olden-days asylum before it was stained by the badly behaved women who were chained up there. *Fine, fine.* I'd fix it.

I took the elevator down again and walked to the curb, relieved that the rocking chair was still there. I carried it home again. I covered it with a sheet. Like something dead. (For example, the body of the feeble old man whose ribs I'd broken because his family had insisted on heroic measures.)

Back at the paint store, I was accosted by someone who worked there. She didn't wear a blue smock like the other employees, and her name tag also included her title: *Doreen, Home Beauty Adviser.* I must have looked like I needed help because she told me—in the assured voice of someone grabbing the elbow of a blind man who is entirely competent on his own but thrown off-kilter by the unexpected assault— that the colour of the year was Hazelnut. (In the real world: beige.) She said, "You can't go wrong with the colour of the year." Or, as an alternative, she'd recommend Lilac Grey. Doreen was impeccably made up, her fingernails painted with tiny stars on her thumbs. She waved her hands as she extolled the virtues of muted pastels. Normally, the number of paint chips she flourished would have overwhelmed me. How could I possibly find the right colour among them? But apparently, I was broken beyond indecisiveness.

"I like this," I said, picking out a red that matched the car I hadn't purchased because mine was still functional. "Does red go with purple?"

"No," she said.

"Great."

I got three cans of it, red like the sun going down on a smoggy day, like the hard cherry candies I'd loved as a kid. When I rolled it on the walls, the colour felt delectable. I soon got into a rhythm with the roller. By the end of the weekend, I'd moved on from the walls to the kitchen cabinets, and the old dresser I'd hauled back from the storage locker, and the insides of closets. I wasn't thinking about Bruno or Ruth or their kids. They weren't even in the back of my mind where I kept things like, *Post an obituary on Vivien's social media accounts.* Maybe it was the colour. Brighter than blood but in the same family, sort of a cousin or nephew. Suddenly, I had to put down the roller and clap my palms to get rid of the wormy under-the-skin sensation I'd felt when examining Ruth.

As I clapped my hands, I felt the sting and heard the sound, and my heart sank. I grabbed my phone, opened my contacts and tapped *Bruno Edery*, then the red button to hang up, remembering I'd been blocked just as I was going over what I needed to say: *Listen to me; it's urgent.*

Ruth's urine sample. She'd provided it before she'd started the antibiotics, and it had shown no sign of infection. That was the point I needed to make, the thing that would sound rational, like I'd put the pieces of a medical puzzle together, and not been startled by a peculiar feeling in my hands. It isn't unusual to prescribe an antibiotic for the most common cause of infection before receiving the test results, only to discover that the particular bacteria involved needs to be treated with a different medication. However, the culture was negative. There was no bacteria.

Ruth didn't have a bladder infection, but she was passing blood and her pain was in the wrong place for kidney stones. Bladder stones—possibly. Also cancer. Her face like grey oak. The overall survival rate for bladder cancer is 77 percent, but that depends on the stage it's at, the type of cancer, whether it's spread and how far. People often don't realize that this number is just a statistic, not an individual's chances, and it doesn't refer to a cure for life, but simply the odds of being alive in five years.

Visible blood wasn't a good sign.

Ruth needed a scope. A friend of mine was a urologist; he might fit her in, and a scope, though uncomfortable, would give him a good view of her bladder from the inside. Also, I wanted her to have an ultrasound. I could give her the requisition so she could get it done right away. If she would talk to me. And if she wouldn't? I picked up the roller and smacked it against the wall, splattering myself with beads of red paint. I'd make her talk to me.

I called my cell provider. Then, after waiting a long hour, I called Ruth.

"Don't hang up," I said. The cat was kneading my lap. He wanted petting. I ignored him.

"Joan?"

"Yes, I've got to—"

"But I . . . Did you change your number?"

"Yes, don't—"

"I'm sorry, Joan. I can't go behind Bruno's back."

She hung up. Snowball butted my hand.

In the morning, on my way from one patient to another, I drove through Chinatown, passing the building where Ruth worked on the top floor. She was excited that they'd been able to take over the whole floor. She was hoping to become a partner. As I approached the building, I slowed down, thinking that if I found a parking spot, I'd run upstairs, and there it was, right in front, a miracle if ever there was one. I stopped the car and walked up all five flights to the top floor because the elevator was out of order and, obviously, God wanted me to do this.

I said to the receptionist, "Could you let Ruth Edery know that Dr. Connor needs to speak with her briefly?"

She dialed a number, repeated my message. I didn't hear what Ruth said, but the receptionist looked at me over the top of her reading glasses and said, "Uh-huh. Of course. Got it." To me, she said something polite about Ruth being unavailable and something less polite about the office being a private one and that meetings were by appointment only. The office was open plan. Behind her was a glass partition. I could see Ruth standing near a colleague's workstation, staring at me.

If humiliation was a reason to give up, I'd never have moved in with my mother.

CHAPTER 20

Bruno was teaching his class at Central Tech that evening. Hoping to speak to him before it started, I drove to the high school after I saw my last patient. A three-storey Victorian hulk built when the area was at the edge of the city, it was now in the midst of it, a twenty-minute walk from Bruno's house. I parked in the teachers' lot. Then I headed to the entrance, dashed up the steps and hurried through the corridors, looking for an office or a map. When I came to the gym, hearing the sound of a ball hitting the floor, I opened the door to ask the coach for directions. Second floor, west. Through an archway, up the stairs, past walls of lockers, I spotted Bruno speaking to a grey-haired man wearing a tool belt. The classroom door was open, and I could smell oil, freshly cut wood. When the man entered the workshop, Bruno turned and saw me. Above his head, a fluorescent bulb flickered.

"Ruth told me you went to her office." His face darkened, and he shook his head.

"She's sick," I said. "You have to listen, Bruno. It could be serious."

"Is this another scam?" He looked at me like I was the guest of a TV psychologist, perhaps someone who faked pregnancy and took money for a non-existent adoption.

I said, "Ruth has abdominal pain and blood in the urine, but no bacteria showed up in the test. That's not a bladder infection."

"So, she's got a virus," he said.

"Rare."

"But possible." He leaned against the doorpost, looming over me, and I stepped back.

"Usually only in a patient who's immunocompromised," I said.

"But she could."

"Please, Bruno. I have a friend who's a urologist, and he can fit her in for a scope next week. But she could have an ultrasound right away." I held out the requisition. He didn't take it. "She can do it in any lab she wants. She can tell them to send a copy of the report to her family doctor, not me."

"We don't have one. That's why she went to the walk-in."

"Then have them send it to the urologist."

"Who?"

"Ezra Feinstein. I've got his contact info for you." I fumbled in my bag one-handed and pulled out a slip of paper. "She doesn't have to talk to me. Neither do you. Forget it's got anything to do with me, but take my advice on this."

"I'm good with forgetting it," he said, but he took the requisition and the paper with Dr. Feinstein's number on it.

I said, "Be angry with me."

"Believe me, that's no problem."

"Just don't let that stop you. Time isn't on your side."

A woman interrupted us, asking if the class was starting.

Bruno muttered he'd be there in a minute. When the woman had retreated, he said, "Are you thinking cancer?"

If he was my patient, I'd just have said that testing was needed to rule anything out. But he was my nephew, and I said, "If Ruth has cancer, and you wait, and it spreads . . ."

"I'll talk to her," he said.

"Talking isn't enough."

He straightened up. "It's not really any of your business, is it?"

An ultrasound works like the sonar used by submarines or the clicks and chirps of bats listening for echoes. It transmits high-frequency pulses that travel through the body, and when the sound waves hit a boundary, say between soft tissue and bone, they're reflected back, and the machine uses calculations of distance and intensity to create the image. A reservoir of fluid acts like a trampoline; sound waves bounce off it, enhancing movement around the abdominal cavity. Pregnant women have an abundance of fluid in their protrusions. The rest of us don't. So, it has to be created by filling the bladder to capacity. The best imaging comes from patients full to bursting; the trick is to hold it long enough.

The last thing I'd expected was to find myself in a clinic waiting room, distracting Ruth from the pressure in her bladder.

She'd texted my new number just as I got home. Bruno must have called her before the class began. I hadn't even got out of the car yet. *Come to the lab with me. Tell me what the ultrasound shows. I don't want to wait a week to find out.* Technicians aren't supposed to discuss the images, because a radiologist needs to interpret them. I was neither a radiologist nor a technician, and a physician is only allowed to treat family members for something minor or in an emergency. Under the ethical rules I'm subject to, diagnosis is considered part of treatment. But the last line of her text: *You owe me.*

In the waiting room, there were rows of padded grey chairs, like an airport lounge. A TV screen was broadcasting its twenty-four-hour news at low volume. The lab was running behind schedule. It's not called a waiting room for nothing; everyone there had been waiting a long time. Across from us, a woman suddenly clutched herself and then got up to run to the washroom. She returned, sheepishly telling the receptionist what she'd done, and had to start from scratch, drinking multiple cups of water.

Ruth was starting to squirm. To get her mind off her bladder, I asked her when she'd left Israel. She told me it was after her military service, which had consisted mostly of filing and answering the phone. Oren, her ex-husband—then her boyfriend—wanted to study overseas. He was offered a scholarship by a Canadian organization; she didn't know he hadn't applied for anything in Europe, where flights home would have been faster and cheaper. To the relief of her parents, who were worried sick that she'd be dumped and alone in a foreign country, they got married before leaving Israel.

Toronto had struck her as new and glistening. No desert wind, no ancient monuments. Eventually, she discovered it had been Oren's intention all along to stay in Canada. He didn't want his kids going into the army to die or be maimed. Also, he was infatuated with the idea of sitting in a café without keeping an eye out for suspicious-looking characters wearing vests that could blow him up. He'd thought she wouldn't come with him if she knew he wanted the move to be permanent. This he'd confessed when she told him she was pregnant. She was in university then too, with one semester left in an urban planning degree. She was livid. She missed her family. She missed her country. But what was she supposed to do? She was busy with school and work, supporting Oren through dental school, and she believed that her child needed a father. She couldn't have known then that another man would be a better father or that he'd restore her trust—Bruno had never deceived her. She looked at me.

I said, "It wasn't my intention to deceive you."

She said, "What part of pretending to be my husband's mother was truthful?"

"It started because Vivien asked me to do it if anything happened to her. She wanted to protect my mother from the grief of losing a child. And she was right. Mom's last months were better. I wasn't trying to get anything from you."

"But you did."

"Not for myself."

"Are you sure?"

"Bruno was glad he got to know Mom," I said.

"But now he regrets it. Not to mention the kids . . ."

"What did you tell them?"

"That Vivien died and that you're too sad to see anyone."

"So, who's lying now?"

"You put us in this position. It's complicated."

I said, "I know."

A technician in blue scrubs looked down at her clipboard, then scanned the waiting room. In medical settings, clipboards are everywhere as if we're still in the twentieth century and there's such a thing as privacy.

"Ruth Edery!" the technician called.

"Here," Ruth said.

I persuaded the technician to let me accompany her by saying I was an emotional support person. She was a kind woman with an Eastern European accent, whose round face contorted with concern—assuming that Ruth had been sexually assaulted or abused as a child. As soon as we were behind a closed door in the room where the procedure was conducted, she said that in her country, when they did the ultrasound with a girl who was still a virgin, they offered her the option of inserting the wand in the rectum. Would Ruth prefer that?

If even now, a health care worker could be that dense, what had my sister faced forty years ago, seeing the doctor when she was pregnant and reeling from sexual assault?

Ruth told the technician to conduct the test as usual. Behind a curtain, she changed into the hospital gown, emerged and lay on the table. While her belly was being smeared with goo, she became chatty, diverting herself and the technician from the fact that one of them was splayed and the other manipulating a wand. Ruth asked if she had kids, which she did, two sons in high school. Ruth said she'd had a daughter with her ex and had thought she wouldn't date again until her daughter was older. It was a friend's fault she changed her mind. The friend wanted to fix her up, and Ruth kept making excuses until finally her friend ambushed her, bringing a tall man along when they met for lunch. Ruth made the technician laugh with her imitation of the friend's pretend surprise that the tall man was there and also a vegetarian like Ruth. The technician stopped laughing as she scrolled through the images to make sure they were clear. I guessed that—like me—she understood the significance of the mass sitting on top of Ruth's bladder. It was the size of a twelve-week fetus and as smooth as a stone.

After Ruth was dressed and the technician had led us out to the corridor, I said, "Do you have time for coffee?"

"I'm heading back to work," Ruth said. "Just tell me. Was the ultrasound normal?"

"Let's talk about it over coffee, please. And if Bruno could come meet us, that would be better."

In palliative care, I'm not the one who has to tell patients the terrible news that brings them to me; I don't see their eyes changing as they take it in.

The food court on the main floor of Women's College Hospital was spacious, arranged for sharing confidences or grief. My mother would have approved of the colour scheme with its white tables and moulded plastic armchairs. Ruth and I had muffins with our coffee, but she only picked at hers, peeling a bit of crust off the edge and nibbling. I asked about the kids, and Ruth replied civilly but briefly, all her chattiness used up. Kids were good. School was good. While she thumbed through messages on her phone, I pretended to be absorbed in my coffee and muffin. Finally, Bruno arrived. By the look on his face, she'd neglected to inform him that I'd be there too. He stopped in his tracks when he saw me, glanced over his shoulder at the exit, then marched resolutely to the table.

"I came as fast as I could," he said, depositing his backpack on the floor.

"That's all right." Ruth shifted to make room as he pulled an extra chair from a nearby table and angled it so that I had a good view of his shoulder.

"What's *she* doing here?"

"I asked her to come with me today. I told you."

"No, you didn't," he said.

"Oh, right, I didn't. Because you would have made me agree not to do it."

I said, "Ruth texted me. I thought you knew. But anyway, I'm here, and you should be too."

"I'm not going to change my mind," Bruno said.

Ruth tapped his hand. "It's not about you; it's about the ultrasound."

"But you've got an appointment with the urologist."

"Next week. I couldn't wait."

Bruno turned to face me then. He didn't want to, but he spoke as if he wasn't enraged, or as if rage mattered less than his wife's goodwill. "Okay."

She smiled and kissed his cheek. "Tell us," she said to me.

"I have to remind you I'm not a radiologist," I said.

They nodded.

"But I did see something in the ultrasound."

"What kind of something?" Bruno asked.

"A mass."

"What do you mean, a mass? Tumour? Cancer?"

"I'm not sure what it is. I texted a photo of it to Ezra—Dr. Feinstein. He'll get the full report in a few days."

Ezra was an old friend of mine from medical school. When he was an intern, he started attending my father's AA meeting because he needed to find one in the Goy-burbs, as he called them, where nobody his parents knew would see him slip into the church basement. Until my father relapsed, he'd been Ezra's sponsor.

Ruth leaned into Bruno, and he put his arm around her.

"The mass is sitting on top of the bladder, but you've had blood in your urine, so that means it must be . . ." I hesitated. In a medical context, except for pregnancy and skin grafts, *growing* is an anxiety-provoking word.

"Bad?" Ruth asked.

"It must have infiltrated the roof of the bladder."

"Infiltration sounds like a spy," Bruno said.

"Pierced. If it's cancer, and like I said, I've never seen anything like this so I don't know, but the type of cancer . . . The ones that develop before they show symptoms are dangerous because the disease is progressing undetected."

"Can Dr. Feinstein tell from a photo of an ultrasound what it is?" Ruth asked.

"He won't give a diagnosis based on it, but he might have a sense of possibilities. I'll give him a call when I get home this evening."

"No," Bruno said. "We'll talk to him at our appointment."

"But if Joan can find out more," Ruth said.

"At least let me talk to Ezra," I said. "He wouldn't refer you to an oncologist until he sees you, but he could think about who you need."

"It's that urgent?" Ruth asked.

"It could be."

"We don't even know what the ultrasound showed," Bruno said to his wife. "You're taking her word for it? Really?"

Denial is the first line of defence, and I'd made it so easy for him. I said, "Okay, you've got reason to distrust me. But I wouldn't lie about something important."

"You've got to be kidding." Bruno pushed back his chair.

"Not ever with a patient."

"So now she's your patient?"

"Take a look at this yourself." I held out my phone with the blurry photo of the ultrasound image, pleading as if I was in sixth grade and my teacher, who'd caught me in a lie about homework, wouldn't believe that I needed to see the school nurse because my stomach hurt, not until someone snickered at the red stain starting to show on the back of my skirt.

"I don't know what I'm looking at." Bruno stood and shrugged his backpack over a shoulder.

Ruth sat a moment longer. Then she said, "Thanks for coming when I asked, Joan," and she got up and left with her husband.

I didn't have time to sit with my worry and shame. I had to see my next patient, the single mother of three children under the age of seven.

Eddie Wong died on Thanksgiving, two and a half weeks after Ruth's ultrasound. He hadn't been back in my care long—his decline was quick.

I'd spent the evening with Larry, who'd insisted that I join him and his wife, the three of his children who lived in Toronto, and the nine grandchildren, who exhausted me with their chatter and excitement over the slideshow of his safari trip. (Maybe less the slideshow than the presents he'd brought back for them.) I didn't get the message about Eddie until I woke up at six the next morning. I dressed in a hurry, got into my car and drove toward the lake. I'd known the end was coming; Nicki—his nurse—had texted me. She'd administered glycopyrrolate for his breathing and haloperidol for nausea and agitation; she'd inserted a line into his port for the morphine pump and shown Eddie's niece how to press the button every twenty minutes.

He wasn't alone—that was the important thing. Cecilia was with him—Niece Two, the one with the voice like a train whistle, who'd urged him to do megavitamins. (When he'd refused, she hadn't spoken to him for a day, but that was all the coldness she could manage.) She'd been at his side for eighteen hours; he'd passed just after four a.m. The other niece and her family were on an airplane to Disneyland. She'd wanted to cancel her holiday, but Cecilia argued that their goodbyes had been said, and her uncle would want her to go.

She told me this while I was taking off my jacket. Through the living room window, I could see nothing but the darkness before dawn and city lights. The day had been mild even for fall, so no foggy breath would be rising from the lake. The coffee table had been pushed against the wall under the window to make space for the hospital bed, but the stack of art books was still on it, his reading glasses askew on the pile as if he'd just taken them off for a moment. Eddie lay on his back, clutching himself as if he'd needed to urinate. His terrier was under the bed, his head resting on his paws. When I'd come in the door, he'd yapped a couple of times for show, and then returned to his post. I scratched him between the ears.

"Uncle Eddie wouldn't let go," Cecilia said. "Even when he couldn't get out of bed anymore. Then I thought he would when he couldn't speak and hadn't opened his eyes for hours. But he resisted, until Nicki came and gave him the shots. He was a stubborn man. Strong."

"Hello, Eddie," I said, speaking to him as I'd been taught when I was young enough to still think about having children.

Cecilia looked exhausted, grey hair puffy on one side and flat on the other. "A couple of days ago, Uncle Eddie told me to pack his wool socks, in case it was cold. He said to tell you—"

"Me?" I wasn't expecting that. In their last days, patients muster strength for their family or sometimes even the nurse who's been at their side every week. Not the doctor. Not me.

"Yes, you."

"What?" I crouched over my bag, removing my stethoscope, hiding tears until I could swallow them. Only then did I stand up.

"He said that he's got his passport and not to forget yours."

"Oh, Eddie," I said, leaning over him. I kissed the bristly cheek, somehow still warm. A tear fell on it. "So, I'm just going to listen to your heart now, but first I have to unbutton your shirt. Is that all right, Cecilia, or would you rather do it?"

She nodded her assent and went to put the kettle on.

The shirt was blue and soft, as if it had been washed many times, and under it, I pressed the drum of the stethoscope against the shrunken chest. It's a terrible sound, that silence. The kettle's whistle was a relief. Cecilia brought a tray to the table as she'd done the first time we met. I drank green tea as I filled out the death certificate. "You'll need this for the funeral home," I said. "Have you got one?"

"The same one we used for Aunt Lucy and my parents. I called and they said to let them know when I've got the certificate, and then they'll be here within the hour."

"Go ahead," I said. "Give them a call. I'll wait with you."

After she put down the phone, she told me that Eddie had wanted me to have the quick portrait he'd done of me the day we painted together, and he also wanted me to choose another, any of them except the one of his wife, which was to go to his nieces. Cecilia said I was free to take that one too, if I wanted—

neither she nor her sister had been that fond of Aunt Lucy.

I sipped my tea, holding the warm cup in both hands, and then walked around the living room, looking at the paintings. Cecilia showed me more in Eddie's bedroom, stacked against a wall, and I flipped through them while we waited for the undertakers to arrive. I put several of them on his bed and stood back, comparing them. In the end, I chose a scene of the frozen lake as seen from his window. Part of the couch was visible, and I could imagine Eddie sitting there, talking to me, being irascible. I lost it then. Light refracted through my tears, forming sparkles above Eddie's body, and I imagined they were beings of light come to take my old friend away. How do any of us know that they weren't? Cecilia came over to hug me, and we held on to each other, weeping, until I hiccuped, and she smiled forlornly.

We reseated ourselves at the dining table. She poured more tea.

"What's going to happen to the dog?" I asked.

"He'll go to Kevin. As soon as they get back. I'll keep him till then."

The undertakers arrived, a youngish man and woman with doleful expressions. Under their topcoats, they wore high-collared suit jackets with a faintly Victorian air, cuffs fraying. I shooed Cecilia into Eddie's bedroom. It isn't pleasant to watch a body being bagged—the sleeping person you love is suddenly revealed as a stiff cardboard figure being manipulated into an oversized duffle. After they departed, Cecilia emerged from the bedroom.

"You kept your word," she said.

I nodded. "A promise is a promise."

CHAPTER 21

Later, when the pandemic locked down the world, I would realize that what was true for my patients was now true for all of us. The catastrophe was unexpected. It made our lives constrained and small, permeated our thoughts with anxiety over an uncertain future. And yet people remained themselves. They found ways to bring whatever mattered most to them into lockdown, and what they chose—my colleagues and friends—made me see them more clearly. My own choices were predictable. I don't think anyone was surprised when I offered to provide palliative care in long-term care homes. But I doubt they could have predicted what sustained me through it.

Ruth Edery   Tuesday, October 15, 08:37 PM
To me

Hi Joan, I want to thank you for being so persistent in getting me tested. We've got a diagnosis. Unfortunately I have urachal cancer. I just thought I should let you know. This is harder on Bruno than it is on me, so please

don't contact us. As I'm sure you can appreciate, I need
to focus on getting well and don't have the energy to
deal with family complications. Thanks again.
Ruth

I hadn't recognized what I saw in the ultrasound images
because the urachus is the remnant of an organ in the
embryo, a channel connecting the bladder to the umbilical
cord. It shouldn't exist in adults. After birth, the stump of the
urachus is normally absorbed. Occasionally, it isn't, and that
tissue—behind the belly button, irritated through a life-
time—can become cancerous in some people, though it's
so rare nobody knows how many. Something in the range
of a handful in Canada at any time. A few dozen in the US.
A couple in Ireland. A couple hundred in India. Before the
morning check-in call, I'd searched the medical journals
database. The problem with a disease this rare is that knowl-
edge accumulates slowly. To make it worse, it's one of those
cancers that grows without symptoms, so that by the time it's
diagnosed, the prognosis is grim.

There was another email, this one from Bruno, same date:

Bruno Edery
To me
Joan, don't tell Ruth about this. I don't want her think-
ing I'm worried enough to get in touch with you, but
I've got questions, and I can't ask her oncologist with
Ruth sitting there. I'll call you when I'm alone. Okay?
Send me your new number.

On Wednesday, I went for a walk in the ravine after work and found a quiet spot, away from the joggers and dog walkers, where I could sit for a few minutes on a bench surrounded by cattails. It had rained, and ducks were enjoying themselves in a puddle nearby. I wasn't expecting Bruno to call; I'd figured he'd have to wait until after everyone was asleep. An elderly woman was sitting on the bench too. She was heavyset and wore a purple coat—the exact shade of my armchair rocker—and she was close enough for me to smell her lilac fragrance, which reminded me of Mom. I admired her coat, and she thanked me and said purple had always been her favourite colour. It turned out that she had an apartment in my building and was involved in arranging for the kids who lived there to visit all the units on Halloween, which was only two weeks away. I said that I might be on call but could leave a basket in the hallway, and she told me not to do it because the first teenager who found it would take the whole thing. She smiled as she got up to go and that's when I noticed her prosthetic foot. I guessed she was diabetic.

My phone rang while I was still sitting on the bench. Bruno said hello, but after that there was no small talk. He sounded scared and angry with me still, but also with the medical system and cancer itself. Ruth was forty and in good shape. She biked to work. He was the one who never got any exercise except for lifting wood in and out of his truck. He said this as if cancer had looked around for its prey and had chosen Ruth to spite him. Her tumour was five centimetres in diameter, which was smaller than urachal cancer often is before discovery, and it hadn't visibly spread to any distant organs, which was also positive, but it was in her lymph nodes and that wasn't good. Ezra had referred them to one of the few oncologists

familiar with this disease. Ruth liked her, which was important. Bruno thought there was an affinity because they were
both petite brown women. Dr. Singh had a chirpy manner like
a smiley small bird. Her tone was too cheerful, Bruno thought.

Wouldn't hearing that the prognosis was eighteen to
twenty-three months be a self-fulfilling prophecy? Could
hope sustain his wife? He pushed on without waiting for an
answer. This wasn't a question for me.

He'd read that the best treatment was surgery, but the
oncologist was recommending chemo because the cancer
had metastasized. Why did she say it had metastasized?

This time he paused, and I asked him if he was confused
because there weren't other organs involved like the liver or
lungs.

"Yes."

"*Metastasized* means it's not confined to the initial
tumour," I said. "It's out there in her body."

"But just the lymph nodes. Why is it Stage 4? Couldn't it
be Stage 3 or 2?"

"What would you want if she was at Stage 2 or 3?" I asked.

"To cut it out," he said. "Get rid of it. I want them to get
rid of it."

"I would too." I got up to pace the small path that circled
the cattails. "What else did she say?"

"I don't remember. You're supposed to record what the
oncologist says. I read that. But I forgot."

"Did she tell you that if it's in the lymph nodes, that means
cancer cells are in the fluid that passes through them?"

"Maybe. I don't get it. Or I don't want to." That's what he
said, but here he was on the phone with me, someone he
couldn't stand, asking for explanations.

"The lymphatic system collects excess fluid from tissue all through the body and returns it to the blood."

"So, the cells could be anywhere."

"Yes." I heard his ragged breathing as he tried to get control of himself. My own voice cracked as I asked, "What's Dr. Singh recommending?"

"FOLFOX. She said that's the chemo they use with Stage 4 colon cancer. She wants Ruth to start it on Saturday. But it's for colon cancer."

"Urachal cancer used to be treated like it was a bladder cancer, but that didn't slow the disease any," I said. "The cancerous cells do look more like colon cancer."

"Why isn't there something for this specific cancer?"

"Because it's very rare."

"So, no one cares?"

His voice had got loud, and I heard Noah calling, "Dad, what's wrong?"

Bruno called back, "Nothing, buddy. Go watch TV. Any show you want."

Noah yelled, "Grrreat!"

"Not enough patients for a trial," I said.

Then Bruno spoke so quietly that I didn't hear him and had to ask him to repeat himself.

"They might do surgery after," he said. "Depending on the MRI."

"When?"

"Next March maybe. Or later in the spring."

"That's a good sign."

"Is it?"

"Dr. Singh wouldn't be suggesting it if there wasn't a chance for more time."

"*Good* should mean Ruth getting well. What the fuck is time?"

I said, "Memories. Sarah's high school graduation, Noah's birthdays, holidays."

"It's not enough."

"It fucking isn't," I said.

"You won't tell Ruth I called?"

"I won't."

"We'll see," he said, and ended the call without saying goodbye.

I had pins and needles along my right arm, as if I'd tensed my neck so hard while holding the phone to my ear, I'd inflamed the nerve. I sat on the bench again, unable to make my feet take me home. My nephew's searing grief hit me as if it was mine. It *was* mine. I sat there with my losses until the sun fell.

Saturday, Oct 26, 05:30 PM
Joan: You want to come over?
Augie: Tonight?
Joan: If you aren't busy
Augie: I'll bring food

Augie helped me write my sister's obituary. We sat on my caramel-coloured couch, feet resting on the ottoman. One of his socks had a hole in it, and I felt tenderness for the vulnerable toe showing through. We'd left the greasy takeout containers, mostly empty, on the kitchen table, part of a vintage set—Formica and chrome. The chairs were vinyl, all in cream and red with dusty roses for accents.

I didn't have plates yet, because I lacked confidence in my ability to hold on to things, and small items were more trouble to pack than furniture. We'd used the plastic cutlery that came with the order and ate out of the containers, since we were already acquainted with each other's spit and had no inkling a pandemic was on the way. Even so, I was feeling the fragility of existence, how a life can be upturned from one day to the next.

As Augie leaned in to read what I'd written, the press of his shoulder and the scent of his aftershave filled me with nostalgia, as if he wasn't really there, as if he'd left and couldn't return. My cat was on his lap.

He said, "You don't have to take that out. *Beloved grandmother* is fine."

"But they never spoke to her. What if I say, *She leaves behind . . .*"

I was writing on a yellow notepad, using the clipboard that had been in Vivien's box. I wore the 1960 penny strung on a leather cord. I hadn't been able to speak with her during her last illness. I didn't know how sick she'd been or even that she had been sick. In the dreams I'd had about my family dying, it was always cancer that got them. "Okay, I think this is it. Should I post it?"

"Wait until tomorrow, so you can read it one more time." He put his hand on my cheek to turn my face toward his.

We kissed. We had sex. When we spooned, I had a hot flash. He rolled away, then rolled back. Sometime in the middle of the night, I woke up to the cat purring in tune to Augie's snoring, and I thought of recording it, but the sound was so soothing, like a kettle bubbling, that I fell back to sleep before I could pick up my phone. In the morning, Augie asked why I still kept the armchair rocker, which was now in the bedroom, clashing with the red walls. I told him that if I discarded everything from my past, he wouldn't be there either.

"I'll miss this when you get serious with someone again," I said.

"I'm not looking, Joan."

While I was in the bathroom, Augie made breakfast. I left him to eat it on his own. Sarah had sent me a message, and I hurried out to the car, my hair still wet.

It was a short drive from my condo to Bruno's street, but the only parking spot I could find was a block up and another over. The neighbourhood was decorated for Halloween, every house more elaborate than the next, and I paid attention as I walked past, so I wouldn't think about what awaited me at my nephew's house. Gargoyle tombstones rose up from lawns. Scarecrows sprawled in lawn chairs. Trees were draped with gauzy strands. Skeletons and grim reapers hung from their branches, mocking death. Someone was testing sound effects—screams, moans, ghastly laughter. It's fun to be afraid when there's nothing to fear. Somewhere, a fireplace was going—I could smell the fragrance of burning logs—and I wasn't thinking about anger or illness or having a home without plates in it. I pushed it all away because that's what it takes to be useful in a crisis: you face reality; you don't succumb to it.

Sarah was waiting for me on the porch. The small patch of yard was brown, the tree in it bare of dangling bones. The house had no decorations, either, except for a sad plastic pumpkin. Sarah was sitting on the stairs, next to the pumpkin, huddling in a winter coat though the day was mild and the sun out. Her dark hair was glossy, pulled back in a ponytail, but the polish on her nails was chipped.

She said, "You changed your number. You told me I had it but I didn't. Some jerk has your number now."

"I got the message anyway," I said.

"I had to message Vivien on Facebook. Why don't you even have your own account?"

"I'll get one if you want me to."

"No. I hate Facebook."

I sat down beside her on the stairs. "Does your father know I'm here?"

"Probably."

"Probably?"

"Dad's in the bathroom helping Noah get washed. I told him through the door. The water was running."

"So, no."

She shrugged.

"I came because it was important enough for you to use Facebook, which you hate, to send me a message."

"Okay."

"So, what's going on?"

"I dunno."

"*You* asked *me* to come over right away," I said.

"It was dumb. Forget it." But she didn't make a move to get up. Across the street, an old woman was sitting on the porch, watching the neighbour's children, a pair of little girls chalking a hopscotch board on the sidewalk. I'd played hopscotch when I was their age.

"I don't much remember what it was like to be fifteen," I said. "Do you go out for Halloween?"

"No. There's a party, but I'm not going."

"I never liked parties."

"It's not really a party. Just some gamer friends having pizza."

"Could be fun."

"Maybe," she said, reaching up to tighten her ponytail. "I don't care. Dad is taking Noah out, so I'll stay home with Mom."

"She doesn't want you to go?"

"I don't have to ask her." Sarah put her hands on her hair and pulled out the elastic, then twisted the mass of it into a bun. "She's sick. You know."

"What do you know about her illness, Sarah?"

"That it's bad. She's got urachal cancer. She feels awful."

"That's normal," I said.

"Like want to die awful?" Her voice caught. It caught like a little grey mouse in a cat's mouth.

"Did she say that to you?"

"Not exactly me," Sarah said. "I heard her talking to Dad this morning. She said it was horrible and she wasn't strong enough, and if she was going to die, everyone had to accept it. Then we all heard Noah crying downstairs. He'd peed himself in the kitchen. So, Dad had to go downstairs and deal with him."

"I'm sure she didn't plan for you to hear her."

"They don't plan for me to hear anything." She picked at the nail polish on her thumb. "Aunt Joan . . ."

"What?"

She looked up at me. Her face was desolate. "If Mom asks you to help her die, you have to promise me you won't."

"I don't need to promise."

"You do! I know you keep your promises."

"Medically assisted death isn't part of palliative care. It's not something I do. Also, I don't think your mom means it."

Sarah looked at me sullenly. Just another adult sliding away from unpleasant truth. There was a time all children visited with death. Not anymore. Not in neighbourhoods like this. No one on this street would drop their kids into a lake without swimming lessons, but they throw them into a mortal life with only denial for a life jacket: *You're safe, I'll protect you with my magic umbrella.* I knew better than that. I should have known better.

I said, "Chemo is hard. When it's working, the side effects can be worse."

Sarah's eyes filled. "What if it isn't working?"

I held her gaze. I said, "We won't know until your mom finishes her six rounds and has an MRI."

Her face was crumpling.

"Sarah."

She leaned her head on her knees, crying. "Mom's going to die and I won't see her again, and Dad won't want me anymore and I'll have to go live with my father."

I let her cry. I gave her tissues from my bag. I said, "No one's dying yet."

"If she stops chemo . . ."

"I don't think she will."

"But if she does . . . And even if she doesn't . . ."

"You're Bruno's daughter. He would no more get rid of you than his own hand."

"He got rid of you, and you're related."

We sat for a moment looking at each other in the harsh light of reality. I wanted to kick it to the curb.

"See?" she said.

"He did. And yet, here I am."

"Outside."

I got to my feet. "Well, I'll go inside."

"Can you talk to Mom? Make her finish chemo?"

"I can't make her, but I'll talk to her."

Her face was so hopeful. I had no magic umbrella, but sometimes there's more wizardry in the right words than in a prescription pad. As I put my hand on the door handle, I prayed to find them. The handle turned.

CHAPTER 22

I didn't blame Sarah for staying on the porch, out of range of her stepfather's displeasure. I was nervous enough myself, hyperfocused on the sound of Bruno's voice as he came closer. Still, I couldn't help but make a mental note of the changes I saw. Garbage bag in the hall. Boy's underwear—not overly clean—on top of the bag. When I'd come for Friday dinners, I hadn't appreciated that although the house was packed with stuff, it was contained. Things hung on walls, were stacked on shelves and enveloped by bins. If someone pulled a book off a shelf, there wasn't a puff of dust.

Containment was clearly no longer a priority. Also in the hall: a random scatter of toys, an overturned blue bin, a juice carton on its side, a broken doorknob, a torn Cellophane packet leaking crackers, a twisted swimsuit and towel getting mouldy. The smell of the house was different. Not herbs and spices, but fast-food grease, dirty laundry, something like spilled soda. Maybe it *was* soda—a column of ants was working on something. Then Bruno came down the stairs. Seeing me, he skidded to a stop. He'd shaved off his beard.

His jawline was my father's. No, broader, squarer—his unknown father's.

"What the fuck?"

"Daddy said a bad word!" Noah appeared in his Spider-Man costume, the sleeves and legs too short.

"Who let you in?" Bruno asked.

"The door was unlocked."

"Hi Grrreat-Auntie!" Noah grabbed me around the middle, his hands and hair still wet from his bath.

"Hi." My hand went to his head. He snuggled in and I scratched it gently.

Bruno yanked his son away from me, then glanced at the clump of red cloth gripped in his fist and abruptly let go. He flexed his hand as if it was a prosthetic he was getting used to.

I see this all the time—not only the people altered by disease moving tentatively, but how the whole-bodied react to a world that's cracked. People behave like reluctant immigrants to an unknown country. They think they can go back to normal, but the body knows. It wakes at odd times; it moves fitfully and with cravings, trying to negotiate a fractured landscape. Eventually, the mind catches up, carrying what it can from the old country to that new place; chasms are filled or bridges are built over them. My mother dealt with stress by destroying her environment before it broke around her, so she could rebuild. Not me—I chose to sit among the broken pieces as if I had nowhere to go. But here I was, inside the house.

The boy looked up, scared and confused as his father told him—his voice tense as he strained to hold in his temper—to go watch TV.

"I'm not allowed to watch TV," Noah said. "I'm supposed to play. Mommy always says, 'No TV.' You play with toys to develop your brain."

"Fine, play," Bruno told him. "Just do it in your room."

"I don't want to go upstairs," Noah mumbled.

"Noah, I'm serious."

"I won't have another accident. I promise, Daddy."

Bruno's jaw tightened.

"I want to stay with you," Noah said.

"I'll come up soon." His father pushed him toward the staircase.

Noah's bare feet left wet footprints as he moved away.

"What are you doing here?" Bruno asked.

"Sarah messaged me."

"She shouldn't have." His voice was stony, his face stiff—not with outrage, not totally. I recognized that look. It hid pain and was meant to block questions. Behind the brushed teeth and aftershave, there was a hint of whisky. He looked just like my father when he was hungover. "I'll speak to her."

"Maybe you should know why she contacted me first." Keeping my voice low came automatically. "She heard Ruth this morning, telling you about feeling at the end of her rope."

"Oh, shit."

"She wants me to talk to her mom about it."

He pinched the bridge of his nose. "She has a—"

I knew he meant to say *doctor*, but I interrupted. "A husband who doesn't let his personal feelings get in the way of using all the resources at his disposal to help his wife. Would you consider that I might know something about what Ruth is going through? A bit more than most?"

He stood for a moment, uncertainty chasing resentment and anger and fear and a tiny flash of hope.

I said, "This is World War II. You're the Soviet Union and the Nazis have invaded. I'm America, bringing you planes."

He shook his head. He said, "I'm North Africa."

"Who am I?"

"A French colonialist. But I'll ask Ruth anyway. Wait here."

I waited for a long time—well, probably not very long, but it seemed an age. I unbuttoned my fall jacket, then took it off and draped it over my arm. Sarah opened the front door just enough to peer inside. When I smiled, she whispered, "Did you talk to her," and I said, "Working on it," and she closed the door. Through the front window, I saw her sit back down on the step beside the pumpkin and take out her phone. A few minutes later, Bruno came downstairs and told me that Ruth said I could talk to her if he made tea for me and, fuck it, there was no tea, so she said coffee, but there wasn't coffee either because he hadn't put it on the list he'd given his mother, who was shopping for them, and he was going to make a quick run to the store if he could figure out where he left his keys.

An array of medications on the nightstand. A pail next to the bed. The metallic odour of medicine. A patient lodged in the bed with a phone, TV remote, water bottle. There was already a guest chair, and on Bruno's side of the bed, a box of tissues and an unopened package of ginger candy. The patient seemed happier than I'd expected. Ruth was propped up on her pillows, smiling when I came in. Light streamed through her window, casting her shadow on the wall, a double Ruth welcoming me with a beckoning hand. She wore plaid flannel pyjamas and knit gloves a deeper red than my walls. The pillow behind her head was gold, her dark hair fanned against it, still thick.

"I'm glad to see you," she said. "I want to get things settled before I go. Come sit." She pointed at the dining room chair that Bruno must have brought upstairs. I pulled the chair closer and sat, jacket on my lap, wondering if Sarah was right and her mother was going to ask me about medical assistance in dying.

"Are you planning on going somewhere?" I asked.

"Yes." She beamed. "I'm thinking of going to Israel."

"Ah." So, not MAID. Theoretically, I'm in favour of there being a choice, but it makes me uneasy. Also, I'd be sad when she died, whether I was a part of her life or not. "When?"

"Soon as I can book it."

"I see." So there wouldn't be any medical assistance to prolong life, either. My heart fell.

"I'd like to see my family," Ruth said.

"Do they know?"

"Not yet. If I quit chemo, I can have a normal visit with them before they find out. I'll take the kids. They'll miss school, but later they'll be glad we had the time together."

"What about Bruno?"

"He's teaching, and we need the income." She frowned. "He'll feel like I'm leaving him, and I will be, but just for a while."

"Not for a while," I said, "if you refuse treatment."

"It's *my* cancer," she said. "I thought you, of all people, would be open-minded."

"Because I've got no opinion?" Maybe my tone was a little testy. If I was still masquerading as my sister, I could express an opinion. Multiple opinions. Contradictory ones.

"No—because you're around people who are dying and it doesn't freak you out," Ruth said. "I thought I could trust you to have an honest conversation."

"So, you expect me to be honest."

"I was hoping," Ruth said. "Yes."

"About what I know or what I think?"

"Both."

"Even if you don't like what I say?"

"I'm not going to like what anyone says—unless it's that there's been some kind of mistake and I don't have cancer."

"All right," I said. "Talk to me."

"A week ago, I felt fine."

"You weren't fine," I said.

"Compared to now, I felt great."

"Okay," I said. "I'll give you that. Chemo sucks."

"I didn't know it would be this bad."

"No one does. The fact sheet doesn't do it justice."

"I feel a little better today, but by the time I can get out of bed, I'll be heading to the hospital for more chemo. I joined a Facebook group, and people are telling me it gets worse with every round. I'm not that brave." She put her hand on mine. I gripped it. "All my friends had natural childbirth. I couldn't wait for an epidural." She said it as if she'd let down not only herself but all women from time immemorial.

"There's nothing wrong with that," I said.

"But I couldn't even take labour pain and I got my kids out of it. My beautiful kids . . . I yelled at Noah." She let go of my hand. "I screamed at him for bringing me a drink that was a little too cold. I told him he was torturing me."

"A living mother screaming at you is better than a dead one who doesn't."

"I'm going to die anyway. I want to leave them with good memories."

"Like a trip to Israel."

She nodded.

"You still want to know what I think?"

"Not if I have to beg." She sounded irritated. That was fine—there was energy in her irritation. I could work with it. Or, for a change, I could just say what was on my mind. What I'd been thinking since I'd sat down.

I said, "Nothing hurt me worse than my mother saying she wanted to die."

"Oh Joan . . . When did she say that?"

"It's a long story."

"I can make room in my busy schedule." She laughed— brought out of herself—and that made me think the story was worth telling, even though it meant opening up more than I would have just a few months ago.

So, I told her about Mom planning to adopt Vivien's baby. How she didn't come out with it right away. First, she spent months getting ready for the baby, obsessed with making sure everything would be perfect: all the clothes, the toys, the crib.

Unfortunately, the people in her life were less than per-fect. Dad was drinking more and more, blacking out and missing work, while Mom kept going with her plan, ignoring him. Looking back, I thought she had to be deep in denial, building a fantasy life no one else knew about. Finally, out it came—the intention to adopt my sister's baby—and there was a big blow-up when Vivien said no. Mom reacted the way she always did when stressed. She started getting rid of things, but this time she went berserk. If Vivien had been considering letting her adopt the baby, the combination of Dad dead drunk and Mom throwing out our beds and ripping up the carpet would have killed that chance. And Mom must have realized it. When she was done clearing everything out of the house, she had a panic attack.

"We all thought it was her heart," I said. "And while I was calling 911, she said, 'Don't—I just want to die.'"

Ruth looked at me, aghast. "I'd never say that."

"You don't have to say those exact words for your kids to get the message."

"The message is that I love them so much I'd rather have a good time with them than hang around sick for a couple of years."

"Is that for them or you? The way I see it, this isn't acceptance or selflessness. It's running scared. If you go away with your kids, you can pretend the disease isn't happening. But it is, and you'll come home to it. When the cancer causes you distress—because it will—you'll yell or do whatever else you're doing now. Let's just hope the cancer kills you with liver failure before it spreads to your lungs so at least you'll be able to talk without oxygen. And please don't wait till the last minute to say whatever you need to tell them. Most people are too out of it for last words. Also, don't worry so much about yelling. That's when it gets scary—when you stop yelling and become selfless because you're letting go of your sense of self. Sacred and scary."

Her eyes bored into mine as I spoke, and I wasn't sure what she wanted to find in them. When I stopped, she looked down.

She said, "I'm scared."

"Of what?"

"Everything. Not being able to take it. Not being me."

"You'll still be you."

"This will kill my mother. Her blood pressure is already too high." She looked toward the window and the view: her bare front yard, a neighbour's tree with its cobwebby gauze and its bouncing skeleton. "I thought if I just take the kids to Israel and we have a good time, then afterwards, when things progress, I wouldn't ever have to . . . It would be like a car accident. You don't have to tell your mother that you got hit by a car and died, do you?"

"That's exactly how I got into this mess," I said. "By not telling people Vivien died, just like she wanted, because my mother was weak and I was strong and Bruno was a stranger."

"It's not the same thing," she said. "You pretended that Vivien was alive."

"That's true. But you're doing what she did—hiding from what you know and letting someone else deal with the fallout."

She said, "You don't understand. I still have plans. I'm going to put rooftop gardens in new developments. I'm thinking Sarah might become an architect—she likes building things with Minecraft—and we could go into practice together. I want to be alive to meet Noah's first girlfriend."

The anguish in her voice was so much like her daughter's. I said, "Okay, tell me this. How's the blood in your urine?"

She looked startled, then thought for a minute. "You know, I haven't noticed any."

"The abdominal pain?"

"I pretty much threw up my internal organs."

"That's the nausea. I'm asking about the pain you had before."

She thought again. "You're right, it's different. Almost gone."

"So, the chemo is working."

"I guess it is."

"There are options," I said. "If chemo is so intolerable that someone can't finish the course of treatment, that defeats the purpose. Your oncologist could reduce the dose."

"No one told me that."

"She will, if you tell her what's going on. It's not uncommon. And you can still visit your family. Usually, there's two weeks between rounds, but sometimes people take an extra week because they need the breathing space."

Her smile was wobbly. "Is a lowered dose of chemo as good as the full one?"

"It should be, if you do an extra round."

"I could do that." She drank from her water bottle, gloves protecting her fingertips. Sensitivity to heat and cold is one of the more unpleasant side effects of FOLFOX. I'd had patients tell me they felt like they were being impaled by needles.

"I had plans too," I said. "I was going to have kids, but I wanted to do it right. When I had everything a kid needed."

The pity in her eyes mirrored mine. She had children; I still had a life. It felt like a choice on my part, but maybe it wasn't any more than illness was a choice of hers.

"Are you sorry you didn't?" she asked.

"A bit. Are you sorry you did?"

"Of course not!" She looked appalled that I'd asked.

"What if the situation was reversed and one of your kids had a terminal illness?"

"God forbid . . . No. And don't ask anything else. The answer is always no. I'm not sorry I had my kids."

"So why do you think you're doing something to your mother? You think you wilfully got cancer just to mess up her life?"

"Because I left!"

I leaned forward, but I didn't fill the silence.

"My mother nags my kids to FaceTime with their cousins, but they don't really know each other, and my kids make excuses not to. My sister's kids probably do too, so that's it. They're strangers. And if they weren't, my kids would have more family. I came here and they only have me and Bruno, and soon they'll only . . . Do you know when my father died?" I shook my head. "Seven and a half months after I left home, in a suicide bombing. Don't say—" She put her hand up as if to stop me from telling her that it wasn't her fault. "I wasn't there to help my mother through it. And why? Because she was annoying, that's all. She worried too much, and I couldn't wait to get away from her. So, I did that. My sister stayed, but I left her."

"In a family, you're always doing things to each other. There's no way around it." I'd pleaded with my father to quit drinking. He'd only gotten sober after my sister ran away. That was the puzzling paradox: doing good doesn't necessarily cause good and being selfish can, but if I were to be selfish as a kind of underhanded way of doing good, it would backfire just like it had when I'd posed as Vivien. "Maybe that's how you become who you are," I said. "Reacting."

Ruth nodded. "Only sisters know what you've been through."

"I wish I'd had the chance to talk it out with mine. You still do."

We held hands then. We both gazed out the window. White clouds hung over smoking chimney tops. The smell of fresh coffee drifted up from the kitchen.

When I came into the kitchen, Bruno had the hangdog look of a man who's hungover and wishes he could turn back the clock. The coffee was made, but he stood idly, as if bewildered by how to get mugs from the cupboard and milk from the fridge. I told him to sit and he did, on one of the high stools at the kitchen island. I bustled about like Eddie's tea-making niece. First, I cleared off the island. Scraped the dried gunk off dishes and stacked them in the dishwasher. The cereal box and cookie box and jam jar went in the pantry, the random raisins and toast crusts in the compost. I wiped the island down. I cleaned the counters. I swept the floor. It was parquet, the cupboards oak, brown as autumn. Bruno sat watching dejectedly. I was thinking, *Nothing to do here but be Joan—all Joan.* In the backyard, there were still a few blue asters blooming amidst the dried-out grass and flower heads.

After a while, he said, "Thanks. I felt bad about leaving that for Mom."

"No problem." I poured coffee into mugs. Bruno drank his black. I topped mine up with milk to cool it off.

I told him how it had gone with Ruth—that she was considering the options she had with chemo, and how her mood had shifted as we spoke. I didn't mention anything she'd said about her family except that she'd like to see them and she could manage that even while she was doing chemo.

He said, "I don't want her to die."

I said, "I don't either."

He said, "She's my everything."

And that was the reason Sarah had messaged me. I said, "Kids can feel that."

He nodded, misunderstanding. "She's theirs too."

So now what? I could either let Sarah down by betraying a confidence or by leaving her to cope on her own. "That's not what I meant," I said. "Sarah's afraid that without her mother in the picture, she won't have a home with you."

"She told you that?"

"Pretty much."

"And she came to you. Not me. *You?* She feels that alone? Why would she—"

"Like you said. Ruth's your everything. And you smell like you're falling apart."

He grimaced. "Sorry, I haven't thought to shower."

I was worrying that what I'd say next would offend him, killing any chance I would have to talk to Bruno in the future, but I might not have another chance anyway, and it had to be said. "When my sister was Sarah's age, her boyfriend was an ex-convict, and a year later she was pregnant."

He looked at me intently. Frowning.

"Sarah's mom isn't available to her. If you aren't either, who's she got? Kids find solace where they can. With whoever gives it to them."

"Oh, fuck." He rubbed his face, eyes closing. "I don't know if I can do this."

"You will."

"Why are you so sure?"

"Because I've been through this with patients so many times. Either you do it alone or with your family. That's your only choice."

His jaw tightened. "It's a shitty choice."

"Everyone has to make shitty choices. I know I have."

"For better or worse." Was that a bit of a smile? He stood and refilled his mug with coffee, then said, "I've got work to do. I'm late with a job."

He walked me to the door, ruefully eyeing the mess in the hallway as if anticipating a scolding from his mother and finding some small comfort in the normalcy of that at least.

Then he asked if I'd come back to check on Ruth after she had her next round of chemo, and I told him I would.

CHAPTER 23

It's with great sorrow and regret that I have to let you know that Vivien Leigh Connor is no longer with us. She died as she lived, bravely and in a place of her choosing. She was an original, always true to herself, and respected by doctors, nurses and patients around the globe for her tireless spirit, her dedication and her fearlessness. She was predeceased by her parents, Sheila and Hugh Connor. She leaves behind her sister, Joan Connor, her son and his wife, Bruno and Ruth Edery, and her grandchildren, Sarah and Noah Edery. She will be terribly missed. May her spirit live on in the caring of others.

After posting Vivien's obituary to Facebook, I composed another message. Condolences were already appearing on my sister's timeline when I sent it to Grace, Oscar and Raoul.

Early this year, Vivien moved to a remote village in the DRC to provide care for Ebola patients. Before she left,

she asked me to promise that in the event she died,
I would take on her social media accounts and pretend
she was alive to protect our mother's mental health.
Last March, Vivien was in a dugout that tipped over and
she cut her leg on a rock. The cut became infected, no
treatment was available, and it spread, causing septi-
cemia. She passed away on March 20. I apologize for
having misled you into thinking I was Vivien. Full disclosure: it was really nice to be someone else for a while—
someone like Vivien, especially. As you know, Mom died
three months later, and I should have ended the deception then, but there were unforeseen complications. My
sister's son came into her—my—life. I want to assure you
that he knows the truth now too. Thank you for your
kindness and love for Vivien. You were her family.

Their replies came quickly. Raoul thought it was
hilarious—so much like Vivien to wreak havoc one last
time from beyond the grave. Grace was angry that I hadn't
taken her into my confidence, but relieved that her suspicions had been validated, which proved to her how close
she and Vivien had been. Oscar was infuriated and posted
on Vivien's timeline:

I thought my mother was the expert in gaslighting but
no. Her manipulation has been surpassed by someone
I believed was a good friend, only to discover that my
friend had died, and her sister—JOAN CONNOR—has
been posing as Vivien. This has been going on for
SEVEN MONTHS. Vivien died in March. We've all been
"friends" with a fake.

Raoul responded with a meme: a man in a tux, holding out a wineglass with the caption *Here's to you, best liar ever.* My sister's Facebook friends were decent people. None of them told me to shoot myself, but there were plenty of vitriolic comments, and I replied apologetically to all of them. Within hours, the number of Vivien's Facebook friends dwindled significantly, many of them blocking her account. It was embarrassing, but I was strangely relieved and went shopping for plates. I came home with a full set of earthenware glazed in blue, bordered with rays of red and gold like the setting sun.

On Halloween, I covered my apartment door with spiders, bats, a skeleton and witches. I had a carton of chip bags and another of mini chocolates to give out. The woman I'd met from my building—her name was Paula Giannis—had organized a costume parade, and everyone on my floor stood in the hallway to applaud the kids as they trooped down the carpeted corridor in disguise, with Paula following on her mobility scooter. There were treats in her basket, and I contributed chips but not chocolate because of her diabetes. Later in the evening, she dropped by for tea, and I boiled the water in my single pot, thinking I should really get a kettle.

It was my first autumn without any family. I didn't realize that it was my last autumn in the world as we had known it. While the weather got colder and snow fell in brief flurries, I saw my patients bare-faced, relying as usual on how much I could communicate with an expression of reassurance or concern. After work, I decompressed by walking in the ravine, careless of how close I got to other people. I saw cardinals and sparrows and mourning doves. I heard a mockingbird imitate the call of a frog, which made me laugh. Paula, who was there on the bench, heard me laugh and came over to talk to me. We stood less than an arm's length from each other.

Sometimes, Augie came for the walk with me. Sometimes, we ate a meal together in a crowded restaurant or saw a movie in a theatre, and there was no jolt of adrenalin if we heard a cough. A few days after each round of Ruth's chemo, when the side effects peaked, I checked in on her. Bruno remained reserved—we spoke only about her condition—but I noticed Sarah's homework spread out on the dining room table alongside Bruno's sketchbook, as if they were now working together in the evenings.

I often ran into Denise. Once, we met in the backyard. She was going to the garage—against the leaden sky, a splash of colour in her red coat—just as I was coming out of it after locking up my bike. I stood awkwardly, unsure of my welcome, but she threw her arms around me and I hugged her back, holding on because I hadn't thought I'd ever be hugged again by anyone in my nephew's family over the age of six. Later, I'd be glad I did; I'd reimagine her hug and Augie's shoulder pressing mine when we sat on the couch, his bare toe poking out of his sock, touching my bare foot. Another time, Denise was putting away groceries when I arrived, and she made coffee for me. It was strong; I had to drink it with half a cup of milk. Denise teased me about it, blaming my Anglo heritage—white skin, white coffee—employing the same half-scolding tone she used for passing judgment on Bruno's T-shirts.

Ruth's hair began falling out. She wanted to visit her family in Israel before it became any thinner, and they planned to travel in December, as soon as Bruno's classes were over, but then her oncologist recommended she wait until she was done with chemo.

The days became short and, in the darkness, blue and red and gold and green LED lights flashed around neighbours' houses and trees. Noah begged for a Christmas tree. He no longer believed that Santa was real, and it wasn't about the gifts—he said if they could have a tree, he wouldn't need any Hanukkah presents. Everyone else had a tree, so why couldn't he? A big, beautiful tree. With ornaments. And shiny stuff. His mom would feel better if there was shiny stuff.

He got Sarah on his side. She said they'd make everything but the lights, and she'd pay for the supplies with her babysitting money. Bruno said no. Ruth said yes. A seven-foot fir tree came into the front room. Denise and George were appalled. The scent of the forest filled the house.

Ruth's fourth round was the worst. The day I checked in on her, the kids were having a respite at their grandparents'. Mood swings are to be expected when someone is dealing with the end of normalcy, but they're also a side effect of chemo. Ruth felt too sick to scream at me, but she did accuse me of manipulating her into continuing chemo when she could have gone to Israel instead, and now she couldn't go, because if she caught a cold and ended up with pneumonia and died, her mother would feel guilty for the rest of her life, and she couldn't do that to her mother, who didn't even know yet that Ruth was sick, and no, she wasn't going to tell her over the phone.

Before I left the room, she signed a form authorizing me to speak with her oncologist about her meds. Then she threw the form at me. She was weak; it fluttered to the floor. When I came downstairs and asked for a glass of water, Bruno said that he'd been yelled at too, and did I want a shot of Dalwhinnie instead? I said I would, and he said he'd join me.

We perched on stools at the kitchen island, each of us with a glass, the bottle—low on amber liquid—between us. We drank, and Bruno told me that he'd purchased a DNA kit from 23andMe. The results had come back—a combination of British Isles and "broadly South Asian." So now he had that in common with Ruth too. Did I know that in World War II, 2.5 million South Asian soldiers fought against the Nazis across three continents? They had units in Algeria, and wouldn't it be an interesting coincidence if his biological grandfather—whoever that was—had been stationed there, beating back the enemy and saving the lives of his adopted grandparents? I pictured it—these grandparents encountering each other and shaking hands in unspoken acknowledgement of their descendants' connections. In the photographs he'd found online, most of them had facial hair, at least a moustache. He might grow one.

"Do you miss your beard?" I asked.

"It was bothering Ruth." We drank some more.

"Feel naked without it?"

He nodded. "And off-balance, like whose face is this? That's why what you did was so shitty."

"What did I do to your beard?"

"You know what I mean."

"Yes and no." I wanted to get up and clear the kitchen counter, which was cluttered with a line of glass jars. I wanted to wipe it down. I wanted to smell bleach. I said, "You mean not telling you about Vivien. Bruno, I also had to protect my mother, and it would have hurt her so much if she'd known. Why is that so hard to understand?"

He shook his head. "You still don't get what you did to me. You take it for granted that you know who you are and where you're from. It's no mystery. No one is keeping it from you. Every time you look in the mirror, you're not thinking about it."

"It isn't necessarily a wonderful thing."

"I realize that; it's what I said to myself too. I only went looking because I was concerned about how a lack of medical history might affect my kid's health, and it was frustrating not to have the information I needed. But that's not the whole truth."

He looked out toward the glass doors. I followed his gaze. The yard was darkening in the early twilight. Noah's action figures on the patio table were posing against the setting sun. Bruno said, "I've always felt like some kind of weird creature with no name, hatched from an egg. Then you show up online, and I'm thinking you're my mother, my birth mother. We form a connection. You tell me things. The pieces fill in. Stuff I didn't know I needed to know, and now I do, and I stop feeling weird. Whoopie!"

He refilled his glass. "And then I find out it's all a lie. You—Joan. Withholding the facts. I'm swimming in misinformation. I don't know what to believe. I don't know anything. I don't know who my mother was. It was all a fiction."

"There was only one lie, Bruno. Mine. You could get to know her for yourself."

"How? Consult a medium?"

"Better. I'll give you Vivien's user ID and the passwords for all of her online accounts."

"Maybe," Bruno said. "But what would I find out? Social media—people curate it. They present an image."

"Her image is no image," I said. "But make up your own mind about it. I deleted all the posts and chats I had anything to do with. Everything that's left is hers. There's a lot of it. You can also go through her email. There's years of it."

The bottle was empty. He stood up and opened the cupboard to take down another. He uncapped it and refilled our glasses, then sat again. "Okay, I'll do it."

"Being Vivien was my beard," I said.

He smiled. I watched the evolution of it—a smile slowly broadening until it seemed to stretch to his princely ears.

I smiled too.

"There's a picture," he said. "But how do you mean?"

"I could say things I never would on my own."

"For example?"

"Do you think you're an alcoholic?"

He lifted his glass. "You're matching me drink for drink. Are you?"

"I worry about it. But so far, my hygiene isn't affected."

"I showered today!"

"So did my father. Twice a day. He thought it made him seem more presentable when he was drunk, but it didn't fool anyone. What I really should ask is do you have an emergency bottle stashed somewhere?"

"I'm just sad," he said, "because my wife is sick."

"And sometimes you're sad for other reasons."

"That's true."

"I know about sad drinking . . ." I pushed the glass away. "Maybe I should have coffee now."

He got up to put it on.

I said, "Some kids don't act out. They shut down instead."

"Better than getting pregnant." He was standing near the coffee maker, leaning against the counter.

"But there's you," I said. "My sister would have been so glad to know you."

"Even though I wrecked her life?"

"I never should have said that."

The coffee maker burbled. The fragrance filled the kitchen.

"But is it true?" Bruno asked. "Did I?"

"No," I said. "She had a good, full life. I just missed her a lot, and I wanted her to come home. I wasn't willing to meet her halfway."

He took mugs from hooks under the kitchen cabinet and placed them on the island. Mine was imprinted with a cartoon boy hanging on to a blue blankie. Bruno's had lettering: *The carpenter saw everything*. He poured the coffee. He sat down across from me.

He said, "When the Pope dies and goes to heaven, what does he eat for breakfast?"

"What?" I asked.

"Ethereal."

I said, "Can I give the kids gifts for Hanukkah?"

He thought for a minute. "We could put them under the tree and give Noah a thrill."

I wanted to know what the kids might like. Bruno wasn't sure, but he thought that Noah was hankering for Star Wars figures or a magic kit, and though he had no idea what would make Sarah happy, she was always doing something with her nails. Then he said, "That chocolate cake of yours. The kids miss it. If you're not doing anything for dinner Friday, maybe you could bring it."

So, on Friday I came with the cake and wrapped presents, which went under the tree. I'd got a magic kit and a gel manicure set that came with a dome-like heater that you stick your fingers under to harden the polish to a lacquer finish (the plastic-faced beautician at the counter had assured me it was their bestseller). I was nervous, but it was only awkward at the beginning.

That was the Friday between Christmas and New Year's. Ruth had been scheduled for chemo the next morning, but it was delayed for a week because her white blood cell count was too low. Nobody was concerned about drawing out her treatment—not yet. I left with a present too. A belated house-warming gift, Bruno said. It was an Easter cactus. It would bloom in the spring when the city was still grey.

At the beginning of the new year, I had a productive conversation with Ruth's oncologist, Dr. Singh. The array of pills on Ruth's bedside table changed, the dosages adjusted, and one nausea medication was swapped out for another.

I wasn't worried about the novel coronavirus, even though an epidemiologist friend of mine said a tsunami was on its way. I thought she was overreacting—in Toronto we'd been through SARS, and we'd gotten by with a lot less fuss than you'd think from the news. But by the end of January, worldwide cases of COVID-19 were already at ten thousand, which seemed a big number at the time, more than all the cases of SARS *ever*. The WHO declared a global health emergency. In February, the first American died of COVID-19. I was watching numbers double every few days. At our downtown office, we held team meetings to discuss how we'd work with our fragile patients, given the predicted shortages in personal protective equipment.

Mid-month, Ruth's white blood cell count was borderline, and she was offered the choice of postponing chemo. When she talked to me about it, I urged her to finish while she still could. And so Ruth had her last round of chemo. Before March break, a doctor in Hamilton—a forty-five-minute drive from the hospital where Ruth had been treated—had unknowingly returned from a holiday with COVID-19, and on her first day back at work had appointments with a number of cancer patients with compromised immunity.

I watched in horror as doctors in Italy wept over having to choose which patients to treat because there weren't enough ventilators for everyone. The NBA cancelled their season. Bruno at last accepted his inheritance and tried to buy airline tickets for Ruth's family to come to Toronto, but there were no tickets to be had. Airplanes were packed with people trying to get home from wherever they had been stranded. The border between Canada and the US closed. As hospitals redoubled their efforts to face the pandemic, Ruth's MRI was cancelled. We didn't know if and when she'd have her surgery.

I felt compelled to tie up loose ends before I was in the eye of the storm. I gave Augie the extra key to my safety deposit box, where I'd placed the will Gary had urged me to make and insurance information. He promised to take my cat if anything happened to me. Then I rented a U-Haul to clear out my storage locker. Sarah insisted on coming along to help. I didn't ask why.

We drove through city streets away from the lake and toward the suburbs as she listened to music through her earphones. Sidewalks disappeared, roads became crescents named after flowers or the developer's kids, lawns broadened. Already, in mid-March, trees were starting to bud, twigs swollen at their tips.

I said, "How much should I pay you for this?"

She said, "I can't take any money. Mom would kill me. You're family."

Family. I let the word settle.

"Doughnuts okay?" I asked.

"Ha. Always."

We stopped at a Tim Hortons and left with a tray that I put on the floor at Sarah's feet and a box that she balanced on her lap. The storage facility was just a fifteen-minute drive from my childhood home. My unit was in the last row, facing the fence around the building. Together, we lifted the door to air and sun and the view of a plane tree that had somehow survived between the fence and the industrial park beyond it. We began sorting. A stovetop espresso maker went into a carton for things I intended to keep, and my outdated textbooks were tossed into a bin for recycling. Sarah made a face at clothes I'd bought a decade earlier in case my mother threw mine out, and condemned them to a giveaway bag. I'd been bringing my old journals, a few at a time, into my apartment, so the wooden filing cabinet was empty enough for us to hoist it, with the remaining notebooks, into the truck. At the back of the locker was an old camping trunk. Sarah grabbed one end and I grabbed the other. We were sweaty by now, and her chin was smudged with a bit of dirt.

"What do you keep in this?" she asked as we lifted it into the U-Haul. "More clothes?"

"My father's old stuff."

Her face fell. "I thought maybe you'd have some vintage."

"I've got his air force jacket." It had been in Augie's attic, hanging in a garment bag beside Uncle Jack's much-used wedding suit.

"Can I try it on?" Sarah asked.

"Sure."

I unlatched the lid of the trunk and lifted it. Sarah pulled out the jacket. As she put it on, she said it was heavier than she'd expected. I told her the thick wool had kept Dad warm in unheated planes. I handed her the military cap, which she tipped back on her head so it wouldn't slip down over her eyes.

We took a break in the storage unit, sheltered from the rising wind. Sarah perched on a box, drinking hot chocolate and eating an elaborately sprinkled doughnut, while I sat in a deck chair and ate an apple cruller. A squirrel jumped from an overhead wire to a branch of the plane tree. I thought I saw a nest under construction and wished I had my binoculars. A bird was singing. The days were getting longer, though it was barely above freezing, and some mornings I heard cardinals bringing in the dawn. I drained my coffee. Sarah finished off her doughnut and looked down at her empty cup, tearing a piece off the plastic lid. She had different colours of enamel on each of her fingernails. She said, "Aunt Joan . . ."

"What?"

"Does it hurt to die?"

"I don't think so. We have good medications for pain. Mostly, it just seems natural—the body gradually shutting down. The people I've been with when they die, you feel the love in the room. And more, something I can't describe. You feel it whether you believe in God or not."

"When our cat died, Noah said that angels took her away. Dad thought he said *angles*. I was really sad, and Noah came into my bed and gave me one of his Spider-Man action figures."

"He needs to get something softer to share. How old was Libby?"

"She was old. Like nineteen. First her paws didn't work, and then she couldn't move her legs. She was afraid of the vet, and she wasn't in pain—that's what Mom said—so we kept her at home. When she couldn't reach the water bowl, Dad gave her water with a dropper. Noah said that when Libby was lying on the floor, he saw sparkles all around her. He didn't tell anyone else, just me. Have you ever seen anything like that?"

I shook my head, and her face fell. "But I did experience something after Vivien died." She looked at me hopefully. "After I got the box with her things in it, I dreamt she was lying next to me, but when I woke up, the feeling was still there. And then I felt her put her arm around me. It was around dawn and I'm sure I was awake. My toe itched, but I was afraid to scratch it in case she disappeared."

She nodded, then crumpled her serviette and stuffed it into what was left of her cup. "You've still just got one pot and one frying pan."

"I don't cook much."

"We could get more before I go home. There's stuff like that at Bed Bath & Beyond in the Stockyards. I like the Stockyards."

I wasn't sure why she wanted to delay her return home, but I agreed. Sarah took off Dad's jacket and cap and put them back in the trunk. There wasn't much left in the locker, and it didn't take long to load it into the U-Haul. While I drove, Sarah was busy with her phone. When we arrived at the Stockyards—a former slaughterhouse and meat-packing plant that had been redeveloped—I was thinking about long-term care homes. The first outbreaks were in the news and I was glad my mother wasn't locked up in one. I parked, and we made our way past Best Buy and Home Depot to the shop Sarah had suggested.

There, I found a set of stainless steel pots with red handles. Sarah approved and asked if I needed towels and sheets. I said I didn't because I had two sets of everything, and she rolled her eyes and told me to get more. Eventually, I picked colours that matched my dishes: gold and blue towels and sheets. I threw in a Spider-Man bolster for Noah—at least it was soft—and for Sarah, an eyebrow care kit. (Her eyebrows looked fine to me, but apparently, they were not.) I paid and we went back to the truck. I needed to return it with a full tank, so after we left the Stockyards, I pulled into a gas station.

After we filled up, and I turned out onto the street, Sarah said, "How did you stand it when your mom died?"

"I just did."

"I guess. She was old."

"I still miss her."

"Because she's your real mom."

"No, because she was my mom, period. Denise is your dad's mom," I said. "My sister gave birth to him."

"But he went looking for her. Because she was his blood relative. And he needed her. Like, I don't know—it's better."

"It isn't." If I wasn't driving, I'd have put my hands on her shoulders and turned her to face me, so I could see her eyes and she would see mine, and she'd know I was speaking the truth. But later, I realized that the only reason we were having this conversation was that our eyes were on the road, her vulnerability unseen.

"Finding out where you come from, that's something," I said. "But it isn't everything, and it doesn't have to be anything. If it hadn't been for your mom's illness, your father wouldn't have contacted me again, and you would have all lived on easily without me. But your family couldn't do without you. Has Bruno ever treated you as less his own than Noah?"

"No, but—"

"No *but*. Love is love."

"You never had a baby, so how do you know?"

"Because I had a stepdaughter, and I can't imagine loving any child more than I loved her. I know that, too, because of how much it hurt when I lost her."

There was silence for a moment. Sarah's voice was quiet. "Did she die?"

"No. Her father and I split up." The wipers swished. Zoe had been eleven when they moved away; she'd be in her mid-thirties now. "He didn't let me stay in touch."

320 LILIAN NATTEL

"Couldn't you have done it anyway?"

"I didn't have a legal right."

"So, my father could get me. If he wanted. Even if Dad . . ."

"Your mom will be around for a while yet."

"You're sure?"

"I am," I said. "And at sixteen, you have the right to withdraw from parental control. You can live anywhere you choose."

She went back to her music, and I drove home in the rain. I took my father's jacket out of the trunk and put it in the back of my car, and then Sarah helped me lug everything else up to my apartment. After I returned the truck, Sarah wanted to walk home, but by then it was pouring, so I gave her a ride. When we arrived on her street, I found a spot across from her house.

Suddenly shy, thinking I'd overstepped again, I said, "Here you are."

"Aren't you going to come in?" she asked, craning her head toward the back seat.

"Should I?"

"Don't you want to see Dad try on the air force jacket?"

Though the trees were bare, the air smelled of spring—muddy and fresh—as we made a dash for the house through the rain. Sarah pulled me in from the hallway, calling, "Dad! We've got something for you!" He ambled down the steps and along the corridor toward us while Ruth came from the kitchen with Noah. She'd regained her appetite. Noah was in regular clothes, the only mark of Spider-Man on the pencil case he was holding.

We all stood around Bruno while he tried on the air

force jacket and cap. It wouldn't have mattered if it didn't fit—that wasn't the point—but the jacket was just a bit short in the arms, the cap perfect. I took a picture with my phone.

"It's yours," I said. "If you want it."

He thanked me. Noah jumped from the couch onto his father's back. Bruno held on to his son's feet and ran around the living room, neighing.

CHAPTER 24

We're waiting. We're waiting for surgeries to resume, for normal life to return, and I wonder if it ever will. Spring has come, and with it a meteor shower and a pink full moon—my mother would have loved that. The trees are green, birds nesting, flowers coming up. I spend my days among the elderly and frail in long-term care homes. Though I carefully suit up and am tested regularly, when I get home, I walk up the stairs to my fourth-floor apartment so that I don't infect anyone in the elevator, and as soon as I'm in the door, I throw my clothes into the washer. I miss Friday dinners at my nephew's. Snowball has grown into his paws, a big cat purring under my chin when I fall asleep.

Sometimes, I think it's okay if I die, because I have no mother, no sister and no children. Just when I've resigned myself to a lonely but heroic end like Vivien's, I get a video call from Noah wanting to show me his latest action figure set-up, and there is Sarah at the table behind him, baking her nails, acting as if it's just chance she's there to say hi. I look around, then, at my wealth, the riches of things that in themselves are meaningless, but in the stories they tell me—everything. The kettle that Paula, my neighbour, picked up for me; Bruno's cactus with its red flowers; the towels I bought with Sarah; the walls I painted while pondering her mother's symptoms; the couch where Augie and I sat, feet touching while we wrote an obituary; the chair where I rocked my stepdaughter.

When she was Noah's age, Zoe was a dinosaur nerd. That's why I thought she'd like *The Adventures of T-Rex*, and I bought the entire season's worth of videotapes for her. What was there not to like? Five singing dinosaurs, identifiable by colour, who also fought crime.

She hated it. She was insulted. "They're not real! Do you think I'm a baby?" So, to make up for it, I took her to the dinosaur gallery in the museum. It happened to coincide with one of my sister's visits, and she came with us, watching, bemused, while Zoe lit up every time she came to a particularly fine point, like the fact that birds are actually dinosaurs. We got thrown out of the exhibit after Vivien ducked under the rope around the T. rex, pulling Zoe with her, so I could take a picture of her hugging the leg bone. (Zoe slept with the photograph under her pillow for a year.) That evening, I drove Vivien to the airport, and she said, "You've got a good kid there. I'm sorry I won't be around for your birthday. I'll call, okay?"

Bruno and I sometimes talk about what he's found in Vivien's digital archive. Yesterday, he drew my attention to an email I'd skipped over. Five years ago, she'd volunteered to take care of Ebola patients during the first outbreak. Terrified she'd die, I had suggested she come home for a visit. She responded with a photograph of herself in a haz-mat suit and this reply:

> My dear, I can't. I wish things were different, but it won't work. Just remember this. You're my only sister. No one can replace you. Somehow, we'll get together, and you'll see everything. Promise. Love you.

By *everything*, I'd assumed she meant her workplace and friends, her car and her room. The sink where she'd rinsed her hennaed hair, the latest man whose hand had been on her shoulder during our Skype calls.

But she knew I couldn't leave Mom and was afraid of flying, so that wasn't going to happen, and I'd dismissed her promise as an empty one, as usual. Only I was wrong. She'd found a way to show me everything that mattered: her words, her pictures, her connections to people in her life— even her son. And she'd done it the only way possible, by making me lie for her.

Today. The first Sunday in May. We're celebrating my fifty-seventh birthday, Bruno's forty-third together on Zoom. Bruno and his family crowd around the iPad on his dining room table. His parents have set up George's laptop in the living room of their house in the north end of the city. Augie joins us from his condo near the lake, and my old boss Larry Klieger is in his home office, disgruntled that his Arctic cruise was cancelled.

It's a Sunday afternoon here, and late evening in Tel Aviv, where Ruth's family is joining us. I'm meeting them for the first time. Ruth looks like her mother; her sister is taller and plump, with a mane of wavy hair. They call me "Shwan," and I imagine myself with a long neck and white wings.

Birthday presents are piled on my table. They were left, wrapped, in front of my door with instructions not to open them until after cake. I thought it was silly to have a cake, but they said I must, so I baked one and stuck a lot of candles in it. Ruth carries in Bruno's cake, and I bring my own. We set them on our tables, and everyone sings. Noah counts one, two, three, and Bruno and I blow out our candles. Flames flicker and vanish.

After we have cake and there's a lull in telling jokes (Bruno), arguing politics (Sarah and George) and singing (Ruth and her sister, who has a beautiful voice), Noah demands pin-the-tail-on-the-donkey. His mother shushes him, but I say, "Let's do it." Donkeys and tails are printed in our respective homes and taped to walls. I tie a bandanna around my eyes and swirl myself around, and everyone laughs as I lurch toward the wall and stick the tail onto the donkey's ear. Then it's Bruno's turn. His wife and kids spin him, their hands on his shoulders and back. I remember when I was six or seven and Vivien taught me the trick of slightly opening my eyes at a friend's party so I could get the prize, which I wanted very much, though I don't remember now what it was. I've started writing in a paper journal again. I don't need cloud backup anymore; the world's impermanence has put me on equal footing with it.

Augie sends me a direct message. He says, *When this is over, can I spend the night?*

I message back a smiley face.

We all pour wine and raise our glasses. We say, "Happy birthday," and "Cheers," and "Santé," and "L'chaim," and "Till 120."

Bruno says, "To Vivien—I wouldn't be here without her."

After my friends take their leave and the kids go off to play video games, I have a sombre conversation with Ruth and her family. She asked me to help her explain her diagnosis and to assure them that she's being given every possible treatment. Her mother and sister weep. Across the ocean and the time difference, I can only sit with them. When the crying stops, in the peace that comes after grief, I am sitting with them still. I think about distance and family, the different kinds of distance, how family can be lost and gained. In my journal I write: *Vivien, I found it. I got it all.*

This morning, I set up my own Facebook account. I did a search. Then I sent out a message:

> Are you Zoe Li, born August 2, 1987? I think you might
> be my stepdaughter.

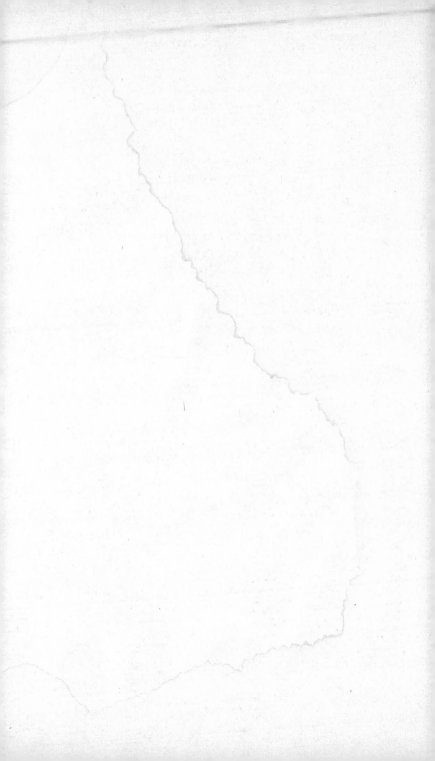

ACKNOWLEDGEMENTS

Writing a novel during a pandemic would be impossible without the support of the people in my life. Hugs have been especially important, but virtual connections have also been a lifeline. At times, we're all tired and weighed down, and yet people are still having babies and writers are writing. All of it is better with help. I've been privileged to work with my peerless editor, Anne Collins, who cannot rest until a book is all that it should be. I also want to thank the entire hard-working team at Penguin Random House Canada. A special shout out goes to Kelly Hill for the beautiful cover and to Stacey Cameron, my copy editor. I am always grateful for the wisdom of my agent, Dean Cooke, who has been a steady presence throughout, and to the dedicated team at Cooke McDermid. Several health-care professionals—physicians and nurses—generously shared their expertise to talk to me about palliative care and other medical issues. They prefer to remain anonymous. I want to express my appreciation for all the delivery people who kept me supplied and safe. My family brought life to our home and wore masks diligently. They are my joy.

Born in Montreal, **LILIAN NATTEL** now lives in Toronto with her husband and two daughters. She is the author of *Girl at the Edge of Sky*, *Web of Angels*, *The Singing Fire* and *The River Midnight*.